Jane Austen and Shelley
in the Garden

JANET TODD is a novelist, biographer, literary critic and internationally renowned scholar, known for her work on women's writing and feminism. Her most recent books include *Don't You Know There's a War On?*; *Jane Austen's Sanditon*; *Radiation Diaries*; *Aphra Behn: A Secret Life*; and *A Man of Genius*. She has published biographies and critical work on many authors, including Jane Austen, Aphra Behn, Mary Wollstonecraft and her daughters, Mary (Shelley) and Fanny, and her Irish pupil, Lady Mount Cashell.

Born in Wales, Janet Todd grew up in Britain, Bermuda and Ceylon/Sri Lanka and has worked at schools and universities in Ghana, Puerto Rico, India, the US (Douglass College, Rutgers and Florida), Scotland (Glasgow, Aberdeen) and England (Cambridge, UEA). A former President of Lucy Cavendish College, Cambridge, and Emerita Professor at the University of Aberdeen, she is now an Honorary Fellow of Newnham College.

Praise for Janet Todd's previous works

Don't You Know There's a War On?

"Lush prose . . . this smouldering novel is a dark and strangely disquieting pleasure." *Times Literary Supplement*

"I love this powerful, brilliant evocation of post WWII life. Strongly recommended." Miriam Margolyes

Radiation Diaries: Cancer, Memory and Fragments of a Life in Words

"Janet Todd's pain-filled interweaving of life and literature is a good book written against the odds – it is frank, wry and unexpectedly heartening." Hilary Mantel

"A stunningly good, tight, intelligent, truthful book and one of the most touching love letters to literature I have ever read. Ah, so that's why we write, I thought." Maggie Gee

"I read it avidly, unable to stop. I love the voice, especially the tension between restraint and candour in its brevities – and yet endearingly warm and honest. It's an original voice and utterly convincing in its blend of confession, quirkiness, humour, intimacy. It's nothing short of a literary masterpiece, inventing a genre. A delight too is the embeddedness of books in the character of a lifelong reader; it is fascinating to learn of Todd's fascinating variegated past. How gallant (like the verbal gallop against mortality at the close of *The Waves*)." Lyndall Gordon

A Man of Genius

"Strange and haunting, a gothic novel with a modern consciousness." Philippa Gregory

"Todd has an enjoyably satirical style; she writes with shrewdness, humour and compassion." Miranda Seymour, *Sunday Times*

"A rip-roaring read." Michele Roberts, *Sunday Times*

"A convincing and entertaining path through Behn's life in the vivid context of her times . . . an effective mixture of historical research, literary criticism and fiction that brings us as close as we may ever get to the truth of this enterprising and enigmatic literary figure." *Shelf Awareness*

"A brisk, entertaining, and richly detailed portrait of a unique woman and her era." *Kirkus*

"Janet Todd guides us with unfailing buoyancy and a wit all her own through the intricacies of Restoration theatre and politics. [Behn's] epitaph seems to suggest her wit is buried with her. Not at all; it is now wondrously resurrected." *Evening Standard*

Jane Austen

"Monumental, powerful, learned . . . sets the standard." Frank Kermode, *London Review of Books*

"Essential for anyone with a serious interest in Austen . . . rendered with razor-sharp clarity for a modern audience – exceptionally useful." Duncan Wu, Raymond Wagner Professor in Literary Studies, Georgetown University

"Intelligent and accessible." *Times Literary Supplement*

"Easy to read and engaging; excellent on Austen's work." *Choice*

"Janet Todd is one of the foremost feminist literary historians writing now." Lisa Jardine, Centenary Professor of Renaissance Studies, Director of the Centre for Editing Lives and Letters, University of London, *Independent on Sunday*

*Death and the Maidens: Fanny Wollstonecraft and the
Shelley Circle; Mary Wollstonecraft*

"Todd is an extraordinary researcher and sophisticated critic. This
biography conjures a vivid sense of a revolutionary and a woman, and
offers precise insights into the progress of one writer's life." *Ruminator*

"A juicy portrait, reconstructed with insight and wit." *Entertainment Weekly*

"Terrific insight . . . Todd soundly and generously reimagines
women's lives." *Publishers' Weekly* (Starred)

"Janet Todd brilliantly captures the absurdity in Wollstonecraft
while defending the view that her life was both important and
revolutionary. Like Virginia Woolf, Todd interprets this life as a
daring experiment. Wollstonecraft is all but resurrected in Janet Todd's
distinguished book: brave, reckless and wide open to life. Virginia
Woolf claimed for Wollstonecraft a special kind of immortality.
Janet Todd has strengthened the case." Ruth Scurr, *The Times*

"The great strength of Janet Todd's biography lies in her willingness
to unpick the feminist frame on which earlier lives of Wollstonecraft
were stretched to fit." Kathryn Hughes, *Literary Review*

"Janet Todd, a feminist, has done ground-breaking scholarship on women
writers. Her work reads quickly and lightly . . . Even Todd's throwaway
lines are steeped in learning and observation. Todd has documented so
ably the daring attempt of a woman to write, both for her daily bread
and for immortal fame." Ruth Perry, MIT, *Women's Review of Books*

Jane Austen and Shelley in the Garden

A Novel with Pictures

Janet Todd

Fentum
Press

Fentum Press, London

Sold and distributed by Global Book Sales/Macmillan
Distribution and in North America by Consortium Book Sales
and Distribution, Inc. part of the Ingram Content Group.

Copyright © 2021 Janet Todd

Janet Todd asserts the moral right to be
identified as the author of this work

A CIP catalogue record for this book is available
from the British Library

ISBN (paperback) 978-1-909572-270
Ebook: 978-1-909572-28-7

Typeset in Fournier by Patty Rennie
Printed and bound in Great Britain by TJ Books Ltd

For Miriam

Part One

I

It is a truth universally, begins Jane Austen . . .

Shhh, says Fran, finger on lips. Not subtle. Money and sex. How many versions before you settled on that flirtatious opening?

The amazing Agafia Lykova, reclusive and garrulous, lives most of her life alone in the wilderness of the Siberian Taiga. The last survivor of a family of Old Believers who fled Stalin's persecutions in 1936, Agafia traps animals and fish and grows potatoes. In a lean year, like Charlie Chaplin in *The Gold Rush*, she eats her leather shoes. Excluding the shoes, the diet's good – in her seventies she retains her teeth, though filed down from cracking nuts. Now a world-famous hermit, she receives numerous letters and presents. The donated modern food may cause tooth decay.

Fran smiles with Jane Austen over this account. I know, she says, the material is so intense we should focus on trifles. Those shoes, the fan letters.

Nothing is trifling in the life of the isolate, the miraculous Agafia Lykova.

Nor in the life of Jane Austen. Both are celebrities.

I am a fridge magnet, remarks Jane Austen. Miss Lykova, I believe, is on YouTube.

Fran looks through her kitchen window. Bare trees and flat, sodden, sewage-coloured February fields below a greyish sky. If the sky came lower – moist, cold and alive – would it squash

3

the mushroom-smelling earth, leave a slug-trail? I may have to learn to live with people before it's too late, she thinks.

You'd be happier if you had work, observes Jane Austen. Your Agafia's busy fishing, digging and praying. You should take up intricate sewing.

Men don't sew.

Men have guns, says Jane Austen (contrary to admiring views, she's not always in universal touch), they get up with the lark to shoot things.

She slides behind the great fireplace as Annie Klein ducks her head to negotiate the lintel at the foot of the staircase.

Annie suspects Jane Austen of haunting her friend.

Not quite, Fran would say if they discussed the matter. The

woman's there, often uninvited, an intruder. Like a dream she ambles in, sits down and won't leave despite a batting of eyelids. Settling where a shadow should be.

Is Fran grateful? Dickens's Mrs Blimber of *Dombey and Son* said, if she could have known Cicero, she'd have died contented. Sometimes Fran resents her Author muttering in her ear.

Mind's ear, Annie might have said.

'The fact is you're too isolated here now you've retired. Wifi and IT gadgets aren't company. You'll get weird if you stay much longer. Well, weirder.'

Though mid-morning, Annie hasn't yet had coffee; it makes her a little severe.

'I know,' says Fran, unable to repress a smile. She's pleased when someone troubles to analyse her.

'Dr Johnson thought solitude and idleness roads to madness.'

'Can't do idleness,' grins Fran, fingering the screwdriver in the drooping front pocket of her jumpsuit. She stares at the drizzle making pointillism on the small-paned windows, then swivels her eyes towards thin cracks in the bulging plaster round the wood frames.

Mice scamper along private alleyways.

To prevent Annie noticing, she speaks loudly. 'I'm planning to write now I've time. Something oblique, a little personal.'

'Writing in solitude's as mad as talking to yourself. Virginia Woolf's room of her own was in a big family house. You'll never have a writing group out here. You haven't even joined a book club.'

Fran avoids looking at Jane Austen, who, she guesses, now smirks by the window. She hears the Author saying (for the umpteenth time) that she never wrote alone, someone was always at home to applaud a sentence, laugh at a witticism. Women do not need rooms of their own, she rumbles on – we're not all in

Bloomsbury. We were a large, lively family, extra young people about, father's pupils, friends, relations.

Just Mum, Dad and Me, sighs Fran. But we were content.

What, thinks Annie, can Fran write about? She has no fierceness about lost life. Those dear dull parents in their warm little bungalow? Then she recalls drowned Andrew.

Fran's an uneasy hostess, forgetting to lay out flannels and bath towels, arrange flowers by the guest bed, but she loves having Annie in the cottage. Annie colours in outlines.

The women sit on Arts-and-Craft chairs with pierced-heart backs and studded brown seats. Annie found them in an auction – Fran wouldn't know an Arts-and-Craft chair from a Windsor. On the deal table remains of a pheasant stuffed with Boursin cheese, accompanied by roasted potatoes, parsnips, carrots and steamed purple-flowering broccoli.

Fran gazes idly at a china pig with a trapdoor in its back, half ornament, half piggybank. Incongruous in the sprawling fireplace, it gleams pinkly next to a child's blue clay owl called Plop: an haphazard shaft of sun catches it between showers.

The cottage meal isn't the imaginative one Annie concocts in her better lighted Cambridge kitchen; still, though conventional, it's good. Waitrose has responded to the new estate (built on a flood plain) by providing prettily illustrated dinners for two or four. Among them plucked, prepared pheasant. The Boursin cheese is Annie's touch.

Fran had forgotten just how much washing-up this avatar of Christmas dinner causes. Thankfully she's not made her lemon surprise pudding with beaten egg whites. More intricate mess with sticky prongs as well as splattered counter. A cold shop-bought tart sits in the kitchen, pulling pheasant smells into its industrial pastry.

*

She and Annie carry the dirty plates the few steps towards the sink. It's under the slanting roof that once reached the ground against the cold and meanness of English peasant winters. Four hungry families inhabited the cottage then.

'It's a comfortable place, not saying,' Annie continues when the tart has dissolved its sweetness in their mouths. It's flowing amiably down to inhabit the stomach, delivering the sugar-high mothers dread in small unrestrained children. The home-made lemon pudding would have been tastier, yet, once en route through tubes, where's the difference? 'But Norfolk's remote. Suffolk's another thing, quaint second homes and all that. But just here, it's, well, very rural. Your garden's fine,' she adds, aware of the labour Fran puts in planting bulbs and bare tree roots in the unaccommodating soil. 'Still I prefer the hustling, bustling streets. You should too. A retreat's good but not all the time, not so you become too moved by yourself and trees – and talk too often to your Author.'

Fran reddens. Annie's been emboldened by speaking of Fran to Rachel, an American attuned to therapy trends: knowing nothing of Fran, Rachel said 'borderline', making Annie laugh.

2

'It's my talk of Agafia that's brought this on, yes?' says Fran as Annie returns from the bar of the Three Geese with a further two glasses of house white. They should be drinking gin, but Fran recoils at the price. 'One can live alone without finding oneself lonely.'

'Naturally.' Annie winces at the pronoun. She'd been mock-ed as bourgeois and (paradoxically) an echo of that fossil Prince

Charles for using it in a lecture at an ex-poly. Now she embraces ungrammatical obscenity while feeling the impatience of a convert. 'Agafia got attuned to isolation early on. She gave it a shape. You said she trapped fish and skinned rabbits. Dirty but probably satisfying.'

'I don't miss teaching,' says Fran. 'It's entertainment now. "We love Colin Firth".'

Annie thanks her stars she's never had to say, 'I work on Jane Austen', then meet the lit-up face of a visiting wife – 'Oh, Mr Darcy!' She smiles benignly at her friend.

'But perhaps I wanted a little chandelier swagger in my life.'

Fran hesitates, 'I wish I hadn't had to work so hard for everything. Much nicer to get it through luck.'

Annie scowls. Fran thinks her lucky, just like her classmates used to do – famous father and posh house – she knows otherwise. 'I've had to persevere for . . .'

But Fran's stopped listening. She doesn't need to hear Annie say again how little she's been rewarded.

'. . . though I've never really made it. Never been in those clubby societies like Apostles, British Academy, never had a CBE or whatever, never had an Honorary . . .' She's tangling in memories of Zach Klein.

'Nobody cares a damn in South Norfolk.'

Alan Partridge's Norfolk is 'the Wales of the East'.

'You'll be retired soon. A Senior Railcard takes you anywhere.'

Old age is an equalizer, Fran means. It can, should they choose, be daisy-time together.

Jane Austen sits in a nook. *I* persevered, she remarks.

Fran stares towards the darkness. She knows exactly what Jane Austen thinks of her virtuosity, her magical tactile density. She also knows what *she* thinks of her Author's faux modesty: those little pieces if ivory she claimed to be writing on with little effect. Really!

Some readers say my books repeat themselves, continues Jane Austen, pretty girl catches eligible man: common romances. Not so. Only a jealous person understands real love, always one-sided. Fanny Price, my heroine with the undiverted heart.

You betrayed her: said she'd have taken another man.

I am a realist. I deal in probabilities.

Pride and Prejudice: the girl who gets it all?

Things exactly as they are, murmurs Jane Austen dreamily from her nook, a crimson horse and blue guitar. She pulls herself back to her time. One must earn pewter.

You created weak Fanny Price to atone for Lizzie Bennet's ludicrous luck – no virtue in being healthy.

Annie regards Fran's twitchy lips. 'You could pretend you're on a mobile phone.'

Fran shrugs, waiting for her friend to mention the future.

'You know, maybe oblique life-writing's a good idea.'

'You mean, if I wrote things down, I wouldn't move my lips?'

'There's a chance.'

Fran looks at Annie seemingly so vivid and confident – yet with failure softly coughing in the wings. The thought swells her fondness.

'Old women do talk to themselves. What cats are for,' says Annie. Fran's six years older than she is: it shows. Six years that counted for nothing twenty years back return to childhood impact: six years marks another generation now.

Fran leans across Annie towards an old woman sitting with two men in an alcove lined with dark anaglypta paper. The men talk together, ignoring the woman as she meditatively sips a brown ale.

'What's old age?' asks Fran.

'Urine,' says the woman.

Unable to bear being left out, one man says, 'People find you repugnant.'

'How strange,' says Fran. 'I'd thought "repugnant" a woman's word.'

The men return to discussing car routes towards the North Sea coast, pitting the sleek A140 against the B1150 with its crawling hay-wains. The woman looks fixedly in the mottled mirror on one side of the alcove; she sees only the top of her head where hair is thinning, she strokes it like a wounded sparrow. 'Disappointment,' she mumbles.

'You just accosted a stranger, Fran. You never used to do that.'

'Yeah, I know. I do now. Like Sebald.'

'What?'

Fran has known very few famous people. She clutches the opening. 'W.G. Sebald. I once told him his posture of sitting absorbed and listening in an East Anglian pub wasn't for women.'

A relevant remark, for they're in the kind of place Sebald might have chosen for the serendipity of a chance encounter.

Not of course *this* pub: he needed a porous edge to vision, a glimpse of North Sea perhaps.

'Remember how it goes. "You're at the bar of the Crown Hotel in Southwold and you get into conversation with a Dutchman – your talk continues till last orders. A woman hasn't the freedom."'

'Well yes,' smiles Annie. The idea of Sebald amuses her. Author of best-selling books lacking irony, plot or characters, a splendid reproof to the creative-writing brigade who get up her nose. (She considers Jane Austen's *Emma* equally plotless.)

Money for old rope, she says – mainly when Rachel isn't in

earshot. Rachel makes good money teaching the stuff. (Annie judges from clothes – unaware her new pal benefits from an ample family trust fund.)

'I think he said old women have freedom unless masquerading as young. I said a droll remark that invites a man into the cosy group of drinkers isn't for an old woman. She's invisible.'

Fran forgets Sebald's response. Encounters with celebrities or royalty are like that: one recalls what one said or might have said; what they murmured back floats off as lightly as a child's balloon.

Annie hopes Fran's finished. She does meander. Comes from living alone. If encountered over the samovar, her Agafia would never shut up about catching fish and planting potato tubers. She'd be a hopeless listener.

'George Borrow, that's the chap Sebald reminds me of,' says Annie. '*Wild Wales* and *Lavengro*.'

'He wrote in German,' says Fran. 'From outside it seems to me life was good to him, so his melancholic pose – OK temper – was if not an affectation then a kind of boredom. Lugubriousness, fame, masculine privilege, a little guilt, and authority: might almost be Hamlet, Prince of Denmark.' A pause. 'His boredom speaks to readers. His work's a sort of pilgrimage into the soul, in its autumn.'

'Shit, where'd you read that?'

Annie hasn't actually finished a Sebald book – or indeed a George Borrow. 'Yup, boredom,' she says, adding, 'I don't believe self-expression's ever authentic.' She strokes the tiny peacock feather on her red felt hat, then twists a black-dyed curl.

Annie's voice is too posh for a rural pub. 'Let's be off,' Fran says. 'Just a jiff, must use the loo.'

As she enters, she finds Jane Austen joining her. You see, smiles Fran, a writer must be absent to be authentic. You knew that.

The Author is uninterested. You would do well to leave the country as your friend advises.

Cheeky. Wasn't it Austenland that made Fran imagine contentment among green fields?

Different were you rooted here.

Sebald wasn't rooted. Yet Southwold has his imprint.

Fran tightens her lips in the mirror over the washbasin, framed on one side by a plastic poinsettia. She's moved by the care taken to brighten up a dingy windowless box of a room. Jane Austen assumes the sardonic look her sister Cassandra caught in the iconic sketch now in the National Portrait Gallery (and worth millions). She's about to speak when Fran enters one of the two cubicles.

A none-too-clean pub toilet's no place for critical badinage.

Fran emerges. Go on, I'm listening. But no one else is in the mirror.

She washes her hands perfunctorily. The air-dryer isn't working, so she rubs them on her stiff hemp jacket. The poinsettia no longer seems a friendly sign. She returns to find Annie by the door, only just restraining impatience.

A mind lively and at ease, can do with seeing nothing, and can see nothing that does not answer, whispers Jane Austen. She channels Emma, a character for whom she has a very soft spot.

Irritated, Fran turns back. Emma never sees 'nothing'. What she sees is half imaginary, the rest just theatre.

Jane Austen smirks. Author and character are imaginists: they see nothing to see everything. She swishes out the door, leaving only the faintest whiff of that wicked narrative voice.

A car speeds alarmingly round the bend. It nearly runs into them as they scramble onto the verge by Carr's pond. You could kill or be killed round here.

'Didn't your Sebald die on the road?' asks Annie as they regain the tarmac.

'He was a ferocious driver, but he had an aneurism. I guess he died at speed.'

The French psychoanalyst Jacques Lacan drove fast. He was proud of being uninhibited, ignoring a red light, a kind of signifier. Where the signifier isn't functioning, it speaks on its own. We suffer auditory hallucinations and crash into pieces, caught in psychotic fantasies.

'Goodness,' says Fran, 'what mumbo-jumbo.'

Mmm, thinks Annie. 'Not really.'

One isn't paid well to be intelligible, whispers Jane Austen falling in with the friends. Every profession has its jargon.

'Do you remember me mentioning my ex-student Thomas,' says Annie, 'the Shelley-devotee? He says Shelley needs speed to feel alive. He skids down slopes, sails through wind, projects mechanical wings and boats.'

On the last lap to the cottage, along a route more bridleway than footpath, they walk single file to avoid hoof-squashed mud. Darkness is pierced by a partly clouded full moon and a dim torch.

Annie returns to Fran's way of life, 'You'll get odder alone. In the pub you guzzled both packets of crisps quite absent-mindedly. As if no one else existed with a mouth.'

Fran stops abruptly, then turns. 'I suppose I could leave,' she says. 'Jeoffry's wandered off, probably found a fishier home.'

'There you are then. Cats are never homeless.'

'It would be an adventure.'

'If you sit in the centre of a seesaw you get none of the fun of going up and down.' Fran snorts: Annie's been in one place and one job these past thirty years.

As they near the lit cottage, Fran senses its comfortable settling in grassy ground. 'I'd miss it. A boat on a swamp. If you pressed a knitting needle through the grass, water'd well up and swish against its walls.'

Not wanting to appear ungracious, Annie says, 'It's been a good visit.'

'Blickling and Felbrigg?'

'Yeah, well, I'm not a National Trust devotee. Even when houses are open.'

'You old Marxist! You and your dad!'

'Nah,' sniffs Annie. Any mention of Zach Klein – even when softened into Fran's demotic 'dad' – makes her edgy. 'They should be care homes, hospitals, boarding-schools, refugee centres – or wrecks after bricks and girders have been stolen by the displaced.'

'Don't care for the rich now or then, but houses have a sort of life – if you burn or knock them apart, they hurt.'

This wistful strain annoys Annie. Identities don't come from houses, places or culture. She calls them – well, when the matter concerns white British – identities of exclusion. She finds a literary palliative. 'Do you know that short story by Virginia Woolf, "A haunted house"? No? About a house with a pulse and beating heart. The ghosts are a couple seeking their old joy where there's the shadow of a thrush and sounds of wood pigeons, that kind of rusticry.' She doesn't add there's treasure in the house: love or the light in the heart. It would only encourage Fran.

'There you are then. You like Anglo-pastoral after all.' Fran unlatches her gate.

'Only in words.'

'You know there's a hedgehog hibernating over there in the pile of leaves.' Fran's eyes shine in the outside light. 'They roll into a ball so spiky only badgers and humans can penetrate it. People tell lies about hedgehogs, collecting fruit on spikes for winter, their dung curing baldness – or is that stewed hedgehog? Suckling cows, so ruining *our* milk. Mating must be stressful with those prickles, don't you think?'

Aware of the surrounding darkness and her damp feet, Annie wishes Fran would shut up and open the triple locks of her back door.

3

In one of the two big bedrooms forming the first floor of the cottage with the great chimney piece between them, Fran sits on her small double bed. She contemplates Jane Austen sidling into the room.

A little perambulating round Southern England but otherwise such stability! How'd you have coped with rootlessness, nomadism without tent and tribe? (Can one envy a ghost?) You needed midwives in life and work. You'd have been a lady writing upstairs on her little writing-table without the handy brothers. Waiting on a curate or pompous college fellow to remove the shame of spinsterhood.

Got that off your chest? sniggers Jane Austen. You are *so* residually Victorian: my sister and I never thought of women as spinsters, surplus or odd. We were ladies – and I, in addition, was an Author.

It's a point of view.

Why do a 'Mary Wollstonecraft': splattered on her path through life by mud from contemptuous boots and hooves? Being what? A poor teacher, companion, governess, hack writer, exhibitionist of women's 'rights'. Surely better loll in a warm family carriage, not your own woman perhaps but always a lady?

I had no command of the carriage, protests Jane Austen. It was not yet the Age of Woman. You can't anticipate history, though you can rewrite it, as your age is doing. I kept it at my back.

Fran's rebuked. She knows as well as Jane Austen (and Annie?) the humiliating lack of control one has over one's life at any time. Does one have a duty to be mutinous?

She goes downstairs. Her slippers edge each creaking step as her hands brush bulging walls. She likes the modest difficulty of ascent and descent. It makes her feel a benign stranger at home.

Annie's boiling a kettle for night-time tea. Fran can no longer drink it without needing to get up three times to pee. Each evening she leaves the cooling tea by the kitchen sink.

As she holds her warm floral mug, Annie watches Fran pouring herself a glass of tap water. She grins, thinking of Rachel and her habit of sipping from a little plastic bottle, as if she were a coddled baby or rare tropical flower needing the constant drip of tepid liquid.

The tap water has mineral and industrial traces; they remind Fran of childhood doses of chalybeate when the family visited mid-Wales and Dad gleefully told them – every time – how health-giving and good this foul-tasting liquid was for body and soul. Mum laughed and spat it out.

Fran drains the glass. It's the kind meant to hold a toothbrush. Her eyes rest on it; she pushes it towards the sink, feeling protective of her objects.

Clutching her mug of tea, Annie glances at the framed photo on a windowsill of Andrew with Johnnie as a toddler sitting proudly on his father's shoulders. 'We did proper mothering didn't we? We didn't knock the hell out of them to create self-discipline. The kids have more self-esteem than we have; isn't that the point of it all? – though my mother'd have said self-discipline's equally important.'

'You don't often speak of her,' says Fran, 'mostly Zach.'

Annie shrugs. 'He was more distinct, as tyrants are.' Her expression grows pensive. 'Sadie was house-proud, but she'd dust round my books to avoid disturbing my revising. Not sure I did it for Daniel and Esther. Come to think, I didn't dust. You know,' she adds seeing Fran's quizzing expression, 'I was so proud when that rat of a husband said he loved me more than he loved his mother.'

She's drunk too much of the pub's cheap wine: she'll regret this talk in the morning. Her disrupted marriage is taboo here. 'But see how well they've turned out. Lucky, I guess.'

Not entirely, thinks Fran. Annie's involvement in mothering was minimal and she, Fran, stepped in when her friend was off at conferences, electing to stay on – just a few days because she'd probably never again see Vancouver or Berlin. So, a birthday would be missed if Fran hadn't carted the three children to some downmarket chain for hamburgers and ice cream. Sometimes – and it's an ignoble thought – she wonders whether Annie's enthusiasm for her buying the Norfolk cottage was to make a holiday home for her kids – and at times herself.

Annie knows what Fran suspects. The cottage is pleasant to relax in, with someone else doing (basic) cooking and cleaning. In abstract, she doesn't like the country, but her memories – buttressed by sun-lit photos with espaliered apple tree or reed-edged pond – are some of her best. Never so happy as when being served – and no Paul in the frame.

Mainly of course, Annie comes for Fran.

You can value a friend *and* find her useful.

'No, we didn't do so badly,' she pursues, putting her mug on the wet spot left by Fran's glass, then pushing it back and forwards with her finger. 'We didn't have daughters who got leglessly drunk or drugged on the King's Road. Yet, maybe we didn't do everything right. All three have edged away, haven't they?' Annie checks herself. She's not been such a bad parent, though she admits taking her youth after the children were born. She hadn't had an earlier chance.

Mother-love asks nothing back, Fran muses; yet there's a nagging undertow: surely some thanks might be returned for so much care, treasure and anxiety expended – however puny or by rights it all seems to the grown child. Had Johnnie left so early because he resented time lavished on Annie's children? He'd never said, neither as man nor boy.

He disliked Esther and Daniel. Maybe he'd wanted his mother to himself. Now he'll be looking from his low, beautiful house at the brilliant landscape of Antipodean mountains and blue lake, thinking sometimes of Fran in her wet little cottage. She could come to live near them and her grandchildren, he's said, knowing neither will wish it.

He'd once brought his family on a visit. Mum was there too, taken from the home to beam from her vacant mind. Johnnie was so gentle with her, while Daphne looked on proudly. Her daughter-in-law (the term would always be novel) talked in a high-pitched voice that grated on Fran, but she was a nice enough young woman. She kept the children pretty as pictures.

How Fran had yearned for these grandchildren! In the flesh, she felt less than expected. She didn't know how to treat them, the little prince and princess who turned up cute noses at toys she bought them at the craft fair. Yet, she felt immense love when she received their pictures; she framed the black and white ones in silver. Leave it at that.

Johnnie had been the apple of his grandma's eye when it saw clearly. She'd listened with pride as he stammered out a poem he'd written while she – Fran reddens at the memory – corrected his grammar. Dad had been proud to find a childish poem of hers in the county magazine, an awful thing of bird-song, hawthorn and high Wordsworthian sentiment. He'd not corrected her – but of course her grammar had been perfect – and his wasn't always.

We can't all be teenage geniuses. She nudges Jane Austen.

The friends exchange glances. Each thinks she shows age a little less than the other, wrinkles round the mouth, incipient or pronounced dewlap, drooping eyelid.

Light in the small-windowed cottage is dim, so Fran has no

constant idea how she looks. 'Do you think I should wear make-up? I'm getting grey all over, face, hair, clothes, everything. Would you remark if I appeared with green nails and a slash of crimson mouth?'

'I would,' laughs Annie. She doubts her friend has the skill or patience to make up a clown's face. 'You look fine,' she says, adding 'to me.' She picks up the floral mug again and drinks the strong dregs.

'I *could* go,' Fran repeats as Annie prepares to leave. 'I didn't say but I've got rats as well as mice. Scuttling behind the wardrobe. I was here for a job. If I'd chosen for solitude, I think I'd have gone to Wales.'

'Oh dear,' grins Annie remembering Alan Partridge. To cover the discourtesy, she continues, 'Thomas wants to pursue young Shelley to Wales. He needs a bit of factual ballast for his book. Did you know Shelley went there?'

Fran groans.

'The rats,' says Annie, 'I heard them in the night. Aren't there rodent exterminators in Norfolk?'

'There's also a hole in the bathroom floor. I think some of my lost rings and things have fallen into it. The rats might be down there too.'

'Nice for the next owners to find if you sold the place. The rings and things, I mean.'

'And bats,' says Fran. 'Would anyone ever buy the cottage if they knew?'

'You could rent it.'

'They'd find out about the rats and bats and the septic tank and want a reduction. Best sell if I were to move.'

'You do know a ghost depreciates a house?'

*

Annie pulls the wheels of her Mandarina Duck case down the second crooked staircase, trying not to knock off her cloche hat where the ceiling slopes. On her lower back is her light-blue backpack full of books she meant to read but didn't. It pulls at her shoulders: she hopes it works on posture like the back-straps Rachel sometimes wears. 'I look like a cartoon burglar,' she remarks as she slithers it against the spongy cream plaster.

'Funny word,' says Fran. 'Robbers, thieves, burglars, purloiners, pilferers, why not stealers? all taking what they want, what's another's. Pirate, highwayman, buccaneer, brigand, biographer, plagiarist.'

'Plagiarism's not a hanging offence,' says Annie, flushing as she recalls its malicious power over vain Zach Klein. Scuppering an honour as fast as paedophilia or the unspeakable n—— word.

Fran begins turning the keys in the three stiff locks, pushing out the naked clematis vine that hangs over one of them. In this bare time, Annie should remember summer loveliness, the earthenware planters of tobacco flowers and fuchsia, violets and blushing dwarf roses; the pink glazed pot of bright-leafed camelia. She *had* admired the summer blooming, though not enough: now she's forgotten it.

Some of the bricks in the path have rotted, perhaps January ice made them flake. It's new laid and the quick decay saddens Fran. 'I didn't altogether choose Jane Austen,' she says. 'Actually' –and she lowers her voice – 'I'd rather have bedded down with someone less commonly admired, someone more remote and intellectual.'

Annie's surprised. A little worried too. The thing sounds serious. As they pass through the wooden gate, she smiles back hiding her thoughts. 'Oh, I think you did choose. Isn't there mileage in having an iconic, branded author to teach and talk about. Never at a loss for conversation.'

'You're so wrong,' says Fran carefully closing her gate. She's had a notice printed and tacked onto it telling anyone who opens it to close it again. The postman ignores the instruction. No matter: the sign is part of proper householding.

'Well I guess I don't do ghosts,' says Annie shoving the wheels of her Mandarina Duck case into the boot of Fran's Mini. Both women are short, Fran shorter, but still it feels cramped.

'Your dad Zach?' Fran says, too low for Annie's ears.

The train stops neatly by the narrow platform. Annie enters, dragging in her case. She stands in the open doorway. 'Don't worry so much about words, dear Fran.'

'We laugh a lot, don't we, Annie? Perhaps not so much this time.'

'Freud says humour isn't resigned,' begins Annie but doors close before she finishes. Her carriage's almost empty, so the books sit by themselves.

I believe your Annie consumes rather than reads books, remarks Jane Austen ambling onto the platform.

You mean she uses and excretes? grins Fran.

As the train starts to move, the friends wave through the closed window, Fran waving that bit longer. She looks where Annie had been standing and steps carefully over the warmed spot.

Climbing back into the Mini, she thinks that, despite her tartness, Jane Austen makes the world a little less cold than it might otherwise be. The most important thing is resilience, she concludes, elasticity of mind.

And virtue, says Jane Austen from the back seat.

Fran ignores her.

4

Two months later, Fran leaves Norfolk to visit Annie. She doesn't show to best advantage in Cambridge. Getting a place at the famous university had been the achievement of her youth: arriving there and leaving were anti-climactic.

On the train, she catches herself in the grimy window, notes the infrequently tinted soft hair and tortoiseshell spectacles. Curious how the artificial emerges beyond the 'natural'. Is what she sees an antitype, a prototype, a duplicate, an image?

Why the recent propensity to see parts of herself – in mirrors, windows, people's sunglasses, even shiny kitchen gadgets in John Lewis? Morbid astonishment – or disbelief – at age, that constant bass note to the trills of life?

Agafia lacks a mirror, hence her contented smile.

Sometimes Fran believes she makes, on first acquaintance, a tolerable impression. Then, seeing through other eyes, she notes her error: acting bouncy forty instead of staid seventy.

She looks again at the dirty windowpane. Without spectacles and one slightly droopy lid – 'ptosis' apparently – mightn't her eyes be thought rather fine? By?

Don't even whisper Mr Darcy.

She turns from the window. Muriel Spark said being over seventy is like being engaged in a war. We survive among the dead and dying. Fran chuckles. Not quite: Annie will always be young.

The train approaches Cambridge. People shift, remove earplugs, click off phones, close notebooks and laptops, drain cardboard cups of tepid coffee before squashing them to splatter drop-down trays. Through the window, the road by the train track is filling with racing bicycles.

They pass glassy asymmetrical buildings in Lego shapes. How imaginative! one might say to a four-year-old if she'd made them. Fran thinks of the grass and sedgy pools these gaudy, rebarbative things displace. The melancholy she associates with old Cambridge envelops the new — until she remembers its orderly urban ducks.

From the rack she pulls down her flowered Cath Kidston holdall, then bustles into her linen jacket.

Good humour and cheerful spirits, says Jane Austen.

Fran and Annie perch on wooden stools in warm early-May sun under an umbrella decorated with beer logos. It shows signs of mould from its wintering. They wait for Rachel to join them.

Soon, Fran hopes, for, back on home territory and with a couple of gins inside her, Annie broods over her broken marriage. 'Idiotic. Paul mistook a bit of sparkle for wit. You know' – not an invitation to dialogue – 'he even gave the woman a "baroque sensibility". Shit.' She yawns as if a flower is opening inside her mouth. 'Really!'

'Oh?'

'OK, I looked at his emails.'

Annie's bleak expression is comically at odds with her mascaraed lashes, bright lips and pink and black hat. 'Someone told her she had "a happy heart". Why would she repeat it? What narcissism.'

'Don't let it travel,' says Fran.

Annie stares. 'Not so easy.'

'Of course. Feels like a morass. But the "happy heart" thing's just pre-formed language, you know it.'

'Maybe, but impossible to erase.'

Notwithstanding ambivalence around Anne Elliot and Fanny Price – would they, wouldn't they accept Another? – Jane Austen doesn't propose a second attachment for Annie. Courting men of a certain age – and, despite Marianne Dashwood's sixteen-year-old perception, this isn't thirty-five – don't always explain their ailments, their hernias, goitres and prostates, their fear of an empty kitchen.

'Oh well,' says Fran, 'borrow skates and scoot along.'

She speaks quickly to avoid being ventriloquized by Jane Austen who's urging patience and hope: how much may a few months do?

'Imagine cooking and eating it on toast.'

Fran spies an olive-coloured young woman talking excitedly to two girls. She wears tight jeans and bright white trainers, a red sweater slung over one shoulder below a long head and slanted neck. Fran imagines her in shiny silver high heels and gold Beauty-Queen swimsuit (pre-1970), then berates herself for so banal an image. Two young men stop by as the girls saunter off. The olive woman keeps talking, gesticulating with long-fingered hands, then throws back her head of stiff massed hair in merriment.

Annie follows Fran's eyes. 'It's Tamsin,' she says, waving. With qualifications in diasporic, post-colonial and global literature, she's become Annie's (temporary) colleague in both Department and College. She swims in warm intellectual waters in a way impossible for the soon-to-be-pensioned-off.

Always so.

Fran frowns as Tamsin strolls over. Lovely, she thinks but 'pert', a word fallen from currency, along with 'forthright'.

'You two look like a literary graveyard,' chuckles the young woman, swinging her slim legs over a bench to the side of Fran and Annie.

Fran whispers loudly to Annie, 'She's thinking we've been locked out of life.'

'Do you know what Tamsin once said?' Annie gives her a teasing smile. '"I don't want to be old. I couldn't bear it."'

Surely Annie must have taken this as a compliment? Though a handsome face makes insolence charming.

The long neck and heavy black hair remind Fran of an elegant praying mantis or a dark bewigged flamingo. 'You want to be just as you are all your life?' she asks. 'I'm Fran by the way.'

'Well yes,' says Tamsin. 'I'm Tamsin by the way.'

'And you wouldn't be you if you had a wrinkly face and drooping eyelids?'

'Not really.'

'If you were like us?' pursues Fran.

'Oh,' says Tamsin.

Fran smiles to see she's not retreating.

Then Tamsin says – as if studying a talking bear, thinks Fran – 'What's it like being old? I guess your minds are firmed.'

'We don't know,' says Annie quickly, seeing the question directed at Fran. She recalls the encounter in the Three Geese. 'No one does. Do sit down Tamsin. I'll get you a drink. Coke?'

While Annie's away, Fran studies her companion. The startling eyes move up, down and sideways, cinema-celebrity-wise. Are they dark brown or hazel? Green lights glint like marbles. Gauzy white sleeves invade the hands when her prehensile fingers gesture down. Something hippy, something dippy, something Pre-Raphaelite. Fran wishes she'd had a daughter, been the mother of this young woman. As well as of dear Johnnie, not instead.

Rachel interrupts the silence. She takes the last free stool, smiling her easy smile. 'Hi,' she says. Fran grins back. Rachel pulls out her mobile phone, deletes a couple of texts, then gets up to seek Annie at the bar. Fran urges herself to speak before Tamsin finds the phone for which she's rooting in her canvas bag. 'What are you working on?'

'My PhD was on ecofeminist criticism using BAME writers. I'm like getting it ready for publication while doing new stuff.'

Fran has an image of Tamsin – truly a very pretty girl – crawling in the long grass by a swift river's edge searching for dark crawling words in the undergrowth.

'Is there much call for it?'

Tamsin laughs. 'For apocalypse, the eco end-time? Absolutely. I've taken a creative-writing course. I'm aiming for a wider market.'

'Wider than?'

Tamsin smirks but doesn't answer. She takes out her cigarettes. 'Do you mind?'

Fran does mind but says no. 'Not so many people smoke

nowadays. Just about everyone who wanted to appear arty or intellectual did when I was young.'

'It's literary homage to Zora Neale Hurston,' grins Tamsin.

Annie returns with Rachel. Fran likes Rachel, though Rachel's unsure what to make of this provincial friend of clever Annie's; as a result, she's cautious. Annie carries a small tin tray of coke, beer and two more gins – Fran hopes they're singles.

Tamsin and Rachel chat about creative-writing courses. Annie checks her irritation. The effort amuses Fran, for even she can tell the future's with Rachel's trade, not the Enlightenment Prose Annie peddles to dwindling students. From retirement, she feels benign towards changes passing her by like an empty train viewed from the stillness of a country platform.

Not radical changes, actually: in 1891 *New Grub Street* described the *industry* of literature, the networking, marketing and dumbing-down needed for success. One character understood the modern reader's diminishing attention: it can't be held beyond two inches (they speak of space, we of time, but the point's the same). He proposes to teach novel-writing in ten lessons.

'Self-expression stinks,' says Annie, intending to provoke with her hobbyhorse. She waves her Gauloises in the air.

That year in France has much to answer for, thinks Fran as the heavy smoke assaults her lungs.

'Sure, if we tried to write ourselves,' says Rachel. 'We write from, not of, ourselves.'

'I suppose people express memories to expel them.'

'Can't see that working,' says Fran. 'Memories go underground. If you pull them up directly, you leave bits inside.'

'Oh, man,' laughs Tamsin swirling her tongue round the top of her empty glass. 'You sound like you speak from experience.'

'Ignore her,' laughs Annie, 'she lives alone. She's obsessed with . . .' Fran's heart leaps towards her mouth – subsiding as

Annie concludes, 'a peasant woman from Siberia called Agafia. She exists totally isolate. Or rather she now, I suspect, lodges with Fran though she doesn't know it, the peasant that is.'

'I quite enjoy reading people's lives,' says Tamsin, 'though many are, like, so totally predictable.'

Annie turns to Fran. 'Remember Geraldine, the waiflike woman who works on Anglo-Saxon cooking and looks like a Kate Greenaway child? – she says her imaginary friend's the Queen. The Queen! She visualises HM in different hats, her stony not smiley face, large empty handbag dangling.'

'Was she serious?' asks Fran.

'Dunno, guess you could do worse. The image might be calming – if you ignore the dreadful family.'

'No one's immune to fantasy friends,' says Rachel gulping her beer. She feels hearty beside these gin- and coke-drinkers.

Annie stubs out her cigarette. One fewer pollutant. 'To answer your question, Tamsin, about what old age feels like, since I'm the only one here with experience – though experience is much despised – I should say the transition from youth to age doesn't happen. The early self-image sticks around however pushy the new one. You forget you're old. Clear mirrors feel like someone else's photos.' She pauses, then adds, 'I think old age is being open, not firmed, mind still on fire, less roaring perhaps.'

'You're like saying you distance yourself from old age and stay twenty-three?'

Before she can mention the body's debility preventing such manoeuvre, Fran senses rising damp from the wooden stool. It adds to the discomfort of the smoky air. She should carry a cushion for separating her buttocks from the world.

Jane Austen pops over to claim the elderly thought. One of my most sensible but underwritten characters warned her daughter of physical not emotional hazards. Wrap up around the throat when leaving a public place, Mrs Morland tells Catherine en route to wicked Bath. Who could counsel better?

Mum warned never to show the top of one's arms or neck. Even a turkey is improved by a silk polka-dot scarf, Fran returns.

Thomas Ashe strolls along carrying a pint of Old Speckled Hen in a tall glass. He stops by Annie, smiles, then glances at Tamsin. 'I like the lad,' Annie'd said. 'Maybe a bit conceited. He's married an elegant Indian of such fertility – though that was his fault too – in so many years they've had three infants.'

'May I?' Thomas nods, then sits on the bench next to Tamsin. He looks round her to greet Rachel whom he courts. He thinks she might have influence in American universities when he needs, as he surely will, to join one for fame and fortune.

Fran gazes at Thomas. Here it is: that moment when the stranger enters the slumbering place and the plot begins – or at least a little mental snap and crackling.

Something to remember, like the first meeting with Annie on the park bench in Christ's Pieces when the public toilets were locked.

Sebald in Southwold.

Shelley spying Mary Godwin in Skinner Street.

Darcy snubbing Lizzie Bennet in Meryton.

5

If there's a young person in possession of some learning who doesn't want to display himself, Jane Austen mutters in Fran's ear, I do not wish to know him.

Tamsin is in love. Had Fran entered her head just then, she'd have told her what being old is like. Not the lightning fall into love – or lust – but its almost simultaneous flickering.

Thomas glances round, then catches Annie's encouraging smile.

'We're discussing self-expression,' she says.

'I'm interested in looking from outside,' Thomas announces. 'Seeing beyond your own body and mind was what Shelley . . .'

'A Shelley-free day,' interrupts Annie, 'but go on.'

'Well, it's a human urge not just to express yourself but to see the self from somewhere else, almost as someone else. OK, forget Shelley, but Milton, Kant . . .'

'Kant-free day,' giggles Tamsin. 'Kant was a white suprema-cist.' Her deep-hazel eyes fix sideways on Thomas. She moves her glass as if sloshing coke, though none is left.

Rachel's sorry to lose Shelley. Appallingly self-involved – aren't geniuses always so? But she likes his multi-coloured visions, his foiled yearning for community. Most of the time she hides her liking beneath interest in Mary, whose novels, including cried-up *Frankenstein*, leave her stone cold. Cultural fashion's tyrannical.

On the fringe of the Academy, Fran need neither follow fashion nor address the squalors of the past. But Shelley (Percy, that is) hasn't lately figured in her mind – any more than Kant. 'Are you describing integrated knowledge, Thomas?' she asks.

Surprised, he turns to her, 'Yeah. People pay it lip service.' Seeing empty glasses, he knows he should buy a round, but his mind is cantering. Besides, the act could appear too masculine. 'All knowledge was once connected. Now we use "interdisciplin-ary" as a magic word. Shelley's "familiar" . . .'

'There,' laughs Annie, 'You can't do it. Shelley's your King Charles's head.'

Does she judge her handsome protégé a bit of a windbag

and seek to save him? Or is this interchange a little maternally inflected flirtation?

Eager to get her rump off the damp stool, her lungs from the fug, Fran must leave – but not before contributing. 'It sounds like a cabbage.'

'What?'

'Cabbage, pieces of cloth left over after making up suits. They were purloined by tailors, so tailors were nicknamed "cabbages". To "cabbage" is to pilfer. You can steal or pirate bits of work and thoughts from anywhere. "Interdisciplinarity", yes?'

Tamsin removes her eyes from Thomas – so svelte and delectable, must be gay – bi? pan, she hopes. 'You get it in *Mrs Dalloway*,' she says, 'Toni Morrison.'

'They know these things by instinct in my creative-writing classes,' remarks Rachel.

Annie bites her lip. Her glass being empty, she can't hide the moment with a gulp. She can light another Gauloises, though.

Momentarily forgetting her intention to leave, Fran jumps in, offering what only Annie will find amusing: 'I wonder would Jane Austen be employed to teach creative writing? She's the mother of the snappy opening.'

'Oh, they've all learnt that,' chuckles Rachel. 'Everyone does brilliant first five pages. Prize judges have to be grabbed by the throat or balls.'

Jane Austen smiles, knowing her best-selling rival Walter Scott would never have made a 'Long List', in fact been unpublishable. My openings are excellent. Perhaps *Sense and Sensibility* might be . . .

The damp stool reasserts itself. Fran stands up stiffly.

Thomas unfolds his legs from the bench and grabs his empty beer glass. 'I have to go too, sorry.' He smiles around, noticing for the first time the amazing vividness of Tamsin's gold-brown eyes and bronze skin.

Fran walks towards the market square with Thomas. Years of teaching dozy students have trained her to listen and not listen – as well as talk too much given an opening.

'I guess I *do* like Shelley's vision of a world that's equal, unclassed, tribeless, and nationless,' remarks Thomas, pleased to have even this antiquated audience.

Tribeless, nationless, pooh! Your Shelley reminds me of shallow Frank Churchill in my *Emma* – tired of England before knowing it. Affection begins with one dear spot, a little platoon of family, then circles out to one's country.

'Mmm,' says Fran, 'a bracing idea. There's a woman in Siberia, Agafia . . .'

Before she can continue, Thomas's mobile phone rings from a pocket in his orange satchel. 'Yes,' he says, 'yes, all good. I'll call you right back. Love you too.'

Though the phone's held near his ear, Fran makes out sharp infant cries and chords of a Mahler symphony.

'Annie tells me you have children.'

'Yes, three girls. Two are twins, not identical but very alike. My wife dresses them the same.'

Poor animal, murmurs Jane Austen. Child-bearing is merciless.

'How lovely,' says Fran, wondering why, with little ones and a job in London, Thomas is in Cambridge.

He excuses himself and goes to untie his bicycle from the railings of a nearby church that explicitly forbids attaching bikes.

What a handsome man, admires Jane Austen, as a young man ought to be if he possibly can. A little formal, a little priggish, perhaps too thin in the lip.

Fran shakes her head. A passer-by assumes she's disrespecting the flowered straw hat she'd worried about wearing; she harrumphs, her face turned towards one of the many windows displaying tourist trinkets.

Still dawdling, Fran encounters Rachel by a flower stall. She's buying sweet-smelling freesias. 'I'm a Shelley devotee too,' confides Rachel, chuckling, 'it's great to find him the icon of the day. We can't avoid him with Annie's Thomas.' She pauses, then continues. 'Tell me about Annie. I like her very much, something magnetic, I think. But, beyond seeing her bitterness at her break-up, I don't know much of her life. She quizzes *me* but gives away little. You are, she's said, an old friend.'

'Old yes, certainly old.'

This harping on age irritates Rachel, but she smiles encouragingly.

'She's what you see. Clever, moody, with guts, without modesty. She's the daughter of a dominating, critical father and an adoring mother, a potent combination I'd say. Zach Klein was big in Sociology, a Marxist, and sucker for adulation. Probably at the root of Annie's failed marriage.'

Oh the inelegancy of summing up a complex friend in simple, fictional terms! But on she goes.

I interrogate even the most innocent adjective, remarks Jane Austen.

'Annie's brighter and more successful than Paul was – is – and she put him down in public. Thought him as impervious as she'd like to have been with her dad. I guess she chose him because he didn't dominate, then felt short-changed he wasn't successful like Zach, not so sharp – or cruel perhaps. Look, I'm just doing cod psychology.' Fran should really stop. 'Paul called her laptop her fetish – she used it even under the duvet in the shared bed. Though maybe she told me this to make herself seem at fault. Better than being a total victim, isn't it?'

Standing tall against the sun, Rachel murmurs, 'Yeah.'

'Paul failed to finish a book over many years, did bits of part-time teaching and not much childcare. He used to sit outside cafés reading, sipping coffee, smoking cigars, looking interesting and needy. A young woman with a "happy heart" responded.'

'What?'

'Something Annie said.'

Fran's thankful Jane Austen has wandered off.

'Has it happened to you?'

Surprised, Rachel replies, 'Not really. I had a long-term boyfriend and then some.' She shrugs and falls silent.

Whimperings, moanings, eyes cried out on the carpet. Goodness! How one debases oneself at such times. An old, old story, a shingle beach not stonier, migraine not more searing. Fran grows sad. 'I guess men always think they can go cleanly. Demand dignity in a whirlpool! Annie has pride, it's carried her through. She's wonderful,' she adds knowing enthusiasm overdue. 'She'll be more splendid without Paul. One day.'

Rachel blushes for Fran and says, 'Yes. I'm sure she'll soon be in a good place, if she isn't already.'

A cliché too far.

On her way home to Saxtham on Friday evening, Fran might stop to buy a Chelsea bun, its sweet perfume breathing into the car's air.

You know how interesting the purchase of a sponge cake is to me, smiles Jane Austen. I never underestimate the importance of syllabubs and jelly.

The bun signifies weekend: next day Fran may walk with a friend or see a film, though she dislikes getting home late – or be alone. But aloneness isn't the mode round Annie. Does she ever travel with the poet Elizabeth Bishop towards solitude, 'the wide, quiet plane with different lights in the sky and different, more secret sounds'? Here in Cambridge they chatter and click in libraries and coffee bars as if silence were a corrosive disease: meeting, greeting, leaving and meeting again, on and on.

Don't be such a curmudgeon, mutters Jane Austen.

'Come visit my place,' Rachel says to Fran, who's made jokes about her septic tank and crooked stairways. 'This evening?'

Their eyes make contact. Oculesics, thinks Fran. Rachel looks down and smiles. 'Must get off before my flowers wilt.'

6

Entering the house, Fran and Annie embrace Rachel in the way now common between women. Fran worries how many times to offer a cheek. Over her shoulder she notes Rachel's appraising eye on Annie's clashing orange, red and blue blouse beneath the shiny black jacket and jaunty canvas hat. To Fran it's all Annie.

Sensing her appraisal intercepted, Rachel says, 'You know, I once wrote a piece for the *New York Times* on costume, the way it gives us our sense of our bodies. It controls how we move and relate to the world.'

'Was it about sex?' asks Annie. She has no problem with Rachel's attitude to her style.

'Sort of. Dress makes people.'

Fran rolls her eyes.

'Nothing's natural. The wearer provoking a sexy response feels the whale bones cupping her breasts, making them nestle so prettily in satin pouches instead of flopping free. Like using the skinny bikini to frame bare flesh. Structure to keep the mind on its toes. Everything talks: scarf, gaudy shirt, thong underwear, jump suit, everything.' Rachel finishes with a grin.

Fran looks towards Jane Austen, expecting a quiet sneer. She's disappointed.

None of my characters goes naked. I never thought dress a frivolous distinction.

Oh fine!

Rachel judges Fran unassuming and prickly, an awkward combination, not uncommon in England. 'I'll show you round when we've had a drink,' she says from behind the counter in the open-plan living space. She's expertly opening the Veuve Clicquot so that its cork does not, as with unpractised Fran, fly off through a window or into the fireplace. 'I've never lived anywhere like it. Sort of a doll's house. Guys in Manhattan do amazing things with fractions of a loft but, Jesus! this beats everything. I guess it's the steep house prices.'

'Yup,' says Annie. She's lavished time and money on her artisan terraced home which would, in a cheap unemployed town, have collapsed or been bulldozed. Here it's prized for old iron fireplaces and industrial mouldings. The high value will enrich the Rat when she buys him out.

'You can't nail bookshelves to wattle walls without pulling the whole place down,' Fran remarks.

'Something magical about this secret life of houses,' Rachel's saying, 'closets turn into bedrooms, cubicles studies. There's a restroom under the stairs, really a broom cupboard, awesome? My neighbour's house is a shoe box till you go towards the kitchen. Then it flaps open like an origami flower. When I moved in here, the wife's sister-in-law showed me the wonders like a little girl displaying her toys. So cute.'

The champagne arrives in tinted flutes. Feeling a bubbly contentment after gulping it down, Fran twirls the slender stem. She gets up and walks towards the window by the vase of freesias. It looks onto a small formal garden of box hedges and white gravel.

'A gardener from Harley College fixes it once a week, back and front, just a few square inches.' Rachel laughs.

Small but labour-intensive thinks Fran. 'A bit feudal.'

Why are they talking houses? wonders Annie. Are they going through a phase? Like thirty years back when you worried whether to buy and then produce kids. Should you, shouldn't you? When? Why?

As she and Annie stroll home, Annie remarks, 'You overdid it. Saying the place was "exquisite".'

'I adopted the word from that excruciating dinner at your College. You think it a word above my station?'

'Well, you excelled yourself,' Annie chuckles. 'You talked about a bathroom in the clouds.'

'I try to please.'

'At least you didn't indulge your overwhelming need to offend. I've seen you do that here.' Annie grins and squeezes her arm.

Fran likes the remark, it makes social failure intentional. As it usually is, in a way, though, when it happens, it doesn't stop her wanting to send a mitigating postcard next morning alerting the recipient to what she – usually she – has long forgotten.

The anxieties of common life, says Jane Austen.

Fran and Annie walk along uneven pavements. Dug up for pipes and wires, to Fran they resemble rutted country paths; she stumbles once or twice before settling her eyes on her feet.

A bullet bicycle whizzes past. Annie hardly registers it. Death, thinks Fran, ridden into darkness.

'Rachel's borrowing the house,' Annie says. 'The owner's English, teaches in Princeton.' She pauses, Fran keeps her eyes down. 'I know you think everyone round here's privileged. Some are, but most are like me.'

Fran represses a grin. A father with best-selling books on Nazis and Weimar, lead articles in every American intellectual periodical, which prized his assured Jewish-English voice – still

Zach Klein hadn't provided his metropolitan-raised, privately educated children with 'privilege'? Really, thinks Fran, really!

'Nice,' she says, 'Rachel's nice.'

In theory Annie wants her friends to like each other. A slight chill touches her when they do.

She's invited Rachel for dinner at the weekend. It consists of French hare-and-orange paté from the fancy delicatessen in the Row, pasta Venetian style, salad of green beans, feta cheese, olives and avocado with strawberry dressing, and dessert of French-pear tart with Chantilly cream. Mostly pre-prepared and easy to serve.

Fran thinks back to the pheasant and parsnips in the cottage, the mound of greasy washing-up. If she ever entertains again, she must remember this expensive, effortless menu. Just end with a choice of Fourme d'Ambert and goat's cheese, plus a platter of colour-coded fruit.

Fruit, says Jane Austen, is the very thing on hats. Strawberries, grapes, cherries, plums, apricots, greengages; almonds, raisins and tamarinds might also . . . her words trail off.

Flowers are very much worn, Fran mutters back as Rachel arrives bearing a bunch of peonies.

'I know that recipe,' she exclaims. 'I smell onions, capers and balsamic vinegar. Italy.'

'Sultanas, pine nuts and spinach too,' Annie sings out.

Fran smiles: how little it takes to cheer Annie when she forgets the Rat!

The disposition to be comforted . . . begins Jane Austen.

Annie loves preparing food, relishing the sense of trans-itory control. Then in the last stages she grows anxious. Is she haunted by Virginia Woolf's Mrs Ramsay and her *boeuf en daube* or Sadie, who never quite pleased Zach when entertaining his Marxist chums in the too grand dining-room in Chalcot Square?

Cooking's the youth of the dish, she thinks, the eating its staid middle period, seconds its insipid old age.

Fran hasn't registered a fourth place-setting, so she's surprised when Thomas arrives just as the three women are about to sit down. While he goes to the kitchen to deposit his bottle of wine, Annie whispers, 'He's on his own here. Family's in London.'

To her surprise, Fran feels disapproving.

Perhaps this single male presence keeps talk general. Thomas deploys the word 'feminism' as if delicately saying 'fuck' or 'cunt', unable to stop himself but eager never to offend.

'We're Second Wave,' says Fran, 'you know, give us a job, abortions, equal pay. Hairy legs and no lipstick, aggressive like men, all very heady.'

Annie smiles on her friend. 'Fran's still riding the Wave on her little skateboard.'

'Why not? There's residue from any revolution.'

'There always will be,' says Thomas grinning, 'until we get a non-binary, ungendered society.' He turns to Rachel, 'Have you read Shelley on Charlotte Corday? No, well, she was attacked as unfeminine for her murder of bloodthirsty Marat. The autopsy pronounced her a virgin, so she couldn't be a whore; the revolutionaries charged her with failing in feminine sensibility. Shelley understood her violence was natural.'

Annie swivels her eyes to Rachel, who smiles at Thomas.

'He makes Charlotte Corday a whole human being, you see, ungendered.'

Fortunately, Jane Austen is absent, or Fran would have had to interrupt this tosh. What is 'a woman' in or out of the 'great glazed tank of art'?

'Olympe de Gouges, author of *The Declaration of Women's Rights*, also had her private parts inspected before her head was detached.'

Annie's busy urging second helpings of pasta and worrying that the *tarte bourdaloue* is too small for the company.

The talk disturbs Rachel. All men want to kill a woman in fact or fantasy. To quash the thought, she says, 'Shelley seems to think anything densely emotional is good. To me, violence in art exists to entertain. True in life, sometimes.'

'I suppose,' says Fran, evading Rachel's disturbance – 'the most violent act is death. Since there's so much talk now about life-affirming, do you think there might be death-affirming? It's a pretty majestic thing.'

Thomas turns to her, 'No, I don't. Children make the difference between thinking of life or death.'

'If it weren't for children, I'd be dancing,' says Rachel.

This makes no sense to Fran: is the tone bleak or genial?

'Parenthood isn't always life-affirming,' says Annie. 'Mothers force clitoridectomy and stunted feet on kids, African men push their infants away so they can suckle the women's full breasts.'

'Daughtering can be cruel too,' says Fran.

Not my subject, intrudes Jane Austen. I preferred the cool love of sisters.

Shush, says Fran, not everyone thinks it was cool.

'You can't be good enough at life, at anything, without loving,' says Rachel, throwing off her mood.

'Even mothering?' asks Fran.

'Sometimes I think I've married, procreated, thought, published, everything, all through its power,' says Thomas looking into his empty glass.

Annie reaches for the opened bottle and pours him more red wine.

Seeking to expunge the self-reference, Thomas says, 'Cultural psychology, nothing personal.' He shrugs.

Annie's relieved that his formality inhibits more candour. Once Thomas admitted to churning inside through long complicated Indian meals and the bustle of family togetherness till his senses dulled. Yet he loves his slender, nervous wife – he just wishes he could always be loyal.

A disconcerting thought strikes Annie: Thomas would have got on well with Zach – they could have lectured alternately. She pats away the idea. 'Shelley,' she says, 'sloughed off one unit of mother and babes to take on another. He was a gentleman, not a bourgeois. Not lowly enough to feel the imposition and demands of family.'

Even the surface of family life is worth preserving, says Jane Austen so loudly Fran winces in case the others have heard. But, of course, I was middle class. Also I had a wide sense of family, not for me the pinching unit of mother and child.

Thomas looks at Annie in surprise; he's proprietorial about his poet. Fortunately, he has anecdotes prepared for sticky moments with his elders. 'My friend Humphrey is writing a biography of the hard-boiled egg,' he begins. 'My father worked briefly in Ghana helping set up an agricultural institute. He said the hard-boiled egg in the pot was given to the honoured guest.'

Rachel, whose helpless mother declared when her daughter moved in with her first boyfriend in Greenwich Village, 'But you can't boil an egg, darling,' says, 'Go on Thomas. We love anecdotes.'

'In long German recitals, audiences ate hardboiled eggs, you had to wade through eggshells to get out of the church.'

At Mansfield Park, Henry Crawford left eggshells on his plate, but Fanny cared only for the pork bones on her brother's.

'Quilp,' says Annie, 'in *The Old Curiosity Shop* eats hard-boiled eggs including the shells. He also scoffs gigantic prawns with heads and tails.'

'Jeeves and the Hard-Boiled Egg?'

'In the US,' says Rachel, 'hard-boiled used to mean someone who won't give money to anyone for anything, no way.'

'The sun's a flaming egg yolk.'

'Go to work on an egg.'

'Enough,' says Thomas. 'I've delighted you all long enough.'

Jane Austen pulls herself up at that. No one should delight but herself and her Bennet girls.

'We haven't even considered the hard-boiled egg as missile, the egg-and-spoon race, egg on the face,' adds Fran. 'I went with Andrew' – the name slips out but no one arrests it – 'to the American Embassy to protest against the Vietnam War. A policeman searching for weapons on the bus confiscated our lunch eggs. I've told this story so often it's got under my skin.'

'Egg under the skin,' smiles Rachel, 'might incubate in the warm.'

'Making an angel. No, a feathery woman.'

'They say you can hear the baby turkey squealing inside the egg.'

'The Japanese or Chinese wash their hair with raw egg.'

'Really,' says Fran, always on the lookout for thrifty hints, 'doesn't it scramble in hot water?'

'I dare say you're unaware,' Rachel addresses Fran, 'an Easter egg's a hidden message or joke in software or computer games.'

'Yup,' says Annie. She gets up to take out the empty tart plate and arrange her expensive cheeses and guava jelly.

While she's away, Fran, having shaken off the slight melancholy that usually follows wine, asks, 'If you were a bird what would it be? I'm an only child, you know, the deep, dark and pitiful thing. I'd have to be a magpie.'

'I'd be a crow,' says Annie, returning with her painted board of cheese and jelly.

'You're right,' says, Fran warmly, 'sleek, choleric and clever.'

Annie laughs, 'Scavenging too.'

'A coot,' says Rachel, 'that's me.' She pauses. 'They bob

45

around.' She smiles, turning to each, adding as afterthought, 'They carry their babies on their back.' She squashes a piece of cheese into some guava jelly, then pops them both into her mouth. 'Yum.'

Thomas says, 'Maybe our chatter sounds to birds like their "singing" does to us, just pulsating sound. No evidence they sit around listening to humans.'

'Some birds must, so they can imitate. Mocking-birds mimic car alarms, telephone rings, squeaking gates. Lyrebirds do camera shutters. Makes a change from same old tweet-tweet.'

Suddenly Thomas announces, 'I think I'm a swan.'

The women burst out laughing. 'That's modest,' says Annie. She glances at his splendid person and thinks, Fair enough.

He means he has a family and must believe in monogamy and shared duties. Like swans, supposedly. After Annie's response, he can't explain without appearing earnest. He cuts off a square of guava jelly, forgets to eat it, and says, 'Birds are like the sky, a sort of empty page.'

'None of us chose a cuckoo or vulture, a bird with a distinctive home life,' says Fran. Aware she started the whimsical thread, she asks, 'Do you think we're like people in that show we used to watch, remember Annie? *Bremner, Bird and Fortune*. There was a dinner party where they said things like, "Which religion would you choose to be?" The Irish woman said she was a Catholic and very lapsed, but went to mass for the ritual – and fear for her immortal soul. I liked the man who wanted to be a Muslim so he could do a Fatwa on the person who miss-sold him a car. Aren't we a bit like that?'

''Course not,' says Annie, 'we're in Cambridge, that was Islington.'

'I watched it with my mother,' laughs Thomas. 'She shooed me out when some woman talked about a seven-hour vaginal douche.'

After coffee Thomas and Rachel leave together. Through the sitting-room window, Fran spies them lingering on the curb near where Thomas tied his bike. The talk is more than farewell pleasantries: he's inviting Rachel onto a possible trip to Wales.

Annie would leave the clearing-up till morning. 'I've got too much Mum in me,' says Fran. 'Can't do it.'

The kitchen cleaned, both tired and thirsty from alcohol, they delay going to bed. Annie scratches her neck, then removes the amber necklace that's been chafing her flesh. She places it on the coffee table as if still circling a neck.

'Did you notice Rachel's discreet diamond ear-rings?'

Fran smiles. She can't tell glass from gems. Maybe if she'd seen more of the latter . . .

'Let's have another coffee, this time from my beautiful machine.'

'OK, though I won't sleep. Won't anyway. Why not?'

Annie handles the shiny pods and begins to froth noisy milk. A cappuccino isn't correct after dinner, but now, surely . . . and such pleasure to make. Fran has no liking for the sudsy confection but enjoys Annie's pleasure in a new toy. Till she thinks about cleaning the elaborate parts.

'You know I met Thomas a few days back and he's interested in my Welsh project,' she says when Annie returns, foam sticking to her upper lip. 'It's not really a project.'

'You met Thomas? You didn't mention it.'

'I forgot. Something intervened,' lies Fran, who's kept the news for a mellow moment. 'He says he might like to go with me to Wales to see where young Shelley stayed – if I'm going anyway,' she limps.

Annie looks quizzical.

'If we did go – for Shelley – would you come?'

'Nah,' says Annie, 'I get spooked by a lot of greenness.'

7

I see myself caught in a reliquary, mutters Jane Austen, surrounded by polished carving.

Which part of you is in the casket? asks Fran. A bit of bone, a finger, a tooth?

Tongue, hand. It's a posthumous feeling: constricted as I am by peacock embellishments. Still, I know life and posterity are mere anterooms.

Mum had a horror of resurrection in either place.

A lapsed Baptist, Fran keeps other thoughts to herself. Jane Austen is a Believer like Agafia. Though nowadays the Church of England barely counts, it's still some distance from secular relativism. Did Jane Austen and Agafia ever doubt?

Once as a child Fran watched faith die, right before her eyes. The minister had a house, a car and a (small) flock from the chapel, all depending on belief in the pentecostal flame. In late middle age, how would he learn another trade? He went on preaching.

Had it really happened in so counter-damascene a way? Baptists love a drama: factor that in. Later, the minister was accused of 'backsliding'. Fran imagined him gliding on his rump down the slippery slope towards the lake of perdition, arms folded.

She doesn't often mention her lax sectarian past to Jane Austen. Despite a generous gesture towards evangelicals in a letter, the Author never cared for Nonconformists. At heart she was a traditionalist, a thoughtful, discerning, critical traditionalist.

Are no probabilities to be accepted, merely because they are not certainties?

What are Annie's inherited beliefs? Marx and (fallen) Uncle Joe rather than the Torah – is that the Jewish book? (Fran's embarrassingly ignorant) – were the deities of her world. They don't appear especially damaging. Annie complains of casual anti-Semitism. Fran's unconvinced. She can be acidic, too sure of her opinions though hedged with qualifiers – qualifiers, not doubts. She's not always endearing. She has useful acquaintances, few intimates.

Fran compares herself with her 'best friend'. (How girlish the term! Perhaps this too is a legacy of the only-child syndrome, the impossibility of dealing with more than one consciousness at a time. Contrary too: such friendship at the end, not the formative beginning of life.) She and Annie may be too judgemental, too apt to dismiss what doesn't conform to their standards. They might say with Elizabeth Bennet: there are few people in the world whom I really love, and still fewer of whom I think well.

Even as she slaps the quotation on them both, Fran finds it true only of Annie. She feels a rush of warmth from head to loins as she contemplates her friend's buoyant self-regard.

No damping down excitement about the proposed trip. Worry too. So long since Fran's been away in close company. Would Thomas and Rachel want her had they known Annie might refuse? But would they be going at all if she hadn't been encouraging? Shelley's time in Elan Valley was brief, the poems he wrote there aren't the masterpieces of his mature years. Yet Thomas likes this raw early stuff: it breathes of wild land and ideas.

No accounting, thinks Fran gratefully.

Thomas will travel to Wales in his roomy four-wheel drive – traded up with his father-in-law's money and insistence. The two women will go by train to Llandrindod: its station (according to Fran) left standing after Beeching's cull. Rachel has quality waterproof gear for feet and head and expects to be dry despite having, with initial disbelief, consulted the BBC weather for mid-Wales. She still hopes Annie will come.

'Annie's chickened out,' says Fran. 'She draws the line at hostelries without ensuites. She'll keep her mobile phone on. So,' she adds, 'you and I will take our first outing together. Our friendship has been quick.' She intends a compliment, then fears her words sound anxious. 'Thomas plans to join us in Rhayader. You two can burble on about Shelley. We'll see his house under the water. It'll interest him though he poohpoohs biography.'

Fran's smile makes Rachel uneasy: she's trying to humour me.

'We must be nice to him since he's young and keen. As for me, I want to see my homeland in company.'

'We've got a TV series called *Homeland*,' says Rachel. 'Fascist sort of term.'

This, thinks Fran, is the kind of verbal sloppiness Jane Austen would mock.

Your 'nice' is no improvement, hisses the Author. Recollect my Henry Tilney rebuking young Catherine Morland for precisely such use.

From Fran's expression, Rachel assumes she's embarrassed at revealing patriotism. They don't haul flags up their garden poles, but Brits mistakenly believe they cover their feelings in irony. Better the good old jamboree of 4th July with ticker-tape parades, cheerleaders and fireworks. Less sentimental.

'We'll go from Rhayader to Elan Valley,' says Fran. 'We can take notes to show we're not tourists.'

Fran visualises herself, Rachel and Thomas in his big car whizzing and honking like Toad in *The Wind in the Willows* down the narrow hill street travelling past the Rhayader workhouse, the chapels, the town clock, Dad's first shop, the rundown manse once inhabited by her grandfather, out to the wild places, to Elan and Claerwen valleys, everyone interested in the many facts she conveys, fascinated by her stories.

What really pulls her towards the unlikely trip? Blood memory, Percy Shelley, Andrew? All or none?

Some years back, calculating her pension after an especially unrewarding day filling in forms explaining – or pleading – to the masters of FE how her attention to *Great Expectations* might provide 'functional skills' for all levels of ability – she'd thought of upping stakes and finding a cottage near the drab little Welsh town. Being born in a place makes it magic: everyone knows it, even governments.

To live near Rhayader is the next best thing to settling on Vesuvius or Stromboli: if an ageing stone dam collapses, there'll be a deluge. Failing that, the town may quietly slide into the river.

'Who'd be looking?' asks Rachel

'What?'

'Who'd think us tourists?'

Fran pauses, having mislaid the remark. 'Other tourists I suppose.'

'You said the place was empty.'

Fran shrugs, preoccupied with the conundrum as to whether Jane Austen will be coming.

Brother Henry said she was 'enamoured' by William Gilpin and his ideas of picturesque beauty. Like the Lake District, Wales inspired this eighteenth-century guru. Sadly, the charming Henry lacked his genius sister's withering irony: on occasion, Gilpin and his rules are ridiculous.

Henry Tilney again – educating Catherine into ignoring the entire city of Bath while they practise the picturesque on Beechen Cliff. As a little girl, Jane composes 'Tour Through Wales'. Her sprightly heroine dashes through the principality noting very little – then hops home from Hereford.

Jane Austen may not come.

Fran visits the Cambridge Library to consult the *Radnorshire Transactions* for signs of Shelley in Elan Valley. Transfixed by the new layout, she stares through a high window on readers in the tearoom. She sees a girl in 1940s ginger ringlets holding her pale-blue phone with little hands that peek like ferrets from the sleeves of a weedy green jumper. At the same table under a corona of grey tangled hair, a man with squashed face sips coffee ruminatively. A fat girl with dark glasses and strands of wheat hair straying across her forehead sits alone. At a table by the wall an old man in a black suit brings his unspectacled eyes within inches of spidery notes. Swishing past him a confident

Chinese girl lets the door shut jerkily in the face of a monkish, flabby jawed man; he's unperturbed, used to rudeness. Round the water fountain the young congregate to meet and hydrate.

Fran's enjoying but not profiting from her 'research'. She's drawn aside by the 1948 issue of the *Radnorshire Transactions*, which laments that the 2/6 charged per copy nowhere near covers printing in post-war times. The county should decide on a coat of arms: might it include both the Welsh pre-Conquest hero, tenth-century Elystan Glodrhydd, ruling his tribe on this patch of land, as well as the Norman Mortimers?

Unlike Annie, Fran's unused to sitting without popping up to turn off a leaking tap, fiddle with a lamp or pinch up a fallen crumb. She fidgets.

Two mornings pass – largely wasted if Shelley's the goal and 'research' more than a mental exercise-bike. Excepting one mention, the *Transactions* are silent on the Poet in Elan Valley. She does however find material on the region's houses – dismaying Jane Austen, who correctly anticipates its use.

Down a side street Rachel and Fran meet in an upstairs coffee shop. They sit uncomfortably on wooden benches, Rachel's head almost touching the ceiling's slope. The coffee's no better and the toilets worse than in the mirrored café chains but, like many New Yorkers, Rachel believes in local business, however cramped. She waits politely.

Fran coughs and drums her fingers on the pad she used in the Library. It remains unopened on the table. 'We can hire a car in Llandrindod and drive to Rhayader. Thomas has to carry his family somewhere before coming on. Rhayader used to have a station. It was opened in 1864 nearby in Cwmdauddwr.' Rachel raises her sculptured eyebrows at the outlandish name but stays mum. 'The line took five years to build over moorland and swamp, then was closed in 1962. Dismantled in months.'

To Fran's relief, Rachel nods. Not because a railway line interests her, but she remembers Annie telling her that, though Fran has held teaching jobs, they'd not dampened a didactic urge. She's warned Rachel, and they've laughed. Didacticism's a no-no in creative writing.

As for Annie, she aims for the Johnsonian mode: teaching known truths in alluring manner.

We all fancy ourselves as teachers, whispers Jane Austen, but can only teach what's not worth knowing.

In for a penny, in for a pound, thinks Rachel in the local lingo. She's of a mood to humour all of them. She is, she thinks, starting to fall in love with this ludicrous uptight country, this overstuffed island quaintly called the United Kingdom. If this is unity, what's disarray?

'We could look round Llandrindod before going on?' Fran suggests nervously. 'Do you want to know about it?'

'How to get my tongue round the first syllable, I guess,' says Rachel.

'No need,' says Fran. 'It's anglicised.'

As Fran begins on the history of the chalybeate springs of Llandrindod, with details of the sulphur smell and the ailments cured, Rachel realises she should have drawn the line earlier. Fran is saying, 'William Gilpin wrote of the "sulphureous springs of Llanydrindod"; he didn't complain about the foul-egg taste.'

Jane Austen falls asleep. Rude considering that, despite mocking credulous cure-seekers in *Sanditon*, she herself took the waters at Cheltenham during her long process of dying. She opens one eye, There's an art to recording boring talk without boring your reader. Mrs Elton, Miss Bates, Sir Edward Denham of Sanditon. She re-closes the eye.

Fran hasn't listened.

Llandrindod-Wells, a mushroom town in the soft green grass of Wales, is not a million miles from speculative Sanditon.

Living in a literary fragment, however, Sanditon avoids the shabby fate of the real spa which millennium funds have not quite rescued. (With a habit of reading words awry, Fran had first seen 'millenarian' on the fading notice tacked to a broken glass pavilion: for an instant she'd thought that, yes, something like the apocalyptic prophetess Joanna Southcott or the celestial king Shiloh from her loins would miraculously put the town back square on the cure-all map.)

She falls silent, tasting in her mouth the sulphurous waters from the chained municipal cup Dad held out to her and Mum . . . she swishes her tongue over her upper teeth furred by coffee. 'I wrote to Melvyn Bragg's Radio 4 programme *In Our Time*,' she concludes, 'suggesting the topic of "chalybeate springs" to the producer. They could use German historians and chemists, and me – possibly. I had an acknowledgement.'

Rachel glances at Fran. What's her tone? And the unopened notepad? Does her new friend write or want to? Is this pad a hint? She recollects the list of Annie's qualities, including the incongruous 'lack of modesty'. Is Fran hampered by too much, so that she depends on encouragement she never quite demands? In one of her own short stories, a nervous Sarah Lawrence girl is reluctant to show . . . Rachel pulls herself back as the bill arrives.

They walk along Trinity Street, noting a new posh restaurant. A homeless man with bulging backpack twists unsteadily, belligerently sticking out his jaw and shouting curses from a little mouth nestling inside a dirty beard. He directs them to the low grey sky, perhaps smelling rain and knowing its ache. Circling in the same spot, he's a parody of the student backpacker. Fran approaches to speak. 'Gissa,' and 'Fuck off,' she thinks he says.

'Yeah, cool,' says Rachel. 'I wouldn't try to engage. We don't in New York. I wonder what could assuage his anger.'

'Defiling snobby colleges and heritage tea shops, setting the whole pile ablaze?'

'Would he be happy then?'

'Maybe. He'd have disrupted civic order. Enough?'

''Course not. What a fraud he'd be if anything was enough.'

8

Fran isn't leaving till after lunch but likes to anticipate. It takes her only a few minutes to grab her things from the gold Victorian hooks on the bedroom door and stuff them into her bag, longer to search repeatedly under pillows, in drawers and beside the taps in the bathroom. Despite such care, she often leaves something behind, a toothbrush, a comb, once a pair of knickers drying on a radiator. Angling for another invitation?

She's bought a second-hand copy of Shelley selections. She intends to study it before the trip, hoping to rekindle some of the adolescent enthusiasm she must once have had: there's a memory of reading aloud to Dad a poem about Euganean Hills, wherever they are. She doesn't recall much of Shelley's life except his fucking Mary Wollstonecraft's daughter on the St Pancras grave.

Annie's making a ham sandwich on sourdough for their last lunch, adding Provolone, rocket, parsley, thyme and a little onion. 'I can help you sort out and present the cottage,' she says suddenly. 'If you really want to sell.'

'Dunno. Country round Saxtham isn't desirable except to sugar-beet and turnip growers, so no rich person will want the place as second home. But I've come to like the flat land and huge sky. The trees tower against it: like hills, one *has* to look up,' she shrugs. 'Now I wonder if I'd find real hills crowding in. Even the Long Mynd, too claustrophobic perhaps. Where would we' – she pauses – 'where would I go?'

'Well you could come here. No hills.'

Fran imagines living on the edge (all she could afford) of this vain town with its abstracted cyclists, postcard centre and drab suburbs of semis and terraces – its Victoria Park, Victoria Crescent, Victoria Street, Victoria Road, Victoria Row. Funny the Empress of India escapes erasure while her imperial subjects are toppled and defaced. She visualises herself struggling to prise Annie away for a cup of companionable coffee. Annie will be busy with friends or old colleagues, while she, Fran, remains in the margins of lives. 'There's a kind of pull from where one grew up,' she says.

Annie carries in the plate of sandwiches. 'Well, London,' she shrugs, wondering what it feels like to be pulled by even less sophisticated places than Cambridge.

For Fran the smell of ham brings with it the great fresh honey-coated hams of her childhood: the grocery shop with its counter of crumbly Caerphilly, cured meat, dill pickle like frog's thighs, and that ham.

Why is she reticent about this warm and lovely place? Is it the common mockery of the grocer above other trades – Mrs Thatcher, a 'grocer's daughter' – a stain, the ultimate putdown, her predecessor mocked as 'Grocer Heath'. In *New Grub Street* an author is writing 'Mr Bailey. Grocer'. Contemplating this low hero, his friends fall about laughing. Imagine, the hero a grocer! 'Grocer' written on her application form to Cambridge which asked what your father did – never mind Mum in her trim clean overall, what exactly does your father do? And nowhere to write, not just any old grocer but a 'Master Grocer' who made the best honey-roast hams in Shropshire, in the country. She loved that man and wishes he would walk into the room so she could say so and no longer wince at his accent. Her eyes feel teary.

The secret of our emotions never lies in the bare object, but in its subtle relations to our own past: no wonder the secret escapes the unsympathizing observer.

Surprised, Fran sniffs back tears. Where'd you say that?

I didn't, says Jane Austen, I quote a successor. I do not write the lachrymose novel.

You've swum down the gutter of time? Or sauntered beside its flow.

Annie lets the quiet dawdle.

'I couldn't move here,' says Fran finally.

Catching her friend's thoughts, Annie responds, 'You're making too much of discrimination and disdain. I'm as out of touch as you with wokeness and no-platforming and all the stuff you've no doubt been reading. Fran, you don't have to be excluded unless you exclude yourself, here or anywhere else.'

How easy it is to be hoodwinked, remarks Jane Austen.

She's arranged to meet Thomas near the station. Since she's carrying her Cath Kidston bag, they've chosen a chain with wide doors. Fran usually boycotts such places because their toilets require a code: more than an inconvenience to the needy public. Now she's stopped working, she makes her own coffee with funnels, paper and hot water. Messy, wasteful and pleasing.

'Are you haunted by Shelley?' she asks over the coffee – and two croissants. She'd bought them to sop up the diuretic liquid before a train ride. Thomas doesn't eat buttery croissants, but he shreds his on the plate to be polite.

'I love his words, I guess.'

'But the man Shelley?'

'Well, he *is* wonderful. A kind of holy innocent, Akhnaten in Philip Glass's opera, asexual and sexual, neither exactly.'

'You mean he's not your type?' Cruder than she'd intended.

Thomas laughs, 'He's beyond me.'

'It's a long way to mid-Wales.' Fran worries Thomas might have cold feet. To prevent his saying so, she adds, 'Do you know the M6 toll road was built on two and a half million unsold copies of Mills and Boon books shredded and mixed with tarmac and asphalt.'

'Best thing for Mills and Boon.'

'Think of everyone riding over unseen, unread words.'

'I have a fast car.'

So, they *would* go. Fran gives a half-pleading, quarter-worried glance towards the café door. As it happens, Jane Austen is looking out, her ramrod back turned inwards. Bonnet ribbons gently flap in the draft created by each entrant. The air is warmish before rain, so it's no great matter. No one will catch cold.

She will want to stay behind, Fran supposes. What did Jane Austen understand of utopia or bliss in wild solitude? All families and shrubberies with her, nature in clothes.

As she walks across the new central space to the station dodging taxis, she remarks, you know your William Gilpin was in Elan Valley? He found the country growing mountainous and 'disproportioned' – too much mountain for too little water. Different now.

As you suppose, murmurs Jane Austen, I don't care for nature without method. Except the sea, the sea . . .

Fran's mind fills with the smooth hills round the swollen rivers of Elan and Claerwen. Agafia could have lived there. She'd have caught fish, trapped rabbits. There are always rabbits.

She stands on the platform of the ugly station. Rain begins, so she enters a waiting-room beside a coffee kiosk, choosing the seat closest to the window. Its table is littered with debris of plastic cups and chocolate wrappings. Inhaling the muggy air, she thinks how much healthier to sit outside and get wet. She stays in, listening to the acrimonious rain hitting the window. Raymond Briggs thanked God it fell on the roof, not on him. She smiles thinking of the old curmudgeon.

Water, wrote a Frenchman, is the key to understanding social progress. Whose is the water? Who owns the falling rain, the sodden clouds? It's a man thing, this urge to possess.

The capture of rain for great reservoirs, the enclosing of water – someone else's water if we talk possession – is the great sign of nineteenth-century progress, the modern world's biggest triumph in the age-old battle of man and nature. How, thinks Fran, will Thomas, Rachel and, improbably, Jane Austen, respond to the great reservoirs of Elan Valley, half nature, half human cruelty?

Think what we do to water: catch it, trap it, doctor it, dose it out of nature, squash it through filter beds and pipes, imprison it in tanks far from where it fell, expecting, as well it might, a quiet life of metamorphosis, a gentle sinking to earth. We humiliate it in sprinkling systems and 'features' by fishing gnomes or frilly plants; we fill baths, over and over, carting off the dirt and filth of humans who, despising its weakness, add fizz to posh bottles from fake springs. Water, a commodity, a demand, a money thing, a slave. How could it stand against all that irrepressible damming energy? Nothing like it in the world since Romans carved highways through Eurasia.

Fran almost misses her train, forgetting she must hurry over a footbridge to a new platform that wasn't there in her time.

Part Two

9

'Have I eaten Mary?' Percy Bysshe Shelley asks. Only the author of *Frankenstein* can answer him. (To Fran's – but not Rachel's – surprise, she's now the prime owner of the Shelley name.)

Thomas quotes the question because for him it expresses the joy of a young gifted pair becoming one entity. An antidote perhaps to whatever Fran, Rachel – and he? – will think of utopian communes in wet Wales. The unanswered question lodges in Fran's mind.

You never had a brother, Jane Austen reminds her. You missed learning early of male self-absorption.

Thomas motors along the A44 on the last lap of his journey, his expensive mountain bike fastened to a back-rack of his Land Rover Discovery. Escapist joy grips him like a second seatbelt. With a few hiccups – errors on his Sat-Nav, insouciant container lorries, slow elderly drivers propped on cushions – he's reached the B&B on the edge of Rhayader near midday. It's dismal and over-stuffed. He made the booking, so has no one else to blame. 'Some sort of show on, so nowhere much was free.'

'Imagine!' says Annie when she hears – Annie who thinks everywhere beyond London and Cambridge a desert. 'Something happening!'

The women arrive shortly after in a small hired Vauxhall. Fran is driving. She took over when Rachel, who's paid for the hire, swerved out of a side road into the righthand lane beside Doldowlod. Nobody was coming, but still.

Fran enters her bedroom, the smallest though each pays the same. Being first there, Thomas moved his backpack and holdall into the largest. Realising the imbalance as he helps the women up the stairs with their things, he offers to change places. Rachel and Fran refuse.

Following behind him, Fran again admires his fine physique, the tallness so important in civilised life – easier to find jobs and mates apparently. People like seeing the strong prey on the weak, all history shows it. Someone claimed a lion hunting a flock of sheep is more poetical than the sheep. Yet, don't we identify with the underdog?

She feels no envy for the strong and tall, has no desire to cross sex and be a man – though she might enjoy transitioning species: she'd do well as a woolly munching sheep, even hunted by lions. Since they bring on sleep, sheep must sleep serenely.

She unpacks her few things onto a side chair, hanging nothing in the elderly freestanding wardrobe. She's tired; she and Rachel have had to set out far too early. Dissatisfied as well – she's talked too much, feeding her companion indigestible facts and opinions.

Would Jane Austen inspire Austenolatry had she let Sir Thomas Bertram drone on about slavery in *Mansfield Park*? If he'd done so, he might have revealed what is most probable, that he was an ameliorist – like her father. An unacceptable position now we see the delicate negotiations of the past in the most lurid light.

Fran surveys herself in the mottled mirror on the inside of the wardrobe door. Who are you? she says. The mirror image smirks.

Though eccentric, the action improves on her habit of staring at Cassandra's crude sketch so fixedly that the aslant eyes swivel to catch hers. That really is naughty.

She grins, sensing that, despite her doubts, Jane Austen has come. She'll not have heard Fran's thoughts on slavery – or she'd certainly have mounted her high horse – and she'll probably not sit on the ground as at the seaside (letting her back be so thrillingly water-coloured by her sister). But you can be sure of nothing.

What are men to rocks and mountains? says Lizzie Bennet, heading for the barren Lake District. She's waylaid by the romantic plot, some strategy – and that luck. But she *might* have gone.

Do you go to a place or does the place come to you?

Jane Austen's busy climbing into the wardrobe ignoring its mirrored door. There are moments when Fran is defiantly angry with the Author and her free indirect manner. Such an easy way to watch others deceive themselves. For now, she simply feels deflated by this quick removal.

Until she thinks: Jane Austen, the Witch in the Wardrobe.

'I didn't really appreciate it was just a reservoir,' says Rachel as they meet for a night-cap, 'I sort of imagined a lake.'

Fran can't believe this. If Shelley's house is submerged, it couldn't have jumped into water and sunk, could it?

Still, Rachel's game for anything. As she says to Miranda back in New York before her signal dies, 'I kind of like it here. Could settle.' Miranda misses the pivotal remark since her seven-year-old son is squawking for full attention – as he always does if anyone tries to share it.

'*Just* a reservoir!' *Cofiwch Dryweryn*, remember Tryweryn in North Wales. A modest reservoir as reservoirs go, but it became a *cause célèbre*, the sign of high victimhood. Aren't we all vying for that?

Cofiwch Dryweryn scrawled on a boulder, vandalised – then, like baby dragons from buried teeth, springing up over rocks and walls.

Capel Celyn, the hamlet (only forty-eight souls and none dead) was drowned for Liverpool – we say 'drowned', not flooded, more emotive – was Welsh-speaking, and in the 1960s the dying of the Welsh language was a potent fear.

'The Welsh do victim in different voices,' said Annie to this news. She can make such remarks knowing that, for victimhood, Jews top everyone, even descendants of slaves.

The Hull poet Philip Larkin, who really might have been Welsh such a temperament he had in him, said deprivation is for me what daffodils were for Wordsworth.

'R.S. Thomas has a poem about it.'

'Who? About what?' asks Rachel, who's considering the different types of Cambridge houses on offer – if she were, just possibly, to relocate. She'd want more than an extended bijoux box.

'Reservoirs. He said reservoirs are the subconscious of a people.'

'Why not the London Tube?'

'He called their beauty a performance for strangers.'

'Sounds Luddite,' chuckles Rachel.

'He was a little OTT,' agrees Fran, 'he smelt putrefaction. The English were scavenging among the remains of our culture, he thought.'

'What an apocalyptic guy – must introduce him to Tamsin.'

'It gets worse. He wanted the English wiped out of Wales – imagine if he'd said Muslims or Blacks.'

'Don't let's,' says Rachel. 'You admire this guy, Fran?'

'Sort of. A misfit lauding a place not quite his. If you listen to him speaking on YouTube, you hear an upper-middle-class Englishman of the past century. He said he'd never have major-poet status because he lacked "love for human beings".'

Fran's glad Jane Austen is in the wardrobe. Loving everybody is hardly the hallmark of genius.

'Liverpool later apologised,' says Fran. 'It didn't return the water.'

Next morning, she proposes to walk the six miles to Elan Village with Rachel. Though she doesn't mention it, a purpose is to see her grandfather's grim stone manse – he so famed for the *hwyl* that his burial slab is marked 'powerful in prayer'. As she passes the house now, a shiver of relief runs through her that faith is derelict (mainly) and that she herself has never lived there.

As one black-stone, slate-roofed house succeeds another, Fran has misgivings about her pedestrian choice. Rachel strides ahead on those bright bouncy trainers Americans wear with every outfit. Such footwear will take her down byways and through any digressions. Fran's feet are already tiring. Why doesn't she have shoes like that? Young Johnnie near died of shame when she'd taken him into a shop thirty years back asking for 'plimsolls'. When did they become trainers?

Rachel's gear looks expensive – though Fran can't actually tell: could be Primark for all she knows. If so, is Rachel rich? The way she claimed that second-best room in the B&B – as a bit of curious slumming – suggests she might be.

The choice to walk wasn't only about memory. Last night Fran had been inhibited by sharing a toilet on the lower landing. Now she fears what John Betjeman calls 'compulsory constipation', that toll on the worried. Walking might be laxative.

A poor idea, she notes, when it does its work. At her leaving drinks in Norwich there'd been a round of tips for retirement. A sozzled colleague offered: 'Never trust a fart.' She grins recalling the advice – and the colleague, with whom she'd once had a post-drinks fumble. Lonesome cowboys farting over baked-bean cans, he'd laughed immoderately.

Just as well Rachel's off in front.

As they approach the reservoirs, the country stretches out like a much-washed Fair Isle jumper: green, purple and tawny, colours muted and smudged, edges fraying, lines between fields and patches vague and muffled; tussocks like pilling wool. Fran catches Rachel to share the image.

Rachel has never seen or worn a Fair Isle jumper in her life; she smiles at the quaint word 'jumper'. Then, intending to please, says 'magical' – a term rather new to her but part of her acclimatising. She looks at stunted thorn and bog cotton, notes tree roots dangling from rocks, water dripping from their hairs.

They make no effort at further chat as they trudge along together. The silence leaves Fran to consider how very unprepossessing Jane Austen must find Shelley. Or is she fascinated by the type – at least in her butterfly time? What *is* Mr Darcy in those early chapters?

They've had this argument, time and time again. (*You* made him the heartthrob with your films. My business is with girls.

Without him you'd be another George Eliot or Fanny Burney. Once you were little more than a high-brow niche interest.

No need to repeat the exchange: Jane Austen always has the edge.)

Thomas passes in his Land Rover, waves and goes on to their meeting place.

By the time they reach him he's unloaded his mountain bike and is dressed for serious moving – a bit of a peacock in his Lycra, yellow cape and normcore. He sits on the car seat, door open, tapping into his small laptop. Two sheep prod his shin, begging for biscuits and sandwich crusts.

'There's something moving and good in Shelley, whatever his errors with women,' he says.

'Is that what you're writing?'

'Some. I do a weekly blog.'

'Really. How?'

'Willpower.'

'You could mention Gilpin,' suggests Fran. 'He was here before the flooding.'

Thomas smiles, closes, then pushes his laptop under blankets on the car's backseat. Getting up, he smooths his fingers along the lines of his intricate bike. 'I'll meet you by the side of the first dam. Go in comfort.'

'Huggy hygge,' says Fran, mistaking its meaning.

I rarely mention a 'hug', remarks Jane Austen. 'Tis an ugly word. Mr Price gives a cordial hug to his daughter Fanny, home from Mansfield Park, then ignores her. From this you discern there's no enthusiasm and warmth in my hugs; so, despite my marketability in most aspects of life – as I'm told – my hugs cannot be commercialised.

'Love that you're here,' exclaims Fran.

'Of course,' says Rachel. She's touched by the warmth Fran's showing towards her.

10

Thomas returns glowing from exercise, rain or sweat on his forehead.

They're assembled. Time to hear of Shelley, the boy Percy when he was The Shelley, before feminism topsy-turvied everything. (No problem with the occasional flash forward in this plot – we know the ending.)

I made no apologies for intrusion in my own voice, remarks Jane Austen. One does not have to be inscrutable. Even an out-of-body narrator has a body, don't you know?

A snigger somewhere, probably from Rachel, who's aware how difficult it is to intrude information in dialogue and action. Clumsy in a short story. Yet she knows more of the nitty-gritty of Shelley's life than the others.

No problem, Annie would shrug, but couldn't you put it in a footnote?

Footnotes are seldom read except by those wishing to poach them.

Jane Austen is amused. I signed off with information, but only after I'd spun my masterly dialogues. I showed Mrs Bennet to be incorrigible before stating it.

So why do both? pouts Fran.

To avoid the possibility of narrative failure, explains the Author, quietly exasperated. Never underestimate the reader's inattention.

'Go on, Rachel,' says Fran.

Mary Wollstonecraft's daughter was not the first pretty sixteen-year-old he'd fancied. Like a vampire he hungered for young female blood, his thin tall white frame needing to be electrified – by spirit, he would say. Adrenalin, laudanum, girl children.

Thomas grins at the hyperbole. Something theatrical about Rachel.

He was born in Field Place in Horsham, Sussex, a snug mansion with no view, a soft and lovely womb blessed by the Established Church. Along with a coat of arms and nannies, what could be more secure? No wonder he sneers at good fortune, pretends in after years he has no family or home.

Like other little boys, he does nature, trapping moths, bats and spiders. In adolescence he thinks himself a farmer in wait-ing, knowing of land and chemicals in soil – how wrong is Elan Valley for his purpose! – but disliking dirt on his shoes and fine clothes. For he's a dandy though careless – needing his shooting jacket and dancing gloves.

At Eton he suffers, dumped from paradise into this camp of class and cruelty, though many testify he brawls with the best when in bad temper.

'Nothing like discomfort after comfort to spawn a poet,' interrupts Fran. She knows a raconteur needs applause.

But with a kindly tutor he reads of ideal worlds. He becomes enthralled by William Godwin, anarchist philosopher of utopia. He can't get enough of *Political Justice*. It preaches against all hierarchies – and marriage.

As Rachel pauses, Thomas walks a little way off waving his mobile phone in the air. As if divine rays might catch and enchant it or wind transform it into an aeolian harp tinkling podcasts and *Guardian* updates.

'I did warn you a signal was unlikely,' says Fran.

'You said it was erratic.'

'A fudge to get you here.'

He returns to the tale. 'Shelley's mind was already full of forests and precipices. He was preparing himself for wilder places than Southern England.'

'You mean earthly ones, I hope, Thomas.'

'Not really. He responds deeply to the physical world in all its stickiness, but he really longs for the immaterial, for pure air and water.'

'I guess we're all stuck in physical moments,' says Rachel.

'I wish I weren't,' moans Fran, taking out her handkerchief to wipe her drizzle-muted spectacles. Her fingers are coarsened by the mucousy liquid soap in the B&B, its coagulated content hanging from the spout: they itch, reminding her of childhood chilblains. She feels the pinching of her black lace-up shoes.

It's important, says Jane Austen, to be appropriately shod. Unless you think with William Cowper, one of my favourite poets,

> When Winter soaks the fields, and female feet,
> Too weak to struggle with tenacious clay,
> Or ford the rivulets, are best at home.

You'll remember Mrs John Knightley's shoes were too thin for the season and my Marianne Dashwood imprudently sat in wet footwear.

Rachel slopes off, a little irritated by Fran's interrupting. Thomas smiles, waiting for her to return. He shifts his feet and looks sideways at his taut calves. He's champing at the bit like a thoroughbred racehorse. The mist covers his way: soon he'll cycle again into nothing. He and Shelley.

If she ignores her friends, Fran could fancy herself back here visiting her Rhayader aunt for Christmas. Frost would mute the ground making tufts of marsh grass stand up like islands in a still lagoon. To a bookish child in the throes of puberty, mist seemed then like the miasma in *Dracula*, a malaria or plague moving silently – or shimmering a gentle blessing on the high fields. Shelley?

Puberty is slushy as well as confused.

She looks at Thomas. Old-fashioned in a way, but also greedy for experience. When Rachel comes back, she says, 'May I tell you both just one story. Mum told it me.'

Fran hasn't mentioned a mother before, just a grim granddad. Rachel's fictional ears perk up. Always aware this drably dressed woman is his admired Annie's close friend, Thomas swivels his eyes to show interest while jiggling one leg. The drizzle is turning to rain. It drips along Fran's nose, mingling with a little snot.

Up in the higher ground where the two valleys meet and the land is tussocky and ragged, there's a cairn of badly piled stones, the grave of Betty Pugh. Late in the last century – whoops, the nineteenth century– Betty was a young farm girl here. On an outing to the bright lights of Aberystwyth – Paris and London to these parts – she found her fresh cheeks and thick hair admired by a sailor. Seduction with promise of marriage was easy. The usual followed: she was pregnant, returned home and waited. Then despairing, she tried to drown herself in the river by Rhayader. She was rescued but, being a determined girl, she hanged herself in a cowshed. Parish churches wouldn't take a suicide, so she was buried where no one lived or worshipped, then given a cairn to warn girls or rebuke predators. In the late 1940s a romantic American, hearing the story, made a wooden cross for the cairn and, before he left, ordered a gravestone. The land was boggy, a stone would sink in. But in time a gravestone was erected with the words 'so sweet, so small'.

'So, they avoided the problem of the soggy bog?' asks Thomas.

'The grave was made of fibreglass. I wonder what words they mumbled over it.'

'They must have shouted loudly,' remarks Rachel. She's warm enough in her expensive fleece but isn't adapting to the bluster.

By now Thomas's ears are attuned to Shelleyan wind rustling somewhere in the newly planted firs behind them, it tugs at the spokes of his mountain bike. He moves his thighs as if riding on the spot.

'Such a lonely death,' says Fran. She wonders if she can mention Agafia in her tundra, watching her family die one by one.

Rachel unwraps a piece of chewing-gum; the story's generic, but Fran's naivety in narrating touches her. She supposes travellers have to tell tales and Fran comes across as a traveller despite the Norfolk cottage. The image pulls at Rachel: a girl buried with the child in her belly.

A mobile phone rings. Amazed to find Annie's voice, Fran pauses after exclaiming. The line goes dead. She swallows away a sudden bleakness. 'I could tell you about the old lead mines,' she says. 'You can still see mine shafts in places up the banks. The quarries seem to be biting the landscape with rotten teeth.'

'Maybe later,' says Rachel gently. 'We're here for Shelley.' She wishes she were more interested in miners and peasants; impossible to mix with English academics without being loudly left-wing. She tries, she really does.

'Mining and Romanticism aren't at odds. Remember Byron and his Newstead mines,' says Fran.

The pain of the quarries overwhelms her. The anguish below her feet, even in this beautiful place, the poor beasts, the boys and men poisoned into emphysema and fibrosis, forced into deforming labour by want and impotence – all for the comfort of a class to which Shelley – and yes even Jane Austen – belonged. She feels a stab of guilt for her mortgage-free cottage and pension. Always two nations, wherever you make the divide.

She clambers out of her rabbit hole.

The rain softens and moves off with a swish over the hills. The whole area could become a lake under this relentless water, thinks Rachel.

A chilling breeze follows the rain. With Thomas away on his cycle again, the two women head for the village café.

Standing outside with their mugs and looking towards the river, Rachel says, 'Time for the Groves, I guess.'

Without preamble.

Charlotte, daughter of Admiral Pilfold, marries Thomas Grove, gentleman; her sister marries Sir Timothy Shelley, son of Sir Bysshe, high sheriff of Radnorshire. As a second home – they have a gentler property in Wiltshire – Grove buys an Elan estate, builds the mansion of Cwm Elan and plans to improve the poor peaty ground. Like other landlords then and now, he hunts and fishes.

Back in the wardrobe in the shabby B&B, Jane Austen lets a comment susurrate along the road and over the hills to the little café: you are troubled by agricultural improvers, I see, like my Mr Knightley, enclosing land from selfishness or good practice. It depends on point of view.

Young Shelley makes boyish love to their daughter Harriet (sixteen), knowing nothing of her inner desire: marriage to a country mansion and fourteen children, as it happens. His impassioned suit, welcomed at first – they were as good as engaged, else why keep a lock of her hair in his diary? – ultimately fails to prosper. Some think this love the deepest of his life.

There's also a son, Tom, Percy's senior by some ten years, a self-important, rather formal lad – Thomas Ashe? The women exchange half-smiles – to whom his father gifts Cwm Elan. He's only twenty-one. Two years later, he brings home a wife, Henrietta; together the couple spend warm summer months in Elan. The poor lady's often ill.

Fran interrupts. How can Rachel speak of weather in Elan? The arrogance of biography. 'Even in August the deep valley can't have been good for a weak chest,' she says.

'Indeed.'

Spurned in love, Percy naturally longs to die. But, why,

without an audience? He finds comfort through his school-girl sisters, who've introduced him to a second, more malleable and younger Harriet. Aged fifteen, she's the daughter of an innkeeper, prosperous enough to send his child to a genteel boarding-school to mix with the granddaughters of baronets.

Not quite a grocer, but not much better.

Full of high utopian thoughts and scorn for families – and, theoretically, class (Rachel nods to Fran) – young Percy in Oxford is desperate to tweak the nose of father-surrogates. A boyhood prank – inquiring of clerics what God was, then publishing their muddled response – blows him out of the place.

'University College makes much of him now,' says Fran, 'it's always the way.'

Poor whiggish Sir Timothy is bemused by this child who thinks obedience a sin against the self.

Percy flees to his cousins in Elan. The mythologically inclined might argue that children get as far from parents as they can to avoid being caught in the gothic horror, paternal strangling.

Fran stares at Rachel. Why the intensity? She rubs her palms together and keeps silent.

Men, remarks Jane Austen from the wardrobe, have no idea of the tunnel of possibilities available to a woman, the adolescent arrogance their sisters cannot share.

Shelley writes that he finds Elan Valley a great bore, he's no interest in purple heather or ochre gorse. A few days later he's more impressed – or he addresses a less laddish correspondent: 'Rocks piled on each other to tremendous heights, rivers formed into cataracts by their projections, & valleys clothed with woods, present an appearance of enchantment.'

Rhayader.
Cwm Elan House

Already Shelleyan, he flings himself down on grass, curls earth with his toes and hears water rushing and roaring through his head. He takes lonely walks, is touched by magic and longs for thunderstorms. Very likely he sports wild flowers in his hair, old man's beard and bee orchids. Self-absorbed of course, because the thingy world is nothing to him.

It was all in all to me, barring immortality, interjects Jane Austen quietly. She hasn't been able to stay in the wardrobe.

I thought not, says Fran. You like a story.

My men tell good tales – Colonel Brandon, Mr Darcy, and handsome Captain Wentworth . . .

Patrician, he's grown up in silk pantaloons. At sixteen he

describes himself as independent, the 'heir of a gentleman of large fortune'.

Jane Austen notes the implied rebuff – a real gentleman's wealth is not precise. Unusually, she blushes.

So, notwithstanding his reading of the lower-class firebrand Godwin, he yet provokes a bill like this – Rachel consults her waterproof notebook:

A Superfine Olive Coat Gilt Buttons 4 8 0
A Pair Rich Silk Knitt Pantaloons 3 8 0
Two Stripd Marcela Waistcoats Double Breastd 2 0 0
1. Pair Patent Silk Braces 0 8 0
A Superfine Blue Coat Velvett Collr & Gilt Buttns 4 12 0

Jane Austen gulps. She thinks of those bonnet trimmings and collar turnings, the tedious mending of petticoats and socks. 'I am a gentleman's daughter' is the proud boast of all her heroines – except perhaps poor Fanny Price – yet it can't equal this. The 'large fortune' you know.

Fran's impressed. 'Did he ever pay for these items?' She knows the answer: not something that concerns a negligent aristocrat.

In my *Beautiful Cassandra*, adds Jane Austen, even as a child I was aware of such carelessness. Eating six ices from a pastry-cook without paying. What a noble fantasy.

At last Fran can proffer her own information, something stumbled on in her days of 'research' in the Cambridge Library.

In 1878 – when Shelley had become a National Treasure – an old woman, who as a girl delivered post to Cwm Elan, recalled 'a very strange gentleman'. On weekdays he wore a little cap but on Sundays to go with the family to church he put on a tall hat. He sailed a foot-long wooden boat in the rapid mountain streams and ran along the bank, using a pole to direct his craft and keep it off the rocks. Once he forced a cat to get in.

There you see him. The man-child sailing toy boats, caring not a whit for a reluctant cat, watching perhaps as water penetrated the wood and the sail collapsed, all losing form, the cat whining piteously.

Legend has it he once made a paper boat from a £50 note – by the way a thing of beauty (as well as immense value) with its intricate engraving.

Jane Austen, who values money no more than is proper but who knows – who better? – the value of a banknote, is appalled.

'He yearns for dissolution,' says Rachel, untouched by the top-hatted, church-going Shelley Fran's creating – or indeed by his careless extravagance. 'Apparently, he swims in the streams, though some record he can't swim. Is he wooing death?' She shrugs.

'If it's a matter of sleeping forever or being awake forever, I know what I'd choose,' interrupts Fran. 'If a decayed body weren't horrid, I doubt we'd be so appalled at dying. Silence and sleep or noise and wakefulness. No contest.'

Rachel smiles. Shelley dresses up oblivion as Elysium. Is he afraid of nothingness?

Fran, Rachel and Thomas are back together at the B&B facing the first dinner prepared by Mrs Price. She's allowed them to bring in a bottle of wine beforehand – and pay for glasses and corkscrew. They decide to drink it in the cluttered sitting room before dinner.

'So, truly, what's so special about Shelley in your view, Thomas?' asks Rachel. She likes to hear him praised.

'Purity. Purity of spirit,' he replies.

'Sex?' asks Fran, forgetting her earlier embarrassment at Cambridge station.

The others ignore her.

'Evil was for him an accident on earth,' says Thomas, 'but it

82

was real and warring with the power of good. To let it in was dangerous to mind and body.'

'Quite a jejune idea,' says Fran.

'Not really. The body and soul were identical for Shelley.'

'Hmm,' murmurs Fran losing inhibition as wine washes her veins, 'and you agree? So much more pleasant for a young, healthy and, if I might say, pleasantly muscular, person to think. In my case I don't want my soul to commune with age spots and dewlaps and leaking orifices.'

Thomas exhales sharply, swallows and goes on. Rachel settles her face into an enigmatic expression. It dispels awkwardness in most reasonable people, though it always infuriated her demanding mother. 'He thought the soul became encrusted with stones, shells and growths, so that in time it became heavy as lead. But these encrustations could be sliced off with a sharp knife.'

'Not too easy with the ageing body, or do you propose plastic intervention?' says Fran.

Thomas tries again to ignore the interruptions; 'shock-jock' swims through his mind and, happily, exits.

'But he thought too the body was frail and exposed, hence the search for eternal beauty and love.'

'In other people,' sniffs Fran, now irrepressible. 'Beauty elsewhere. Other people had to measure up. Where he could grumble and rumble, he did.'

Thomas gives her a steely look. Annie should have come: she'd have kept her friend in check.

'He was always anxious about his own health. One moment he worried about typhus, at another syphilis and consumption. He called himself a feeble, feverish being. He read up about disease and tried cures. He'd have had a field day Googling.'

Thomas smiles at Fran. A generous man, he wants to include her if he can, despite her infuriating ways. 'Mercury, Cheltenham salts, Scott's vitriolic immersions, poultices of caustic, warm baths, Mesmerism and leeches. He ate little, weighed what he ate, and filtered his water through a stone. Butter horrified him. When years back he visited Wordsworth's friend Southey, Mrs Southey's buttery biscuits stuck in his throat.'

Jane Austen usually avoids commenting on other shadows, but can't resist nimbly descending the stairs to whisper to Fran, Your Shelley's a hypochondriac. Had I known this, I might have lodged him in Sanditon and dosed him with asses' milk.

JANE AUSTEN'S
SANDITON

I do agree, Fran whispers back. He could have been mates with Sir Edward Denham and talked high poetry. They both giggle.

Thomas assumes his allusion to butter biscuits has provoked this response. 'But, seriously, it was the world's slow stain that affected him. A poet of his calibre is indeed more delicate, more sensitive than others.'

I fancy, Jane Austen continues, I'd have had little time for him in life.

And he less for you, thinks Thomas, who has a strange tickling in his head that makes him recall, for no reason he can see, Jane Austen and her inflated self-satisfaction, her now outrageous popularity. He feels an urge to provoke.

'The materiality you so like in, for example – and it's a random choice – Jane Austen, is more a female thing in art,' says Thomas turning to Fran, who hears a snigger in her right ear.

I like a glass, a good fire, yes butter too.

'We don't have to pit Shelley against Jane Austen,' says Rachel. Back in Cambridge Annie had mentioned Fran's habit of quoting and channelling the novelist. Rachel's been on the look-out but feels nothing ectoplasmic.

'Well we're here braving wind and rain. Instead of settling by a log fire in a comfortable boutique hostelry in Austen's Hampshire.'

'Nothing comfortable about log fires in summer. They bring on asthma,' says Fran.

Rachel hopes this niggling will stop tomorrow when they're by the lakes. 'It's an image of comfort. Make another if you want – perhaps hot tea and buttered toast.'

Jane Austen hears that. My delight, she says, especially when a little on in years. In *Sanditon* I wrote of a family cosily by a summer fire, buttering toast. A faraway look enters her eyes.

'Shelley was vegetarian, as I am,' Thomas concludes.

'Ah,' says Rachel, remembering him avoiding Annie's cheese but demolishing her hare and orange paté, 'we're having Welsh lamb and new potatoes for dinner.'

'Let me quote Shelley on the carnivore: "as Plutarch recommends, tear a living lamb with his teeth and, plunging his head into its vitals, slake his thirst with the steaming blood . . ."'

'Jeez,' exclaims Rachel catching Fran's eye, 'vegetarians are so aggressive!'

'I can compromise,' says Thomas. 'Eating meat isn't eating human flesh. Anyhow, Shelley was inconsistent. Sometimes he demolished bacon and veal chops. I'm actually vegan, like my wife, but I know the concept is too advanced for our landlady.'

A young leveret, a brace of partridges, a leash of pheasants, a dozen of pigeons, mumbles Jane Austen.

'You wouldn't perhaps mind, Thomas, if we ate the lamb while you toyed with the veg and avoided the gravy?' says Rachel.

'I love gravy,' says Thomas, 'always have.'

I I

'One good thing about this road, no roundabouts,' says Thomas next morning as they drive together towards Elan Valley. Sun streaks through a benign rain. 'Today will be better.'

They arrive at Garreg Ddu by way of the café, Cwm Elan deep below. They get out of the car.

'Bleak,' says Thomas looking round.

'Labour suffered here,' says Fran. 'Miners and farmers living in miserable conditions. The gentry in their mansions chose to see the picturesque and beautiful, not the industry their comfort rested on.'

Rachel smiles, 'I agree, Fran. Whatever his love for the lower orders, Shelley's never anything but upper class.'

Fran looks at Rachel's boots – how many different types of footwear has the woman brought? She wriggles her toes in the same old lace-ups.

'Privileged perhaps,' says Thomas flicking his tongue over gelled lips. 'But Shelley can still feel grief at seeing and losing the ideal.'

Fran raises her eyebrows at Rachel, who turns away.

Thomas tries again. 'Shelley glimpses something transcendent, then mourns the loss.'

'Just Romanticism, surely,' says Fran not unkindly.

'Maybe, but Shelley catches our feeling of imprisonment more than any writer I know. He makes us feel how we're manacled to systems.'

And duty? That London flat? All those babies?

Sensing Fran's thoughts, Rachel nods encouragingly to Thomas. 'Go on.'

He recites:

> All things are recreated, and the flame
> Of consentaneous love inspires all life: . . .
> The balmy breathings of the wind inhale
> Her virtues, and diffuse them all abroad:
> Health floats amid the gentle atmosphere,
> Glows in the fruits, and mantles on the stream.

Holding Thomas's eye, Rachel pretends to whisper to Fran, 'The place is unsettling him.'

Sensitive to women's asides, even when facetious – his wife and mother-in-law speak in low tones while cooking –Thomas grunts, 'OK, let's bring in Harriet Number Two, Harriet Westbrook. That's what you want.'

'We do. It's my cue,' says Rachel, twirling each booted foot to ease her ankles. 'Let's talk and walk over rough ground in Romantic manner.'

Having seen the pretty schoolgirl, Shelley is smitten. Young and unformed, this Harriet may be saved from convention, groomed into a noble soul. Her headmistress tears up one letter breathing liberty and atheism, others get through.

'She should have been more vigilant.'

Perhaps she smells an advantageous match. As for young Harriet, she's deferred to a sister twice her age most of her life; easy to switch to a handsome, charismatic, sexy – some might say over-sexed – youth of nineteen. She swallows his stories of family persecution. As good as romance.

She hates school, she writes. What fifteen-year-old doesn't? It's enough. A mere four months since he'd been sent down from Oxford, weeks after quitting Elan Valley, Shelley plucks Harriet from her cosy life and thrusts her into his own erratic orbit.

He urges free love, she holds out for marriage. She has that much sense.

They're hitched in Edinburgh in August 1811, neither sets of parents, trade or gentry, consulted or consenting. The marriage register names the groom a 'Farmer, of Sussex'.

'And all the while,' adds Rachel, 'he's writing to his friends how much he hates "matrimonialism". An ineffable sickening disgust rises in his gorge when he thinks of monogamy.'

'He's only following radical thought,' urges Thomas. 'In his 1790s *Political Justice*, William Godwin wrote that marriage was an affair of property, and the worst of all properties.'

'It's coming back,' interrupts Fran, finding it hard simply to listen with the place intruding and Jane Austen muttering in her ear. 'Godwin changed tack later, I remember. After marrying Mary Wollstonecraft.'

'Yeah. He revised the work. He was soon on his *second* marriage.'

'But Shelley stays with the first edition.'

'The young can never bear their elders' common sense,' mumbles Fran.

Comic, thinks Rachel glancing at Fran, that simultaneous urge to talk and not be heard.

Eager to make a revolutionary of the loving little girl, Shelley takes Harriet (and her older sister) to Dublin, where he prints copies of a pamphlet *Address to the Irish People*. Priced modestly at 5*d.*, it's intended to 'awaken in the minds of the Irish poor a knowledge of their real state'. It offers 'a rational means of remedy'.

Of course it fails: Ireland never cared much for English saviours. By April 1812 the Shelleys are at Cwm Elan.

'I haven't heard everything,' interrupts Thomas, 'too blustery. I take the social vision more seriously than you, Rachel. Tom Grove mocks his cousin's habit of rescuing people from comfort; but, even if comfortable, Shelley's waifs have dull lives: he lets them see beyond, want something more. So, with Harriet. Not so despicable.'

'Well,' says Rachel, better pleased today than yesterday, having drunk a stronger brew of coffee at Elan village café than the B&B served, 'I expect it's Shelley himself that Harriet and her successors want, rather than "something more". Sadly for them he tends to rescue and move on.'

'I dislike charisma,' sniffs Fran. 'Usually just immense self-centredness.'

'Old-lady speak,' laughs Rachel. 'We all have heroes.'

'Back to Harriet,' says Thomas flexing his shoulders. 'There *was* real love. In his first long poem, *Queen Mab*, Shelley writes a moving tribute to her: "thou wert my purer mind;/Thou wert the inspiration of my song".'

As they amble over the wet ground by the water, the rain unsure now whether to go or stay, Fran mulls over heroes. Is Rachel right? Isn't it Shelley's life, that predatory, destructive, overwhelmingly glamorous life, that's brought them all here? Her memories and tale of poor Betty Pugh are adding little.

'Jane Austen might have read *Queen Mab*,' she says interrupting her own thoughts. 'She's writing *Mansfield Park* when it was published.'

'Nope. Never distributed. He stored most copies at William Clark's bookshop in London, where – and even you must admit this, Thomas – with his ability to get everyone else into trouble, years later they're discovered and sold on the black market. Clark is imprisoned for publishing blasphemous libels: by then Jane Austen and Harriet Shelley are dead.'

'Truce,' says Thomas. 'Shelley's views on revolution change: he tries to suppress the sale. Not his fault.'

'Mary Shelley is better at suppression. When she prints her dead husband's poetry, she omits his tribute to Harriet. I'll go on.'

Sir Timothy is outraged at the imprudent match and won't fund it. Yet the young couple don't live badly. Shelley can point tradesmen towards his expectations (none anticipated Sir T's extraordinary longevity). A carriage is ordered, used and not paid for. Claims of creditors are fatuous, evaded by skipping town.

Rachel nods to Fran, who's reluctant to expose her prim, lower-middle-class soul again.

'Yes,' says Rachel. 'He drinks the best green tea and keeps his hair back with the finest tortoiseshell. Aristocrats are gilded flies' – as they walk she's rubbing her hand along the soft green moss on some standing boulders, enjoying the sensation – 'but oh the deliciousness of being one as well as scorning them. For all his revolutionary tendencies, Shelley knows what's essential for a gentleman.'

'OK. If you follow Shelley round Britain, you usually find his house by looking for the best in the neighbourhood.'

It saddens Fran that Thomas and Rachel aren't more excited about Elan Valley. Can't they see with her eyes? She feels tender towards the trodden ground.

'Maybe we'll do that one day,' says Thomas, struck by a sudden joy at his freedom. He coughs to show he's been ex-clamatory.

After an hour or so of silent walking, the three settle on separate rocks, sheltered by a bank shiny with dripping water.

The youngsters are summering in Cwm Elan with Tom Grove and Henrietta. This time Shelley's so enthusiastic about the valleys he determines to stay. He hears of a fine mansion for rent, seat of the Lewis Lloyds, maybe a mile and half further into the hills along steep terrain, close to a meeting of streams.

Only Fran visualises the house, Nantgwyllt – Welsh for wild brook. 'Go on, Rachel,' she says, not attempting to restrain her eagerness.

To some eyes, the house with its flat grey façade is too austere; others find it elegant. All admit its magnificent setting: framed by trees, with a lawn falling towards the bubbling water. The projecting spur on which it sits forms a sort of island.

'Shelley loves an island,' adds Thomas. 'Such an enclosed and cut-off place haunts his imagination all his life.'

Round the house mountains and rocks make a barrier which 'the tumult of the world may never overleap'. To Shelley it appears the very place for his commune, the utopia of 'ami-able beings', 'asylum of distressed virtue', 'rendez-vous of the friends of liberty and truth'.

Rachel, Thomas and Fran stare over the reservoir. 'Somewhere there,' says Fran. It's a guess.

Everyone must come – including William Godwin. Amazingly he's still alive. Bring his family of girls. A Miss Hitchener too, a schoolteacher some ten years older than Shelley.

'I remember her,' exclaims Fran, 'a grown-up among children.' Throughout the courtship and bedding of Harriet he's been writing intense erotic letters to her; she's his soul-mate, his soul-sister, will be the star of the commune. Sadly, when he sees Miss Hitchener in the flesh, he finds her ugly; swiftly she's demoted.

Only pretty women in this story. Too many characters spoil a plot.

'Young men demand physical as well as intellectual beauty,' remarks Fran.

But not the other way round, intrudes Jane Austen. You'll remember Henry Crawford in *Mansfield Park* appearing plain to the Bertram girls till his charm makes him handsome.

Lizzie Bennet? She isn't the belle of the ballroom when (on a second attempt) she attracts rich Mr Darcy with her sparkle.

Try to remember *I* created them, chuckles Jane Austen. That's the point.

All Shelley needs is £98 for rent and near £1000 for stock. His name's persuasive in the area: there are, at first, no impediments to credit. Before paying a penny, Percy and Harriet move in. Their baggage trundles up the valleys. It includes boxes of books for arranging in the grandest room, a library of classical and radical texts.

Like ailing Henrietta Grove in Cwm Elan, Harriet finds bleaker Nantgwyllt bad for chesty ailments. Ill when she arrives, she's slow to recover. The house is often cold and damp even in summer.

'But,' interrupts Fran, looking at Thomas, 'the bleakness which hikers and bikers so like wasn't so extreme then. Many of the bottom slopes were densely wooded with oak, ash, spruce and Scots pine. Still, no denying, it's a harsh place. In winter, snow lingers in the deep valleys, the house is unreachable. Shelley visited Cwm Elan in spring and summer. Not hard to imagine how he'd fare through the cold claustrophobia of a winter in remoter Nantgwyllt.'

Rachel smiles at Fran – a little loftily, Thomas thinks. He smiles too.

'The suicide rate in Radnorshire was always high,' adds Fran. 'It was a local boast, along with having the fewest people per square mile in England and Wales, and the most sheep. Shelley doesn't sound a winter person.'

Rachel shrugs, 'He was all light – light moves fast, is never fixed.'

Yet, the young couple are happy. Shelley's sincere in his desire to make Nantgwyllt their home. It's poetry, inspiration, muse, and would-be rapture.

In the tundra Agafia still awaits her Rapture, struggling, starving, praying, always on the edge of eternity.

Shelley and Agafia, two sides of a coin.

'The rapture was presumably down to Harriet,' adds Rachel. 'But no place can compete with heaven. Shelley may try but Elan Valley won't be Eden; it must fail. Like Harriet.

Fran is picking her nose, a habit indulged in the cottage; she stops as the others glance at her, then moves her finger against her cheek pensively. She feels the discomfort of the rock prodding her buttocks.

'The poetry he writes here is intemperate, but temperance isn't Shelley's style. It's unstable, but so's time. He says he wants a glass eye, a steel hand and a soul not formed to feel. But he feels with every fibre of his being.'

Fran's glad Jane Austen is off walking somewhere. This kind of talk lacks the wryness for which she's so renowned.

Exactly, says the Author from far away, I am very fond of a long walk. Wordsworth and I find it useful for ordering narrative.

Thomas stands up. He's growing weary of what he calls (privately) this 'silver cynicism'. He wants to mount his bike again and race like lightening up and down hills as Shelley dreamt of speeding his body and words across oceans.

But he wills himself to listen to Rachel. She may not be the key to America, yet she'll have influence. Besides, he likes her. Not far from his mother's age – though light years from her clinging garrulity. Less sharp-tongued than Annie.

As usual, there are money problems. Shelley's still a minor. His furious father and sympathetic cousins withhold a loan, none liking his social schemes. Political rumblings too: a private box of papers sent from Ireland is opened in Holyhead and judged seditious. Money dries up.

So, miserably for his poetic enthusiasm and plans for utopia, Shelley must leave the gloomy, roomy house of Nantgwyllt. After all that bother of moving.

'That's it,' says Rachel, 'end of story! Still, the perishing fire-fly might enjoy a longer life than the tortoise.'

Only a fool fails to secure money before marriage or removal, snaps Jane Austen.

'It couldn't have worked,' says Fran, stretching stiff ankles, 'that belief in possibilities outside the real world. Shelley creates a cosmic drama and, though he says he wants to make things better here, now, his surreal vision would always spoil it.'

Thomas shrugs. 'His goals were beyond families and society. Transcendence is about raising up the individual.'

'You do know, Thomas,' grins Rachel, 'that Shelley's friend Thomas Love Peacock imagines him the author of a work called *Philosophical Gas*?'

12

For some deflated days Shelley and Harriet stay at Cwm Elan with the Groves, then they leave Elan Valley for good.

Rachel chuckles. 'We've travelled a long way to reflect on a few drafty, dreamy weeks.'

'Intense though,' replies Fran, trawling her eyes over the hills. Her companions regard each other as they walk on chatting.

Next year Harriet bears a daughter, named Ianthe after the Fairy's tutee in *Queen Mab*. So young and inexperienced, she leans even more on her forceful elder sister.

Bad move: men never like it – the older sister, best friend, mother-in-law.

'So much to process,' remarks Thomas flexing his left hand as if pushing aside heavy words.

Soon Shelley comes to loathe the sister and, where he loathes, he's cruel. Bewildered by his swings of mood, poor Harriet falls to reading the lovely dedication to *Queen Mab*, heeding old words instead of present angry looks.

'It's hard to believe someone once trusted has changed,' ends Rachel turning to Fran, her voice muted; 'takes time for the mind to catch up with the senses.'

Harriet is persuaded not to breastfeed, a common route for genteel ladies. So, little Ianthe sucks on a wet-nurse. Shelley is outraged: alien milk will infect his child.

Through the ages Christian artists have found breastfeeding picturesque, erotic, intellectually interesting, the suckling of God. Shelley? Well, nipples enthralled him – or he wouldn't – later – have hallucinated Mary's nipples as eyes. Another, all-mothering woman within his woman? No wonder he shrieked.

Before Thomas can interrupt, Rachel goes on, 'One day he snatches Ianthe from the wet-nurse, tears open his shirt and forces the tiny mouth against his own pure masculine nipple.'

'Unmilky too,' says Fran.

'We don't know the size of young Harriet's breasts. Biggish ones, I imagine, in fashion again after the passing Empire vogue for pubescent contours.'

'Did Shelley claim lactation? A man who could ask his wife if he's eaten might believe anything.'

Thomas pats away the question. 'Shelley thinks all bodily parts and fluids integral to a self. Milk from one body is trans-ferred into the being of the other taking the soul with it. The baby's sullied by contact with a hired nurse *paid* to mother.' Thomas pauses, but can't resist going on though he risks blame for mansplaining. 'Shelley thinks earthly existence corrupts children: nannies and parents, then schools and governments. In *Queen Mab*, the newly born is a stranger-soul peeping from its new tenement at desolation.'

'Sad Harriet,' smiles Rachel, 'how many exacting tests she failed: she's all flesh, not the Fairy of *Queen Mab*. Her babies live on earth, not in the sky.'

Shelley *does* have a rather incorporeal sense of infants. Like Wordsworth imagining the child trailing clouds of glory into a fallen world, he toys with the notion that pre-birth memories may be recovered. As a student in Oxford, he snatches a baby on Magdalen Bridge and stares into its ignorant eyes. Then he dangles it over the river while demanding of the stricken mother whether the bundle he holds can tell us about pre-existence.

'A large class-element to this tale,' suggests Fran.

Indeed. A privileged youth, equipped with gown and mortar board, the mother most likely a working woman from the town. She'll think the young man mad, so she'll be cautious. Shelley's response – gentlemen don't explain or apologise – was 'provokingly close'.

We all know what's coming, no need for second-hand story-telling.

Harriet is pregnant again. Shelley abandons her and sets up with Mary, daughter of William Godwin and Mary Wollstonecraft, another sixteen-year-old virgin (with a sexy younger stepsister, not a bossy older one). Desperately unhappy and alone, Harriet drowns herself in the Serpentine in London's Hyde Park. Unlike Shelley, with his pistol-waving, poison-touting and folded arms in capsizing boats, she meant business. She's pregnant for a third time, Fran presumes by Shelley, but keeps the opinion to herself. She looks angrily at Thomas as if he channels the Poet – as if he and Shelley between them have done for Harriet and poor Betty Pugh.

At least Harriet lives on in someone else's story. But it's no compensation.

Responding to Fran's mood, Thomas says, 'Shelley wasn't a stone. He tells the legend of St Columbanus who hung his garment on a sunbeam, and adds, "I, too, have tried to discover a ray of light to fasten hope on it. The casualties of this world come on like waves, one succeeding the other."'

'He takes the miseries he caused as natural phenomena. Everything's about *him*, the genius whose thrilling chords are ignored by a deaf world. What arrogant self-pity!'

'OK,' says Thomas, 'OK.'

They fall silent. Fran is still gripped with emotion; swallowing, she looks away. Thomas recognizes these moods from life with his mother – and mother-in-law. A temperament of female old age perhaps? To ease the moment, he asks, 'If the lease on the house had been possible, how quickly before the commune failed?'

Puzzled by Fran, Rachel welcomes the opening. 'If it hadn't at once and if they'd stayed *en famille* in the harsh winter, young Harriet wouldn't – at least so swiftly – have been abandoned, since Shelley wouldn't have clapped eyes on Mary Wollstonecraft Godwin – who' – Rachel can't resist so fertile a counterfactual – 'without this fall into Shelleyan history, wouldn't have written *Frankenstein*, so denying the enemies of democracy, science and technology their handy metaphor.'

Fran and Thomas laugh. 'Yup,' agrees Fran, letting her mood evaporate. 'If he'd raised the cash, mightn't the commune have had a chance? Doesn't everyone want it, at least anyone dissatisfied with their own little platoon by birth, or without one?' No one answers. 'Shelley's very habit of including everyone, the way he's only briefly infatuated with a single woman, might

have worked – romantic love's not especially good for community living. But' – and Fran wants to belittle her place to mitigate
her friends' insensitivity – 'I guess it needed a better climate than
mid-Wales, something on Lake Como or the French Riviera. A
house with fountains, ferns and verandas, mirrors in orangeries,
majolica tiled walls, flowers spilling from urns, peacocks on
velvet lawns.'

'Whoa,' says Rachel.

Thomas looks at Fran, surprised.

'Just pretend,' she shrugs. 'Prettified, Nantgwyllt would still
be a sort of landed spaceship on a promontory.'

'Best keep it mental,' smiles Rachel. 'Coleridge's stately pleasure dome for Kubla Khan, built with opium inside a warm den.'

Donwell Abbey in its gentle valley suits me, observes Jane
Austen. She's enjoyed her walk alone up the steep road. Now
she takes Fran gently by the elbow, hoping to steer her from
illusion and information.

Rachel and Thomas prepare to move.

The rain that's held off a while begins to roll down Fran's
cheek onto her chin. 'Or a fantasy like a glass cathedral or opera
house in the jungle,' she says.

Thomas looks questioningly.

'I wonder,' continues Fran, 'if Shelley had stayed and written
better poetry here, would his house have been a shrine like
Wordsworth's Dove Cottage in the Lake District. Would Elan
Valley have been flooded to provide tap water for townies?'

The idea intrigues Thomas. 'At least Shelley poeticised what's
drowned. Washed away like him. How do you see it, Rachel?'

'Let's fill Nantgwyllt,' interrupts Fran. 'We came for the place
and the poet but also for his vision, the commune of kindred
spirits.'

'It would have failed,' repeats Thomas.

'Of course, everything does in the end,' says Rachel. 'But

while it lasted . . .' She shrugs. 'An experiment – non-possessive affection, equal sharing – ignoring for a moment the havoc desire always causes.'

Exactly.

Agafia had a sexually predatory 'neighbour'. Modern interviewers light on this, not Agafia.

'Think of Shelley's hangers-on: Harriet (a good housekeeper, by the way – he disliked dirt), her organising sister, not so bad when diluted, Ianthe and the next baby, the young Shelley sisters, earnest Miss Hitchener. Plus – and Shelley needs men to avoid being 'tranquillized' into domesticity – Peacock, maybe an Oxford friend or two, then of course –though this might be hazardous given the factual – old Godwin and his girls: Mary, her stepsister Jane and half-sister Fanny. With so many women, Shelley can flitter attention from one to another, sultanlike. Perhaps then he wouldn't have descended like lightening on handsome Mary and stayed too long. How many bedrooms did you say?'

'Seven. Women share.'

You confuse family with friendship, intrudes Jane Austen; one may compensate for the other's absence – perhaps by the end of my life I took such a view. However, friendship lacks the resilience of blood.

Recalling the touch of a wet oar in his hand, strong male knees on his back, Thomas frowns before entering this female game. 'The earlier Romantics imagined secular utopias too. Southey and Coleridge dreamed up Pantisocracy in primitive America. Shelley called on Southey just after marrying Harriet.'

'Aha!' exclaims Fran. 'Mrs Southey's rejected butter biscuits.'

'The bloody end of the French Revolution put most people off experimental living,' continues Thomas. At times he feels older than the women.

'That implies Shelley's an anachronism,' says Rachel. 'I think people yearn to be solitary *and* in company. Communes appeal in any age, even if you haven't the temperament.'

'Wasn't there something called Oneida in America?' asks Fran wrinkling her forehead in a way that reminds Rachel of Disney's White Rabbit. 'Free sex, gender equality, etc.: heaven on earth because Jesus had already come.'

Waiting for a future Rapture, Agafia can never experience the disappointment these communitarians feel – nothing to look forward to.

Jane Austen dislikes the talk. A religious mind is sustaining, but one must be equal to what life offers.

'Harriet's babies would have had many mothers.'

'There'd be children crawling everywhere. Free love, youth is fertile.'

'All living on Shelley's money or rather his father's. A counterfactual too far?' Thomas interrupts. 'No one thinks of doing paid work outside the (notional) tilling of soil. With all his gifts, Shelley doesn't write for money – as Jane Austen and Keats – and Byron – do.'

'Ianthe would have toddled by the brook and never fallen in, so many watching female eyes.'

Fran's puzzled. Often mordant in tone, Rachel softens at the touch of a child.

'Mothers, then grandmothers, and great-aunts; the men of course would have scuttled off.'

If he hadn't resolved to humour them, Thomas might have mocked emotions so typical of seventies' feminists. Was Rachel old enough to be part of that naive cohort? He's Googled but not discovered a birthdate. More success with Princeton. She's in receptions with the President, who shares a surname with a reviewer in the *New Yorker*, who nods brief praise at her novel of nineteenth-century Philadelphia. He turns on Rachel the ingratiating face that charms Annie.

It helps that both are tall, nearly on a level. He refrains from saying the obvious: the eyes of every communitarian would have been on Shelley and his delicious authority. Without him, they'd lose their purpose.

Observing Thomas and Rachel engaged and moving off, just for an instant Fran plops down on the damp bracken, untying the strings of her wet hood like the ribbons of a bonnet. She looks towards the water, straightens her back.

I was not, murmurs Jane Austen, taken unawares when my dear sister sketched my likeness. I knew exactly what I was presenting: Cassandra and I had excellent posture. And we didn't sit on wet grass.

In her seventies Agafia loads bales of wood on her back. She doesn't care what she looks like to others. She's blessed with a strong spine as well as good teeth.

Fran stands up. No one has seen her. Only sheep move the wet green and copper fronds. She gazes on the lake. Fake of course. Without Shelley it's nothing. Without memories: a reservoir anywhere. She picks up a stone, throws it far out, watching concentric rings ripple, mingling wind and human force. When the sun peeps from behind the rain cloud, it dazzles her.

Shagreen and tortoiseshell, says Jane Austen gently.

Maybe I was channelling a sheep, not you, grins Fran. Then she exclaims, Shit, not sheep either: Enid Blyton, *Five Go Off to Camp* and sleep on bracken!

She catches up with Thomas and Rachel, who open to let her in – she feels a child between grown-ups. Or a hippo between giraffes.

13

That night Fran phones Annie from the B&B. Her room may be the dingiest – she's over her (very slight) resentment there – but, by waving her mobile through the top of its dormer window, she traps a signal.

She's glad Annie hasn't come. The few natives they've seen – probably Mum's fourth and fifth cousins, well her blood anyway – would have smirked at the hats and Pretty Ballerina boots. Shelley never passed unnoticed. Also, Annie might not have been enthusiastic enough. One thing in Rachel and Thomas, another in one's Best Friend. Be unaware in a Norfolk garden if you will, not here. Homeland, you know.

She visualises Annie scrabbling for the phone under the pillow or, if she is still in her study, among piles of papers. Fran rehearses an apology for calling so late. By the time she finds the right words, the phone demands a message. She presses Off.

Still too early for sleep. Or, rather, her brain rejects the hour, ambushed by an evening of unaccustomed company. She reaches for her second-hand copy of *The Vale of Nantgwilt* by R. Eustace Tickell.

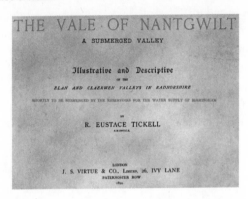

She'll use it next day, rain or shine, to make her companions see what they're ignoring with their chatter: the erasure of place and people, dead and living, the colossal feat that caused the catastrophe. Thomas loves Shelley, the projector, the scientist, the speeder. Surely she can lure him into marvelling at the engineering – the vast acres involved, the gallons of water syphoned along aqueducts, through tunnels and pipes across half the country. Shelley and Thomas. And Rachel?

She takes hours to drop off, but, when achieved, sleep is deep. She wakes refreshed and determined. 'May I tell you the future of the house? Of Nantgwyllt. Before the flood, and after,' she says when they meet in the hallway.

'I'm a cultural historian by early training,' says Rachel. 'I relish antiquarianism, well some.' She's come to breakfast in another set of matching sportswear.

Thomas has also slept well, his mobile silent on a bedside

table. His ears prick up at Rachel's remark. Should he enquire which university she attended? Would it be too direct?

'Bryn Mawr,' she says to his roundabout probe, 'and elsewhere.'

This morning Mrs Price offers scrambled eggs with bacon and sausage. Thomas urges his vegetarianism again and stays with toast and jam, no butter. Better read in modern fiction than Fran, Rachel is ambushed by John Updike's image of a man jerking off into scrambled egg, then eating it with his new bride at their honeymoon breakfast. She asks for poached eggs, annoying the landlady, who daily regrets her decision to open a B&B after thirty years of council work. The poached eggs arrive half drowned.

'I find it very poignant,' says Fran enjoying her fry-up, especially the sausage. 'My turn for telling, yes?'

'Not till I have real coffee inside me,' says Rachel.

Do try to edit, whispers Jane Austen.

The three assemble on a picnic bench outside the Elan café holding paper mugs of coffee.

'Did you ever see anything like that statue of Shelley over there? Usually it's girls who push their heads winsomely to one side – or St Sebastian. The women clutching the manly body are his muses not his harem, I guess.'

'There's no statue to the dispossessed of Elan,' says Fran.

To remember Tryweryn, a small sculpture of a rising bird was proposed. Someone objected it looked uncommonly like the Liver Birds, symbol of marauding Liverpool.

Rachel grins, 'You sound a quarrelsome people.'

Fran enjoys being from 'a people' – sometimes she suffers from ethnic-envy.

The owner of Nantgwyllt, a later Lewis Lloyd, kept a large household of gardeners, servants, coachmen and cowmen, also a do-gooding sister Gertrude who ran a school for local children and provided material for poor women to make frocks and breeches. Every deprived area needs its Miss Gertrude.

Fran pauses to mutter to Jane Austen: she's the kind of woman you never treated with proper respect – unlike your Victorian successors.

The comment annoys the Author, who moves away. She's sick of people telling her what she should have depicted: pushy authoresses, mixed-race hoydens, gleeful lesbians, cunning bastards, abolition of slavery, industrial reform, horrors of enclosure, war, famine, imperialism, death, sex, masturbation, philanthropic ladies . . .

Life in the cottages was cold but cosy, bodies packed close. In autumn the squire's mill ground grain to provide oatmeal for flummery and mess for pigs. After a good harvest they celebrated round a bonfire.

(Rachel has a vision of Fran enjoying Morris dancing and folk fairs on muddy East Anglian commons. She's warming to her new friend.)

Christmas was a carnival upside-down time, the poor waited on by ladies of the House – to whom they curtseyed even in the lanes.

Rachel chuckles, 'If Harriet and Shelley had stuck around,

they'd have been so way out with their free love and commune of spinsters and schoolgirls.'

Hetty Price, a child in one of Nantgwyllt's tenant farms, when in her seventies remembered prelapsarian Elan – well, Elan before the Flood.

Like Tom Grove and most squires, Lewis Lloyd was a hunter – though few foxes roamed the upland valleys. Once, catching a foxy scent, his hunt galloped over hills and moorland, across streams and rivers, beyond Elan Valley and across the Wye and even across the Severn –

'I don't have geography enough for this tale,' objects Rachel, sipping her coffee in hopes it'll mask the taste of poached eggs.

'Never mind, the point is to think far away.'

Local huntsmen and hounds joined pursuit, riding on to Carno and Caersws – No, I don't know where they are either – finally cornering the poor beast by a railway bridge. The squire couldn't resist showing off his fleet hunter by making him jump a last fence. The horse obeyed and died. Lewis Lloyd sent his hounds back to Rhayader on a goods train while he carried home his saddle and bridle.

'That's a dreadful story,' says Rachel.

'You see, there was a train then,' says Fran.

Thomas is jiggling his leg again. Fran, whose short legs never behave like this, rejects the message. She continues. 'There are other stories with an edge too, the informants being retired peasants.'

'Can you retire from peasanting?'

Lewis Lloyd exploited the locals as all squires do or they wouldn't be squires for long. His rivers flowed for guests to catch salmon.

Youths tried to outwit him by dressing as girls and luring fish with lights, then killing with spears. He set his hounds on them.'

Listening from down the road where she's dawdling, Jane Austen knows Fran's thinking of Messrs Knightley and Darcy. As landowners, they're problematic for leftie readers. Come on, she mutters, inequality is a fact of life. No one should be blamed for past beliefs and systems.

Not waiting for an answer, she rushes on. How sure you are your age owns supreme virtue! But how will your great grand-children judge your treatment of farm animals? Of your parents? You are tenacious of your own merit. Do you think time will have no further operations, nor the human mind change again?

'Is that it?' asks Thomas.

Fran shrugs. 'Just a glimpse of local life, the usual tension of rich and poor, one thieving, one defending. Moral complexities change,' she adds, *à propos* of nothing Thomas can see.

They walk away from Elan village. 'Shelley'd have liked this violent construction. He was obsessed by energetic machines,' says Thomas, wishing his buttocks were squashing his bike seat.

'And firearms,' adds Rachel. 'He shot at Welsh sheep. He called them maggoty and mangy. To me they look clerical and prosperous, especially the ones nosing into your car, Thomas. I guess they were thinner then.'

In fact, Welsh sheep are famed for their symmetry, sound constitution, and delicately tasting flesh.

'Shelley could have been a projector. Just before he died, he was building a steamboat.'

'Devising schemes for extracting sunbeams from cucumbers,' laughs Rachel as they cross the road.

Thomas breathes heavily. Even Rachel can exasperate. He'll be silent about the iron machinery ordered by the poet for his last boat.

He returns to the car to unhitch his bike. While Rachel and Fran continue to walk by the water, he rides off along the bumpy tracks towards the remains of the Cistercian abbey of Strata Florida, once landlord of Elan Valley. He's on an exhilarating high of speed, a Shelleyan flight. By the time he meets up with them again, he feels genial and accommodating. His face is rosy, the hue of an older man.

All three stare across the sombre lake, each thinking what an ill-assorted but comfortable trio they've become. They hear the croak of ravens, cries of buzzards, curlews, plovers, water ousels, herons and sandpipers. Names flash through Fran's mind, though she can't recognise the different sounds, as Dad could. Far off up the other bank they see wild mouse-coloured ponies galloping.

'So, an end to the history of these hills and valleys, the struggles to extract lead from rocks, rescue snow-felled sheep. Nothing left.'

'"A tingling silentness",' quotes Thomas.

'Awesome,' says Rachel, forgetting her resolve to jettison the word. The Hoover Dam flashes through her mind: America invariably overtops in scale and enterprise. Even though it isn't raining and there's an intermittent, quite thrilling sun, she isn't transported. But she's content enough. She watches a floating leaf saturated with dark water, sinking.

Fran's about to mention the appalling treatment meted out to water; Thomas prevents her. 'When he was young, Shelley thought that, if water could be manufactured, the deserts of Africa might be transformed into rich meadows and vast fields of maize and rice.'

Rachel walks off, letting the lake lap the rim of her Le Chameau boots. When she returns, she says, 'Shelley loved water. He was always looking for it. It was a mania, he had to be near it.'

'Gazing into it, I bet,' says Fran. 'Like Narcissus.'

The women exchange smiles.

'Shelley liked it flowing and restless,' says Thomas briskly. 'This water here travels fast to Brum. It's the kind of engineering project he'd have admired. Steam and mechanical power. They change the world as his poems should.' He turns so the wind won't banish his words, 'You know this enterprise – forcing land to give water to a thirsty city – beats what the gentry did in England, making lakes and rivulets for private viewing.'

Now scrambling around on the edge of the road, Jane Austen is raring to contribute. I always mocked the efforts of improvers who wanted to fell avenues of limes, move cottages to enhance a vista, that sort of thing. So vulgar and ostentatious.

Fran can't leave this alone. You really did like a great estate, though, didn't you?

Jane Austen says simply, I loved beauty.

A few fuchsia rhododendron clusters lean towards where a fast-flowing brook tumbles into the lake. It's framed with delicate ferns, jittering like butterflies. Behind rise dark leaden rocks, lichen and moss – scraps of hair on an old head. A skirting of deciduous trees, fir above, then the barren moorlands beyond.

To Fran it's achingly lovely. She feels air condense into droplets on her exposed hair. She looks up. 'A red kite I think, they're so fast swooping I can't be sure.'

'Pigeons are faster than eagles except when they dive, did you know that?'

'Swifts are faster than pigeons,' says Thomas.

'Stands to reason,' laughs Fran, 'with that name.'

'I love engineering,' Thomas continues, 'the audacity of men and machines. Napoleon carving a carriageway through the Alps.'

Forgive me for absenting myself, says Jane Austen into Fran's ear. Not really my interest. Politics and people, yes, but when brother Edward spoke of drainage and ditches in Kent, I admit to yawning over my excellent wine. I attributed it to the warmth of the fire, of course.

Righto, murmurs Fran uneasily. Do go back and I'll hurry on. Honest.

The date is March 12, 1891.

Wales is ripe for submerging, Birmingham and London greedy for water, for other people's rivers and rain. A proposed London scheme includes three of the Wye's tributaries, Elan, Claerwen and little Ithon. Why not? They flow through (almost) empty acres. London is nearing six million.

But Birmingham, a greater wen, more sudden in growth, is sickly, its white and rickety people prey to typhoid and cholera, both water-borne diseases. Their state is deplored by philanthropy as miserable, by industry as inconvenient. Birmingham wins with a more modest scheme.

In 1892 it begins. Solid masonry walls will back up the river to form three dams, the head of one reaching the foot of the next, with a submerged dam retaining water. The highest will be over a thousand feet above sea level, its water flowing through a tunnel bored into sheer rock.

Why object? South Wales is pitted by coal mines. The great magic mountain of Snowdon, where Wordsworth saw the perfect image of a mighty mind feeding upon infinity, is about to be scarred by a tourist railway. Anything can be exploited and sold, water or beauty.

People too. Like Jane Austen, Agafia is now a product, a brand. Lykova tours have been created round her Siberian hermitage. Do you pay more for a glimpse of the celebrity and her old, old icons?

A handful of Elan shepherds become construction workers; the rest are evicted without compensation. (Lewis Lloyd sold Nantgwyllt for £140,000, an excellent price.) No one made the fuss that smaller Tryweryn provoked years later when identity politics was just beginning.

'OK,' says Rachel. 'After this rehearsal, we really need to do more walking and looking. So, I will ask you what happened to the displaced tenants, then we should move on.'

Drill down for a tender anecdote. 'Boys struggled to carry their home's prize possession, a great oak four-poster bed, up the valley to a neighbour's house. You can see it now in St Fagan's Museum in Cardiff. Some found work in Rhondda coal mines, discovering the accent sharper there, repartee quicker. One took to his bed intending to die. Don't know if he did.'

Where are Shelley's revolutionary words when needed? 'Rise, like lions after slumber . . . Ye are many – they are few!'

The 'peasants' sleep in their chains. Admittedly, they are 'few'.

In short: to benefit Birmingham, seventy square miles of land containing the mansions of Cwm Elan and Nantgwillt, eighteen farms, a school, chapel and shop, riverbank and amphibious creatures beyond mention – water rats, otters, rabbits, badgers, shrews and voles – all suffered rising death.

'Yet,' adds Thomas, 'magnificent though it all was, the people of Birmingham in the twentieth century were less served than the inhabitants of Rome in 100 AD. I got this Googling *The Times*. Reporters used to be educated.'

14

Let's plough on. Talk and walk. Wordsworth composed most of his poetry while moving his metrical feet below his ugly (but serviceable) legs.

For its time the dam was a massive enterprise. Material and men arrived along a new railway: stones, steam crabs, blasting machines, itinerant navvies – fifty thousand over the thirteen years of building – rough men needing, like an army, to be controlled. To house them, the valley was terraced and a town of wooden huts with tin roofs erected, along with a school (no records except of an evening 'entertainment' in which young-sters dubbed Elan Snowflakes 'blacked up' – oh dear!) and a hospital for men crushed by great stones, blinded by explosions, drowned by sudden waters – or depressed into madness from harsh labour, the want of drink and women. New arrivals were purified, cleaned and disinfected.

Cold baths and temperance: as if creating a dam were a reli-gious ritual requiring purity of mind and body.

'Tin Town' was a model village, an austere type of commune. Bramwell Booth, founder of the Salvation Army and expert on housing vagrants, advised on its making. It's not of course to our libertarian taste, but there are advantages: the great smallpox epidemic of 1896 never took hold here, under the regime of quarantine and surveillance.

No trace left now. It was scooped up in a pall of dust and sold to the Ministry of Defence in the Great War.

There were dams to show for this commune. Nantgwyllt left what? Poetry.

No. **12** No amusements in the house	Amusements in the house are strictly prohibited. No music, singing, juggling, reciting, gambling, card playing, playing dice, dominoes, draughts, marbles, shovel-penny, or any game either of skill or chance, will be permitted in the house.

'I guess we'll be talking about Shelley places soon,' smiles Rachel. She's happy to indulge Fran, but those eggs – they still weigh even after coffee and ham sandwiches.

OK. While planning their destruction engineers and officials lodged in Cwm Elan and Nantgwyllt. 'I imagine,' adds Fran, 'they cared not a fig for Shelley and his dreams. Not being gentry, perhaps they felt out of place and welcomed the vandalism, a deserved lashing out at what they'd not had in class-ridden England.'

When they chased off Ascendancy landlords, the Irish despoiled the great houses of fitments, velvet curtains and brocaded chairs, mahogany mantelpieces, bed hangings, and lead guttering. You find remnants now in local pubs and cottages. Unlikely here: the evicted were long gone.

Did the engineers smoke pipes and stare proudly as a little river rose and turned into a bloated brown mass before its sludge settled on houses and farms?

In 1932 Francis Brett Young wrote a best-selling novel

imagining an Elan Valley mansion sinking like the *Titanic* under water, its five clusters of smokeless chimneys the last to go. In fact, walls were knocked down, so there would be no elegant sinking, just the drowning of a heap of gentry rubble.

Why? Is there something too terrible about great houses where – whatever you think of the man – a major poet, one of the titans of English Romanticism, stayed and wrote, being submerged intact, water flowing in and out their windows and rooms? Would they, one future day, have tempted an unhinged poetic diver to glide into a sacred space and settle?

Small remnants of Nantgwyllt's walls *do* remain, appearing in the odd drought year. Fran saw the heap in 1976 but says nothing. An odd, hot summer troubling to many people.

'My grandmother lived in a mansion on Long Island,' remarks Rachel. 'She had zillions in the bank, but the house rotted round her. She wouldn't allow in workmen. This drowning's better than letting a house be abandoned to damp and decay, so it looks like a leper.'

Thomas notes the zillions. Momentarily puzzled, Fran continues, 'You see now the point of my Tickell book. Supervising the middle dam, he knew what was here just before the valley disappeared. He was an artist and made sketches of what was about to go under. A pity, he wrote, if it should pass away without a record. Two hundred copies of the book were published in 1894.'

'Less than the print run of *Queen Mab*.'

'Not a great circulation,' says Rachel, aware of the gratifying success of her latest short-story collection.

(Her monograph's poor sales – despite the good reviews – would have kept Annie mum.)

Of course, costs overran, hitches occurred. The aqueduct was ready, the filter beds weren't. Let's try a little pomp and circumstance.

In July 1904, their majesties King Edward VII and Queen Alexandra arrived at Rhayader station to inaugurate the Elan scheme. They were met by the Lord Lieutenant of Radnorshire and other county and railway dignitaries, as well as the Lord Mayor of Birmingham. Herefordshire Rifle Volunteers formed a guard of honour, Radnorshire having nothing suitable.

King Edward responded to the loyal address, pleased that he and his Queen had an opportunity to see their Welsh subjects – more than half a century he'd been Prince of *Wales*. (Fran's a signed-up British republican, but pities the Royals going through their dreary routine of greeting trussed-up subjects rendered tongue-tied by a gloved royal hand.)

Jane Austen nudges her. I made my views known through hyperbole for those clever enough to read me. Remember my dedication of *Emma* to the Prince Regent? OTT as you would say.

No comment on King George, though, or were your remarks burnt by Cassandra? Fran whispers back.

I respected madness.

A special train dragged the royal entourage between river

and road, flag-waving subjects lining the way. At the filter beds locals on ponies watched the inauguration from crags. All went well. His Majesty symbolized peace: great works like this were among the 'victories of peace'. (Pity his peace hadn't extended to the Empire, where the murderous Boer War had just ended, or indeed to his nephew's Great War waiting in the wings.) The royal hand turned a wheel releasing an automatic shutter in the filter beds. Water rose. The Bishop of St David's blessed the enterprise.

Then they were hauled further to see the 'monotonous' waste of moorland (the adjective comes from *The Times* reporter). And, finally, here's Shelley.

The royal gaze was directed across the water to where he had stayed. No longer the tiresome visionary of the early nineteenth century, Shelley was now a National Treasure. For ten minutes – apparently – the King and Queen contemplated the gigantic dam, the romantic scenery and the Romantic Poet.

They'd arrived in Rhayader at midday, they left after three and were back in London by eight. 'You can't do that now.'

Rachel's about to express relief when Fran goes on. 'But Birmingham continued to grow. Never enough water, until all of Wales is flooded for the benefit of England.'

'Steady on,' says Thomas. Even in modest states like Scotland and Wales, victim nationalism isn't attractive.

'Let me finish,' begs Fran.

Jane Austen groans.

'To be honest,' says Rachel, 'we only care about the Shelley mansions. I'm enjoying the walks and I'm grateful to you for bringing me here. I can imagine more now.'

'Hang on. I'm in the story. I was visiting my aunt and was given a Red Dragon to wave.'

'OK,' says Rachel, 'OK. No appeasing a real witness.'

'We'll drive up to Claerwen and I'll be brief.'

Birmingham has its eye on the wild moorland above Nantgwyllt where the Claerwen surges with winter rain and melting snow. Once the Second World War is over, capital projects are fashionable, politic response to national bankruptcy and decay.

Claerwen will be a great concrete dam (though dressed in stone – to match its fellows), holding almost as much water as the three Elan ones combined. Construction begins in 1946. It's finished in 1952.

'We don't need the details,' says Rachel, 'but we want to hear your part, naturally.'

Like other subjects of Empire, the post-war Welsh are less loyal and quiet than their fathers and grandfathers. Before the proposed royal opening, an explosion damages an aqueduct. Security is stepped up. The dams are floodlit, police guard entrances and exits.

The opening of Claerwen goes ahead on 23 October. Elizabeth is queen but uncrowned. The old Elan train is gone and the royal pair detrain in Llandrindod. Much reduced from its Edwardian pomp, the town hides its shabby station with smart blue-painted boards. It installs a royal lavatory: the monarch with youthful bladder has no need to visit it.

'I was there,' says Fran, 'my aunt made fairy cakes to sell, with icing-sugar crowns. She got me into the group of local children waving Welsh-dragon flags on the roadside between Llandrindod and Rhayader. It was cold and wet, and the royal

car sped past like a rocket, so they didn't see us. Our black cardboard hats were sopping.'

'That's the source of your republicanism?' laughs Rachel.
'I'd feel the same. No politician would ignore little children. But
I guess hereditary rulers can.'

The pretty young Queen (with her dashing Duke in tow) is
welcomed to what the mayor calls 'the Lakeland of Wales' – the
name never caught on. Like her great-grandfather fifty years
before, she lacks skill with words and reads her speech in those
strangulated vowels she'll have to loosen over the seventy years
of her reign. Like him, she praises a region she never sets foot
in again (favouring tours to warmer, though more truculent,
imperial possessions).

Unlike in 1904, the weather's awful. Heavy rain raises the
water level too high for picturesque foam to cream the surface:
when the royal hand pulls the lever, nothing happens. This time
no one bothers with Shelley.

Seagulls are diving round in the air that's again growing chilly.
Fran feels it crinkling and wrinkling the skin under her layers
of clothing, though her jacket is tightly buttoned. Rachel and
Thomas stroll off leaving her to her feelings as they look over
Claerwen.

She cups her hand to hear herself, then turns towards the dead
people and houses under the water. A few yellow leaves are half
submerged where lake meets mud. She's been holding Shelley
at bay, not knowing so much of him as Thomas and Rachel, but
words from 'Lines Written among the Euganean Hills', his great
poem of self-puffing, dissolution and depression, flow through
her mind. The drowned city he imagines is Venice and by the
time of writing he's a better poet than the youth who set toy
boats floating on Elan river, but his vision of a flooded town
haunts wherever his life is led:

> The fisher on his watery way,
> Wandering at the close of day,
> Will spread his sail and seize his oar
> Till he pass the gloomy shore,
> Lest thy dead should, from their sleep
> Bursting o'er the starlight deep,
> Lead a rapid masque of death
> O'er the waters of his path.

The sun comes out in a rush and the slight chill withdraws. Between the scattering of rocks on the verge the grass is pea-green.

Fran rejoins the other two. Thomas is raring to get on his bike again and do something more with this barren landscape before they leave for good. He likes his companions well enough but is a little tired of ferrying them about.

'It's a forlorn place to some,' says Fran. 'For me it's less place than moment.'

Oh dear, Rachel thinks, finding again this home-love too sentimental by half. Her 'cabin' in the Poconos is in a beautiful woody setting, but she never lets it saturate her mind. Fran's enjoying her memories, Thomas is gloating over machinery: suffering phonelessness, Rachel isn't sure she wants to hear more of either. The land's too bare for humans to cope with, its hills fold in on themselves instead of coming out squarely as mountains.

Fran turns away so Rachel and Thomas don't notice her staring. Here, just here where the small river flows into the lake, here Andrew said he wanted something.

But he was never clear. Kind, methodical, nebulous Andrew. Because he was so often silent, she'd thought him insensitive. Yet on that hot cloudless day he'd commented on a spindly tree with just a few sprouts of life, its bony branches leaning out over the little river. One there now. Fran doubts it's the original. It doesn't matter. She's been here and seen a tree.

Jane Austen pats her shoulder lightly, Remember, what are men to rocks and mountains?

Irony may be true.

Back at the B&B it's what the landlady calls 'fish 'n' chip' night. They eat the vivid peas and soggy chips, while Fran and Rachel also attack the crisp batter armouring small slivers of dry fish.

'Grass is pea-green but peas are never grass-green,' Fran remarks.

Rachel eats with the circumspection Fran used for her first meal of raw Japanese swordfish. Surely she's had fish and chips before, though perhaps never as dry and fatty as this. Then she understands: Rachel is simply sapped with tiredness, her eyes almost shutting as she chews. She's unused to boisterous weather thinks Fran guiltily. She's forced her to walk and stand around while she, Fran, rattled on. 'Tough it out,' she smiles prodding the batter.

They retire early, before the yellowish light of the long evening is quite gone. Demented ideas speed round Fran's throat, which feels stuffed with paper handkerchiefs. Out of the blue she imagines Rachel young and in leather catsuit. 'For God's sake, get a grip,' she says aloud, thinking of her gaudy flash of fancy with Tamsin. She's glad Jane Austen is sound asleep in her wardrobe.

Next morning, she packs up night things and washbag, then, before leaving the room, tries Annie again.

'You're all identifying with Shelley too much. It isn't healthy.'

'I can hear you swallow after you said that,' mocks Fran. 'I don't care for Shelley any more than you do. I prefer the thingi-ness of Wordsworth touching "the hem of Nature's shift" – as Shelley put it, rather indecorously. But Shelley was here. He saw the Elan and Claerwen rivers roaring before they were tamed into quiet lakes.'

'Now you're identifying with him *and* the rivers. Poor Fran, soon you'll be going out in moonlight searching for his ghost. Best come home.'

Fran switches off the phone. Her memories have stirred no one else, her stories, her facts and fiction, just used-up air. Why tell them? Dr Johnson said (according to Annie) a story should make us enjoy life or endure it. Rachel's unanchored tales are better, more believable. Fran thinks of her cheerful aunt, the cakes, Andrew, depressed – she now supposes – in all this whir-ring air. Words shuffle about.

Will the place remember her? That moment when she sat on

a tussock of springy turf, like Jane Austen on the seaside path? Did young bookish Frances once sink down on that very spot: does it hold her youth? She fancies the dead from the mansions and cottages rising like crocuses in spring, their stable consciousness travelling down the centuries. Or herself, young and old, with them as pebbles at the bottom of the lake.

Jane Austen is preparing to leave too. You have to foreclose, you know. Learn to speak, cut, and edit – lives and words.

Fran feels deflated as she drags her holdall across the landing, bumping it down the stairs. Wrapped in a fluffy towel inside, Tickell can come to no harm. She feels the rasp in her throat and fears a cold coming.

I have little compassion for colds, says Jane Austen sidling by. Someone always has one; best make a joke of it. How shocking to have a cold, she mocks.

You said you felt languid and solitary when *you* had one, barks Fran to the retreating back.

Relieved of the Authorial presence, she hazards a little more melodrama when the friends meet outside. 'It feels like the flooding of my own life somehow.'

'Why, just because you were born in that grey village? Come off it!' says Rachel, happier now she anticipates a signal on the road home.

'OK. I just remember it as wilder when I was a child. We came in a Morris Minor. We had to get out to let Dad drive the car up the steeper hills. Grass and flowers seemed brighter, granite rocks more sparkling. Just young, I guess.'

'My father fished,' says Thomas. 'I envied him because he got away from Mother's talking. He'd sit looking at no one and nothing but water. He was a silent man except when infuriated by fish farms and maddened salmon. I remember his trout rivers, very sparkly for a child. Seem nothing special now.'

'Wordsworthian,' chuckles Rachel, 'the splendour only the child sees before the shine fades.'

'On the road, everyone,' says Thomas.

Does Fran discern a tender look between him and Rachel? Impossible, she's decades older, he's married. Her heart slows. Doesn't do to be surrounded by lovers. She's about to bat the idea away when she finds herself smiling. Tenderness and love aren't necessarily – not even primarily – excluding. Don't they overflow?

Wear pattens and keep your feet dry.

When you said the intimacy between Harriet and Emma must sink once they're married, she whispers, did you mean sex trumps affection or friendship can't exist with marriage? Or is it class, now we know Harriet's stain of illegitimacy is unbleached by nobility or wealth?

Jane Austen shrugs, then smiles slyly. You believe the reader's in charge, so answer yourself.

Thomas fixes his bicycle to the back of his Land Rover, while the women pile their baggage into the hired Vauxhall. Abruptly Rachel says, 'Perhaps we might all go to Venice for Shelley. Annie'd come too. Nice hotels, prosecco, *baccalà*.'

As Fran starts the car, the phone signal cuts in. A text arrives.

'God, I know why you're there, Fran. Crass of me not to see it. I'm on the next train.'

She texts back: 'No need, we're just leaving. Anyway, no train.'

Then she remembers: that anecdote she'd told, of the car unable to climb the hills – it was with Andrew not Dad. A VW, not a Morris Minor.

Part Three

15

Andrew? A soft scar not a wound.

Fran regrets saying he disappeared at Elan Valley. Annie was curious and the idea tumbled out. Annie, who prides herself on being rational, added poetic detail. Why not leave her the tale?

Sometimes memory is retentive, serviceable, and obedient, parrots Jane Austen, sometimes tyrannical and controlling. Sometimes you remember little. I myself . . .

Who's talking? What of motivated forgetting?

Fran resolves to take herself less seriously. She reaches for a notebook in the drawer of her rolltop desk, one of a diminishing pile pinched from the FE college. If the marvellous, tragic Mary Wollstonecraft could write her life as a comedy (sadly, husband William Godwin destroyed the manuscript) then the comic mode opens for us all. Fran stares through the window at leaves no longer freshly green.

Try practising what daffy Julie recommended for 4 a.m. glums: list good things – 'counting blessings', Mum called it. Home, food, small pension.

Jane Austen clears her throat. I made near £600 from my work. Possibly it would have been more had I handled my own affairs.

You are always about money.

Food too is a blessing, if not in excess: the mountain of wedding leftovers in my 'Lesley Castle' after all that roasting, broiling and stewing; Dr Grant of Mansfield dying from three

institutionary dinners; hampers of apples so kindly sent us from
Kintbury are covering . . .

Sometimes Jane Austen rabbits on as much as Agafia.

Again Fran thinks of Julie who never ate sugar, salt or
improper fats. Where is she now? Each week she drove to Sea
Palling in the early morning to 'dispel toxins' through shouting
at the top of her lungs from a clifftop. Once Fran went along,
carrying a message for Andrew inside a rinsed Heinz Ketchup
bottle: she'd intended to fling it out to sea but it stayed in her
anorak pocket. She was refreshed by the yelling until, spying
a knot of twitchers, she recovered inhibitions; Julie continued
balling.

Maybe her crystals and meditation, therapy, shouting, yoga,
circle dancing, diminished diet, colonic irrigation, and expensive visits to spas and beauty salons (a lucrative divorce), had
delivered the nurturing, romantic, rich, handsome man Julie
craved, and she'd abandoned 'negativity'. Fran had laughed
about her to Annie, but the woman knew what she wanted and
pampered herself till she got it.

She did laughter therapy too. Gelotology, the study of how
laughter affects the mind and body: a striped ice-cream of a word.

When not empty and habitual, laughter is, it's said, a sudden glory from thinking ourselves superior to someone, something, or (occasionally) ourselves at another time.

Jane Austen's laughs are joyful, sexy or vacuous but never solitary. Only drunks giggle alone. Fran stifles a chuckle as the wicked teenage tales of murder and comic mayhem flood her mind.

So, now to try a little grown-up autofiction, a modern mode. In the Three Geese Annie said one's feelings lack authority. We've exchanged self-knowledge for self-preoccupation, she'd added.

Yup, agrees Fran. She grins at her friend's certainties before the hummable tune of 'Amazing Grace' intrudes.

She's no urge to Social Media, the cats, flowers and bakery snaps of elderly sharing. But in a notebook with sharpened pencil surely some use of her past might answer – more than her other retirement 'projects': the study of Dylan Thomas and R.S. Thomas, an unlikely combo if ever; dying from the dyer's perspective – no editing possible if using experience, of course (ha ha!). 'You haven't died yet,' Annie'd objected. 'Anyway, been done. Sylvia Plath said she did dying very well.'

She hadn't though.

What can Fran call herself? Retired teacher? Mother of course, for there's sweet distant Johnnie, seen now mainly in lumpy face 'chats'. What else? Andrew had every right to disappear, but she'd prefer being a proper widow, not a fading-out Penelope weaving fibs – with no bereavement cards. Self-spoiling, certainly, yet distinguishing too. A disappeared spouse separates one from run-of-the-mill divorcees and widows. It just lacks a word.

Johnnie doesn't talk much of it. Only Fran knows he'd be another man had he folded his clothes neatly and brushed his teeth after every meal, with kindly coercive Andrew watching him. Now he imagines colourful scenarios to bury the absence: one clear blue day in New Zealand Dad shows up from South America with a native wife and lithe grown children to give him the family his mother tried unsuccessfully to provide through her friend's conceited kids.

Maybe the problem's simply retirement. Near a year without even a part-time job unmoors a body. Fran doesn't miss work. The excel sheets, benchmarks, outcome-based success measures, longitudinal education effects. Usually she sides with Lady Catherine de Burgh in her dispute with unschooled Elizabeth Bennet (so impudent to her elders and studious sister Mary). But, occasionally, she wonders at the efficacy of any tuition. Has she left traces on the FE college or its students? Probably waters closed even before her colleagues walked their separate ways from the Brigands' Arms following her leaving drinks.

On her first day there, she'd been given a shared office with her own desk. In the drawer she found an empty crisp packet. Salt and vinegar. So her predecessor was a traditionalist, female – mainly women teach English Literature – or literacy, as Annie once mocked her trade. Did this woman voluntarily walk away? What story in the crisp packet, left carelessly, or purposely, when files and handcream vanished?

Has Fran impinged on anyone? She recalls a clever boy who'd failed in school, then slouched his way to her: a beautiful adolescent – beauty can be found anywhere, nothing improper to know it. At first, he seemed stupid, his head having played no conspicuous part in his life. His time would come, she'd thought. His mother was everything to him; on an Open Day, she saw this mother was indeed something. Jamaican, a flamboyant Pentecostal, she seemed to live in a sequence of sun and twilit evenings. On 'benefits': her gift was to benefit the world. 'Fair do's', as Mum used to say. When Fran praised her, the boy replied, 'Not like you, eh?'

Some element in their many encounters urged her to speak of herself: I wanted to be a writer, she'd said. Or rather I *am* a writer, the label really means a detachment from your actual life, well semi-detachment.

She was boring the boy. 'How do you remember your dead great-grandfather?'

He shrugged. 'Like Grandad, s'pose.'

But he's not dead.

'Same thing.'

She accepted she'd lost the boy.

After all, it was routine, she paid to teach, he to learn, his last chance. So, if she had a tie to him, it was no enchanting affinity.

He'll be grown up now, seeking revenge like the rest of us, making joy and discontent with his beauty. Perhaps he resembles an Aubrey Beardsley drawing, gorgeous and deliciously debauched. She'd have liked to learn he became something traditional like a poet, a violinist, a painter on wood – she was still old-fashioned there. It made more sense he'd become a star of some media with his honey skin and mother's radiance. She could probably find out by searching the Internet, but let's leave him in his golden adolescence, with so much inchoate promise.

She goes out to walk round her pretty garden. The weight of clippers and trowels in kangaroo pockets pulls her baggy jump suit towards her crotch. It makes her feel both free and prepared.

The garden isn't finished. What garden is? Nothing living can be. Just books. That's why novels are so dangerous, they give false ideas of permanence. For readers, that is.

I love a neat garden, says Jane Austen, flowers, fruit, borders.

Back inside after dead-heading a few roses and pulling up some towering weeds by the greenhouse, she writes, 'My name is Fran, widow – possibly'. She scratches out the word and substitutes 'probably', then obliterates that too – 'daughter, mother and friend.' After less than a minute staring at and adjusting her sentence, she exclaims, I need dialogue.

You've learnt something, sighs Jane Austen. 'Alone' always has someone else. She gives one of those particular smiles. Something always serves, nothing will sometimes serve.

Oh fuck, says Fran. She tears out and crumples her page. A great eraser and cross-writer, Jane Austen scowls at the waste of paper.

Piles of books lean against the wall. They've travelled with Fran, she owes them loyalty. But they've bred without her consent.

'I'll drown my books,' says Prospero.

An over-dramatic response to unwanted volumes, even magic ones that can uproot pine and cedar.

Her books are paperbacks, yellowing faster than antique lace, hardback unread biographies and out-of-fashion poetry, a few brown crumblies.

Instead of scribbling or sifting books, Fran decides on deep cleaning. She scrubs the dirtiest parts of the kitchen floor, then attacks the smudged, fat-stained stove. From time to time she looks through the little window to see if the regular blackbird has come.

It hasn't, so she listens instead to the cooing and plonking of pigeons. The stove is now brighter but still smudged; it shows up the grubbiness of counter tops and wooden cabinet doors. Annie suggested distressing them.

With all this desire to clean, clear and remember, at once speak and be silent, is Fran having a late mid-life crisis? An old-age crisis? She regards her gardening hands. Thin paper skin stretching like poor soil over rocky veins.

Jane Austen doesn't see housework as 'work'. Never mistake my life for yours, snaps the Author. We women always had servants, a goodly number, even at our poorest. You have transport and can go where you wish, but I, with only a donkey-cart, was always served. I was never on my knees in a garden or on a kitchen floor.

To avoid more coffee after her cleaning, Fran makes a cup of Celestial Seasonings tea, then sits cradling the mug. The taste is nothing, it's the comfy bear with the cat on the box that makes her infuse and drink.

She sips, thinking of the trip to Venice with Annie, Thomas and Rachel. By turns she's excited and apprehensive. They'd come to her place, she'll go to theirs – to Shelley's and Annie's: Annie with her luscious colour schemes is a walking Venice. Fran will be the odd one out, she must expect it and prepare.

Jane Austen closes her eyes, exasperated, Why not seize the pleasure? How often is happiness destroyed by foolish preparation!

Sometimes Jane Austen has a point.

Fran imagines them in Cambridge now: Thomas, Rachel, Annie and a gaggle of confident youths, perhaps buoyant lovely Tamsin. Doing what they do there, day in, day out. Reading, writing, talking, talking, sipping strong coffee, sherry, wine, walking from courts to panelled rooms, cycling imperiously through ambling tourists and townsfolk, served good free food, talking again into phones and to themselves. Paid for it, entitled for the moment whatever their race or gender – or even original class. (Why not add 'age' to the potent trinity? The biggest category, in time including everyone not prematurely dead.)

She returns to thinking of the town itself, the Backs, King's Parade, Petty Cury, no longer full of fish and odd smells but chain cafés and cheap shoe shops, the low swampy parks good only to cycle through. Cambridge does spring better than anywhere, but it's high summer now – time for trippers and roistering parties, the sluggish chalk river a fairground dodgem-track of swollen punts, pink canoes and colourful kayaks.

Should she ring Johnnie? The hour's always wrong. She never knows what she's barging into. He'd say the right thing, as always, but would she? She'd hear the alien life in the background, the children's strange New Zealand vowels.

Johnnie – burdensome after Andrew 'left', but the warmest loveliest, most soothingly disturbing burden a life could have.

She wishes she could speak to her own mother. Too late. If she looks in the mirror, she sees a version of her but not to talk to. Poor Mum, she'd begun sinking almost at once without the man she loved wholly or at least needed wholly and probably loved, though Dad's indiscriminate benevolence, his kindness to all and sundry, riled her. With no elm to cling to, she's forsaken ivy, trailing her thoughts limply in a 'home'.

Silly to think like this; dementia doesn't come from life's vicissitudes or weaknesses, it's a disease in the brain, not an eviction of mind. Dad would have coped, dressing his once capable wife's body each morning in proper clothes – ironed blouse, straight skirt, and stockings – propping it in a chair, and replying to the polite phrases still rattling round the emptying skull, and even, when the worst arrived, changing pads and wiping a drooling mouth, but never letting the indignity obliterate their past, never as long as he drew breath and his arm worked, banishing his wife to a 'home'.

This, thinks Fran, is coupledom at its best. Annie and she had never got the hang of it. Or was the model hopelessly old-fashioned?

Oh well, Andrew, we didn't make such a hash of it, did we? Johnnie is a good boy.

She looks through the window and this time the blackbird is there, on the patch of grass in front of the holm oak, stabbing the ground with its bright beak. Over and over in the same place, as if its bird brain has no memory.

16

Fran's bedroom has what Charles Dickens called sad-coloured curtains. She finds them soothing as she lies under the summer duvet anticipating the order of inshore waters in the Shipping Forecast. A depression over Iceland apparently. Some minutes later she learns that in South Norfolk it will be a mostly sunny day: high cloud and an easterly breeze. Contrarily, she imagines snow falling.

One year, it fell long and hard over the Long Mynd. Everyone worried about the ponies; then, as it continued, about themselves.

Down into the steep valleys and along the main roads and rail lines it fell, disguising them as the fields they once were. It was Boxing Day, the beginning of the deflated season after too much sugar. Especially *this* year, for Mum had made trays of mince pies to give to visitors. Since none came because of the weather, it was a kindness to gorge as many as possible.

Dad tapped his barometer. Knowing the sad consequence of snowfalls, he was excited nonetheless. The war had been good to him, as he to it; dangers, extremes, made his heart race. Mum was from Radnorshire; snow meant frozen hens and buried sheep.

Years on, this particular winter will become famous as the coldest one since – well, some time, forever. The educated said 1683 or 1739, though Fran doubts measurements were accurate enough for anyone to be certain. The proof comes from art: lighting fires, roasting oxen, and making mayhem on the Thames with cartoon phrases flying from mouths. We know how false art can be when it proposes to tell history.

Andrew, big quiet Andrew, came to stay, arriving on one of the last trains. He brought off-kilter gifts, a wooden pocket puzzle for Dad, a daisy candleholder for Mum, and a long-playing record for Fran, whose little gramophone took only 45s.

Jumping the gun as usual, Mum thought him too big. 'You're too short for him,' she said, 'child-bearing would be trying.' 'Honestly,' she'd replied as she often did when exasperated at her parents' simplicity. 'Honestly!'

Andrew was studying Geology and there wasn't much talk to be got from that. He'd fallen for garrulous, cheerful Fran and pursued her even though she'd had her eyes – hopelessly in the event – on the boy sharing his rooms off Grange Road, a show-off poet intending to amaze the world; he was exiled in Selwyn when he should have been at King's.

Mum and Andrew did their best to chat. Neither best was enough. There were silences whenever the two were alone. Unless the corgi was there; then Andrew patted its square rump and admired its yappy spirit. The house was warmer than his own centrally heated home in Twickenham, for the coal-burning stove in the kitchen was unregulated and splashed its heat through the whole house. Bigger than all of them, he was uncomfortable in the suffocating chairs and sofas bought to accommodate smaller folk. He wasn't used to the steep-sloping ceilings of the attic rooms; they could hear him banging his head every time he climbed to his bedroom, then suppressing his groans where each of them would have cried out, not using naughty words of course but variants, Gosh, Goodness, Heavens Above, My Giddy Aunt. Though, since she started at College, Fran now regularly said Fuck.

His ways were towny ways, not theirs. Yet everyone had the greatest good will and sometimes, when all together, they got on amicably, with Dad and Fran doing most of the talking. The telly was a fine source of topics. Andrew said the London smog reached even Twickenham. Mum said yes, she'd heard that on the news. There was a lot of mist when she was a girl, but she supposed that was different. Andrew said it was. Smog was man-made. 'They will stop it by stopping coal fires completely,' he said. 'Oh,' said Mum, we love our coal fires, don't we, John?' She stoked the sitting-room grate which augmented the big stove. She'd been cold most of her childhood and was grateful for a marriage that brought such warmth. Years later, Fran realised her own wheezing had as much to do with her family's heating methods as with the corgi. Both gone and her parents in a modern bungalow with no grate in the sitting room, she breathed normally. But she missed the corgi and the blanketing, coal-sucking heat.

Sometimes in the past, thinking back, she felt shame for one or other of her parents, their gentle efforts to make Andrew feel 'at home' or 'bring him out of his shell'. (Mum annoyingly called him Fran's boyfriend.) At others, she was ashamed for Andrew. Now she wondered at her own graceless feelings.

After a couple of days, Christmas would officially end above the little shop. Time for Dad to start taking stock and look through accounts, and for Mum to check outstanding orders before they opened again and welcomed the High Street. So many orders there were: people ate more on Christmas Day, but why after? Mum kept herself trim and exclaimed over portly customers and their extra demands for chocolate, syrup, Welsh cakes and potatoes.

Then, just as everyone was wondering whether the visit, lovely for the young people but a bit of a strain, might now be over, and Andrew's own parents and brothers missing him in Twickenham, it snowed again. It went on snowing. Gales whipped up a blizzard. Power lines tumbled down. Villages, remote houses and the few farms to whom Dad delivered his special ham and groceries were cut off in drifts. Coal wasn't delivered either, many houses had no back-up of wood to burn.

'Poor people,' said Mum. And they were. They'd eaten their turkey and Christmas pudding and were isolated in cold parlours full of aunts, uncles, grandchildren, and all the unskilled stuff of

Christmas. Trains weren't running, so there was no question of visitors going home.

Under the snow and wind, the awkwardness in the warm house diminished. Andrew felt its cosiness although he still bumped his head on the attic ceiling and knocked into the occasional table placed where Mum left her glasses and keys, well below the eyeline of someone over six feet. It was all right: Andrew was furniture now.

I know, so cosy, intrudes Jane Austen. At Randalls in the Westons' Christmas party, as snow falls and Emma . . .

Shhh you weren't there yet.

Snow drifted up the shop window making the High Street with its steep cambers into a flat untrodden plain.

No chance of opening the front door, but the back stable door on to the sloping courtyard might be possible. Dad and Andrew pushed and pushed against its thickness till they forced a crack in the bottom half which, after a further greater push, they could squash through. They began shovelling snow out through the big back gates that led from the courtyard over the rough path to scrub beyond, Andrew piling his snow with almost artistic neatness. Mum and Fran watched, Fran suddenly aware how short Dad was. She knew about Mum, but Dad was a surprise. She offered to help, but there were only two big shovels. It was before feminism and she didn't insist. Besides, she didn't like the cold.

While the men shovelled, Mum baked scones and sponge cakes and made meat pies to 'feed the workers'. They weren't short of food – how could they be? – a whole shop to eat their way through and courtyard lofts full of grain, oats, rice and sweet-smelling Bramley apples stored for crumbles and charlottes during the dreary months of January and February. They could have lived isolated for years and been well fed. Even with big lanky Andrew, who, Mum said, must need 'building up'.

'The Jenkinses,' Dad exclaimed, 'the Keelings and Eveleighs, how will they cope without my delivery?'

Still snow fell and ice hardened between layers. The low front shop-window grew darker and darker with cold padding. The telly was intermittent but, when it worked, Mum watched with her ironing board set up in front. 'The sea's freezing,' she said.

'The news is always sensational,' Dad replied. Fran thought he remembered the War when he said this. She imagined him being rescued from destroyers that sank under him, then jumping back into the ice of Scapa Flow to pull out bodies. He'd remark, when praised, it was nothing 'sensational'.

'We have to do deliveries,' he said.

'It would be madness, John. You'd be lost in a snowdrift in no time.'

'We must, all those people depending on us.'

Andrew was on the sofa away from the fire. 'I can drive. I've passed my test.'

'Madness,' said Mum.

'It's a big van, Andrew,' said Dad, 'but maybe together.'

'Sheer madness,' said Mum.

'The farmers will be out of pocket,' said Dad, 'the tubers will freeze in the ground. It's that cold.'

The telly fell into its night-time silence. When it came on again in the morning, it showed people skating on the Thames.

'Do you live near the Thames?' asked Mum.

'Twickenham is on the Thames,' said Andrew.

'Oh,' said Mum, 'that's nice.'

Andrew and Dad scraped snow off the van. It took them best part of the freezing morning. At first the engine wouldn't start, but after coaxing it sputtered and came to life. 'It's a grand machine,' said Dad.

Clucking disapproval, Mum made up outstanding orders. Telephone lines were down, so she and Fran packed up other ones, assuming what might be wanted. Mum kept the score. 'Prices will go up, it says so on the wireless. New supermarkets will be raking it in.'

'No need for us to do that,' said Dad.

'You always were a soft touch, John.'

The women stood watching as snow continued falling and the men set off in the van, the great shovels packed in the back for clearing lanes where snow ploughs had failed. Both were calm, matter-of-fact.

They returned way after dark. Mum was baking again to pass her anxious time. Fran was reading.

'They were so grateful,' said Dad, 'the Keelings all came tumbling out of the farm when they saw the van coming. They pressed tea and cake on us everywhere we went, they were that pleased.'

'So they should be,' said Mum wiping her floury hands on her housecoat.

Andrew's eyes were shining.

The snow went on through the next weeks, but trains were soon running again, with signalmen pouring boiling water over the signals to force them up and down.

Andrew left. Had his mother or a brother phoned, were telephone lines restored? Perhaps he just went because the 'holiday' was over. Everyone liked him by now.

'I couldn't have done it without that boy,' said Dad.

'You could do worse,' said Mum to Fran.

She'll get up and ring Johnnie, even if his vowels have changed and the hour is wrong. 'I love you,' she'll say. He'll pause a moment, then reply, 'I love you too, Mum.'

17

The Master's wife appraises Annie's embroidered, purple-sequinned décolletage, edged by the black gown on which – against all propriety – she's pinned a glittering purple brooch. She whispers publicly across the table, 'My dear, you have such style.'

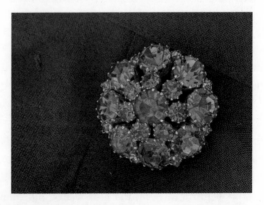

Annie smiles. She intends her eyes to be cool but they reflect the sparkle from the brooch.

Next to her a small plump Fellow tries to regain her attention. In a deep voice she wonders could ever carry in a lecture hall, he says, 'You might be interested to know that Nero watched gladiators through an emerald. Possibly it helped his short sight.'

'Really,' says Annie, looking demurely at her plate.

'And, of course, spectacle-makers invented the telescope.'

She turns her gaze on him, a sequin flashes in the candlelight. Outside the closed curtains, it's still daylight.

'They had bifocal lenses in the eighteenth century. Benjamin Franklin mentions them. After a certain age everyone needs spectacles.'

'If great readers, perhaps,' says Annie, whose reading glasses are tucked into her beaded evening bag.

'Everyone who reads at all.'

The plump Fellow senses the Master's wife regarding them both, pencilled eyebrows raised. He shifts his buttocks inside their black trousers and thick gown. Sweat settles round his testicles. 'More quackery in optometry than almost any other area,' he continues. 'Have you heard of iridology and supposed ways of reversing myopia? No? As if exercising the eye and eating special food could affect a lens!' While he laughs, his nose leaks just a little. 'A man called Bates told people they could throw away their spectacles.' He shakes his head in disbelief, a small droplet leaves his nose to land on his black tie.

A pity, thinks Annie, for the timbre of his voice, though low and gravelly, isn't unpleasing. That droplet is a killer.

A mousey woman – of course, his wife, this is the one feast of the year to welcome spouses – pulls at his arm from his other side. She's no more minded than a fruit fly on his thick jacket.

'I thought it was a useful exercise to cover eyes with your palms and try to see blackness,' says Annie glancing towards the Master's wife now talking in skinny animation.

'Indeed yes. It has merit but won't cure myopia and cataracts.'

Her neighbour's warming again to his subject. 'As I say, many quacks. One authority recommended putting small eye-stones under the eye lid.'

'Hmmm,' says Annie thinking involuntarily of Paul and frowning, 'people can be so gullible.'

'I'm boring you, I fear,' he says, loudly enough to startle his irritated wife.

'Yes, goodness,' she says, 'Annie won't want to hear all that stuff about optics.'

He gives her a withering glance before Annie can lean round to say, 'No, really, it's fascinating.'

'Robert Hooke, the great promoter of microscopes, argued that such new optical instruments could restore perfect eyesight not seen on earth since Adam and Eve fell.'

'Hope it wasn't a disappointment,' replies Annie. Then she adds, 'Blind eyes are more terrible than seeing ones.'

Before he can articulate surprise, she leans back in her chair and remarks, 'I think your wife needs your attention.' She's putting them both down, but why not? We're all outsiders, as Fran would say, trying to make the smuggest bits of England a little less smug. The wet patch on the man's tie is almost dry: it leaves only the slightest outline of a stain. His wife will have the right kind of chemical in a bottle to remove it.

Across the table the Master's wife is saying, 'I abhor vivisection or any cruelty to animals.' The benign Nobel Prize winner next to her, pats her thin arm in its tight emerald sleeve and says, 'Yet such research does so much good for human beings. Think how much suffering of children will be alleviated by the pain of a few rats.'

Annie doesn't hear the rest. The poor man forgets the Master is childless. His wife has two silkily flowing Afghan hounds.

*

That night in the house lined with bookshelves Paul painted green, Annie waives her rule of smoking only in the garden. She does however open the window. The weather's balmy; the scent of something flowery wafts in. Lilac and jasmine are gone, it's too late for wallflowers. Is it honeysuckle? Surely too strong. Roses? But hers, inherited from previous owners of the house, are red and blowsy, with blemishes and weak scent.

Did this mixed ostentation and uselessness mean they'd been bred for disease? Oh rose, thou art sick.

In his fatal illness, Zach Klein had said quite clearly, despite a clogged throat, 'The invisible worm.' A phrase from Blake's poem 'Sick Rose', it had to be; yet she'd never known he loved or even read Blake. Was it the morphine? But drugs can only access what's inside. Or is there something Jungian out there, a cloud of fragmentary quotations from well-known poetry, songs, snippets much used and strummed through a million mouths – to which anyone may let their consciousness or dreaming mind have access?

If any Blake lingered in Zach, it ought to be the image of Nobodaddy, the great blind Bully in the sky. Zach thought browbeating his family droll. Yet for Annie, as much as for her mother and stupid Josh, it had been deadly, the only difference being – they went on admiring what crushed them. Was she so different from her pathetic brother? In adult years, while hating him she'd accepted no man came up to Zach, held a candle to his showy brilliance, certainly not ineffectual Paul – though, now absconded, his act of desertion puffed him out of old recognition. For all his antics, Zach Klein had, to Annie's chagrin, never left the family home. When she said a variation of this, Fran greeted it with, 'Take a BA in the blindingly obvious' – and, on her birthday, gave her a mug decorated round its middle with an irritating Austen quotation: 'So much we don't know of ourselves . . . Very seldom does complete truth belong to any human disclosure.'

The flowery smell still assails her nostrils. Is she smelling the garden as it used to be when Paul tended it? She blinks to dislodge bitterness – the garden, the house – done up with *her* money.

She stubs out her cigarette in an ornamental alabaster ashtray kept pristine till now. She gets up, unzips her dress, lets it fall to the floor, then tries to expunge both Paul and Zach with violent yoga postures. She succeeds better by thinking of Fran and Rachel.

She'd had no desire to go to Elan Valley, indeed still doesn't know exactly where it is. A Londoner through and through, she's familiar with every street and dead-end that could be breached in Camden, Hampstead and Islington (privately, she regards Cambridge as little more than a provincial cow town).

Yet she wishes the others hadn't gone to this outlandish Welsh place without her.

'Are you allowed to drown in drinking water?' she'd asked Fran in their last phone-call.

'Can't even fish in it. Sorry, Annie, it's so long ago. Dead past. I've finished settling it.'

Annie sits and smokes, then stubs out her cigarette and picks up her discarded dress. She phones. Fran will be in bed but not sleeping, so it's all right to disturb. 'Nothing settles,' she says. She's still impatient with anyone not experiencing her own fiery distress. 'You reinvent your past. Quite a skill.'

'Well,' Fran wants to mollify, 'when Johnnie reached his dad's age, he said he thought he should maybe create some excitement in his easy life by having a mid-life crisis.'

That's a giveaway, thinks Annie. Unable to shrug off her own ache, she exclaims, 'Poor Fran.'

Gulping back annoyance, Fran sits up in bed. 'You will get through,' she says. She's weary of repeating herself, but that's friendship.

'I won't,' says Annie.

Why tell people what they should do and will feel? It makes them unhappy and you disliked. In grief we become toddlers.

I know what you mean, whispers Jane Austen into Fran's right ear. Think of petulant Marianne responding to Elinor's sound advice.

Just as well Fran's silent, thinks Annie. If she can utter such triteness, losing Andrew can't ever have been much. Or is Fran making a point that she, Annie, is more needy?

'Sorry, Fran,' she says. 'On edge. They're having a baby.'

'Bound to happen.'

'That should teach her. "Happy heart" doesn't sound the kind of woman to scrape shit off a sleepsuit.'

'Were we?' murmurs Fran. 'Must try to sleep.'

18

Annie gets up late from a dream-disturbed night. Can you dream wrongly? Again she smokes by the open window, an empty coffee cup beside her. She's thinking of Rachel who's not yet quite real to her. How is she teaching creative writing with only one unremembered novel? Rachel had patted away her (discreet) enquiry. People may write in different genres, she'd implied. Under different names? Multiple personae? Where then is truth in the memories she shares? Does she fib like Fran?

They say you can make something true by imagining it intensely: can you make it go away by energetically forgetting?

Not yet. Moths fly in a jar.

Zach said he was relieved when her childhood was over. The misery of that memory almost chokes her. Vomit it all up, she orders herself. No masticating, swallowing then regurgitating; just spew it straight out.

What had the man wanted from her? Reverence, admiration? He got them from her mother, the woman he forced to become feeble and of little use to her daughter.

Why fuss? He's gone and Paul is gone. So let's clipclop through this finite life.

When Thomas Ashe was still her research student, Annie asked him a searching question to prod him further in his study of Shelley and the numinous. He'd answered, 'Dum-dum.' It made them both smile. Dum-dum, she says to herself now.

Fran's no scholar, more a feral academic. She loves the byways and fusion of words, her mental hodgepodge, her galli-maufry. Giving houseroom to Jane Austen is weird, but a little of the imaginary may not be so bad. Conan Doyle, creator of the rational sleuth, believed in fairies. Embarrassed by his credulity, we say that, like so many Englishmen of his time, he was emotionally battered by the First World War, so turned to magic and spiritualism as exit from horror. But perhaps no need of four years unrelenting bloodshed; a more modest battering or bruising may explain bizarre sightings. Is this Fran's situation: Andrew's disappearing a bigger deal than she's let on? Yet, that self-righteous Author of hers is no fairy.

She stubs out her third Gauloises in the ornamental ashtray, leans back in her Fritz Hansen Egg Chair and stares through the window. Dum-dum has failed, the ghost returns.

Even in death Zach was lucky: throat cancer silenced his poxy voice, so he hadn't lived to see his beloved Marxism roll out like Matthew Arnold's Sea of Faith. She might any time have equalled the old goat, become an intellectual superstar herself: demotic firebrand one day, high-and-mighty scholar the next. Isn't the world better for her reticence, her refusal of crude journalism? She's said as much to the chaps on College high table. In my day, they chuckled, if you had anything to communicate, you did it over port. Yet still she seethes at failures only this man could knead into her heart.

To spite him, she'd settled for girlie EngLit, an autopsy of a subject if ever. (The alternative of throwing herself violently away took more guts than she'd ever had . . .) When she'd flung Zach a fine review of her first monograph on political writing of the 1790s – OK by a colleague in Chicago – he sneered,

> See, ladling butter from alternate tubs,
> Stubbs butters Freeman, Freeman butters Stubbs.

That monograph had more citations than most of those re-maindered by fucking Academicians who'd turned her down – not once but three times. (She hasn't told Fran that – Fran who soothes her when she complains of her world, Fran who loves and, she thinks wrongly, envies her.)

Why, her friend once asked, doesn't she protest openly? She's spent years combing history for rebels to hurl at the forever elite purring and preening at the top of everything from land to culture. Why not shout out at the present?

In 1819 Byron's friend John Cam Hobhouse wrote an article on the 'Six Acts' Parliament passed to gag radical newspapers and prevent large meetings in order to stop the French Revolution spawning a second English one.

'What prevents the people from walking down to the House, and pulling out the members by the ears, locking up their doors and flinging the key into the Thames,' asked Hobhouse.

'The horse-guards down the road,' responded Lord Byron.

Exactly.

Annie smiles, thinking that Fran is simply less aware of horse-guards than she is.

Fran never met Zach Klein, so can never know Annie as Annie knows her. For Annie has been to Fran's parents' little bungalow, just before 'Dad' died. Not smelling of the honeyed ham Fran mentioned when she occasionally spoke of childhood, but still having about it the air of a cosy little shop, with everything offered at a reasonable price, the quaint parents living to serve themselves and others. Fran feared Annie would be condescending to them, gracious in an upper-middle-class way. But Annie felt moved that Fran was sharing with her these good people – though she wouldn't and couldn't for one moment have imagined herself being their child. Now Fran's 'Mum' has gone, drifted off into a place where no one's buying or selling, while she, Annie, has lost mother and father. It brings them together. Both orphans.

When Josh and she went to pack up the now expensive

Chalcot Square house and sell the books – discovering that old Sociology, even by inflammatory Zach Klein, wasn't worth what they'd hoped – she found the place grimy and rank: laundry stank in the basket and kitchen fumes lingered on dining-room curtains, while the cluttered study swirled out a stench of cigars and full-bodied sickly red wine. Nothing like this was allowed in her mother's time, though Zach's personal habits must always have been grubby. Sadie had hardly been noticed, but she'd kept all these rooms pristine where now they were dirty and decayed. With her absence, had vain Zach realised he was not a coper, not an independent self-reliant man after all? She doubted he'd had such awareness, even as his clothes and rooms began to stink.

Yet, something animated remained in the showy house – which Oxbridge Annie had once judged lacking the shabby, refined gentility of the established academic tribe. A kind of residual hubbub from Zach's talking, loose gravel on the underside of a shoe, though no words could be made out.

The property was in a 'good neighbourhood' with access to an exclusive little railed garden. As children, she and Josh played in this Goldengrove – with no great enthusiasm, having nothing in common. He'd seek out insects to kill or maim while she studied people walking outside the railings. Perhaps passers-by were envious of those within, allowed to feel grass instead of tarmac under feet, while she imagined herself beyond her caged existence into the little family groups that armed each other and wheeled pushchairs, dragged poodles and waddling dachshunds.

When she visited Chalcot Square from Cambridge, she found this garden with its iron gate the ultimate symbol of everything wrong with the country, her family and childhood. Now, if she were inside the railings, strangers would be walking with headphones clamped to their ears, removing them far from excluding patches of grass.

With a little renovating and much disinfecting, the 'family home' brought in a tidy sum. Most went to Josh who'd never held down a job but had taken on a wife with children already clinging to her. OK, Annie wasn't in financial need then, and what she got was more than enough to pay off a mortgage and fix up the Cambridge house for herself, Paul and the kids, throwing out the back wall in the common way of the neighbourhood. Yet it wasn't 'fair' when you thought about it. Josh had even taken Zach's only picture of value, a portrait by von Neff of some rabbi from Estonia. Not that she cared for the subject – was she the only Jew utterly uninterested in forebears?

Still gazing through the window, she thinks of Fran's delight in her visiting blackbird. Where Paul had made a raised bed to grow lettuce and rocket, a pigeon now hops among the ragwort and dandelions as if hobbled. It looks too heavy to fly and yet, with what seems an enormous effort, it pushes itself into the air. It's borne up to land inelegantly on a cherry-tree bough that bends under its portliness. But it *has* flown, thinks Annie, looking out for analogies in life.

Not waddling but flying.

19

Latish summer and Fran comes again to stay with Annie to finalise the Venice trip. The train rolls over the low wet land beyond Ely, boats below road banks and lonely blank houses across open fields. She's considering Odysseus, the cunning storyteller, striding out of the known into so many new worlds and words. I too, she thinks, am going into new worlds. Do I have enough material to entertain the natives?

Want of material never stopped me from writing, announces Jane Austen.

Once more, Fran and Rachel sit in the independent café where they planned the Elan trip. They know each other better now. Fran moves her chair to settle her legs, wishing she had more bulk in this pokey upstairs room. As usual, the young govern the air with their enormous limbs and laughter, taking more space than is decently theirs.

'I just wanted to tell you I liked our Welsh jaunt,' says Rachel. 'Even more in retrospect. It's helped me come to a decision to stay.'

'In Wales?' Fran shifts her eyebrows which, Rachel thinks, would benefit from some threading or tattooing.

'No, 'course not, but in Britain, here, not going back to New York. I was on secondment for the writing course. I could be renewed.'

Fran finds this notion of choice invigorating – in jobs, country, even it seems in age, for Rachel must be in her mid-sixties, older? Here she'd be pushed out to grass – or kept on part-time as last resort for an emptying classroom.

Rachel is looking away. Enabled to stare with impunity, Fran registers again her companion's polished, groomed, manicured appearance. She's handsome in that synthetic American way, yet, underneath the high gloss, a little perhaps dilapidated. Maybe the wind and rain in Wales had disguised both gloss and worn underlay. Or was there a perforation below the surface?

'Even if I weren't, I could just stay.'

'Without a job?'

'I have a little family money.'

'Righto. So, in Venice you kip at the Danieli while we pig it over a taverna in Mestre?'

Rachel shrugs. The idea isn't preposterous.

*

'Are we all going?' asks Fran later, meeting the others for another coffee perched on spindly metal chairs by the market flower stall. 'The whole caboodle?'

'If you mean me as caboodle, then yeah,' laughs Tamsin, 'I'm in; they'll have WiFi and I can like apply for things if I have to on my iPad. Besides, I have to go to Italy for research.' She smiles slyly at Annie, who's adjusting her purple and mauve scarf caught in the twists of her dangling birdcage ear-rings. 'African-Americans scootered all over. Italians liked them and they liked Italians till the Fascists marched into Ethiopia. Bet you guys never heard of David F. Dorr and his book *A Colored Man Round the World*?'

'Right there,' says Annie, 'and you'll tell us about it.'

'Nah,' replies Tamsin. 'Out of my period – 1852 – but you can like read it. Usual story. Dorr went to Italy with a Louisiana plantation owner who said he'd free him when they got back and didn't. So he ran off to Ohio and wrote his book. Not that interesting to be honest, I'm more like into divas of colour. It's a sideline,' she adds as Annie looks quizzical. 'Everyone loves a singing-dancing diva and, man, do we breed them: Mattiwilda Dobbs, Ellabelle Davis, Leontyne Price, Katherine Dunham, Maya Angelou.'

'Oh,' says Fran, wondering how Tamsin gets the tints on her lower eye-rim. What would happen to the iridescent greeny-blue if she cried salt tears over those vivid tawny cheeks? She'd have to suck them back. Can an eye suck in like a throat or a nose sniffing? If other orifices can withdraw expression, why not an eye? Not an ear though.

Tamsin shrugs, 'Of course I can be doggo if you prefer.'

'My grant,' Thomas is saying, 'lets me track Shelley in Venice like in Wales.'

'What about your family?' Fran shouldn't ask.

'Kiran never wants to stand in the way of my work.' Thomas

pauses before adding, 'She's happy for me to go with you.'

'We thought we were going with *you*,' says Fran.

'You know,' intrudes Rachel, wanting to move off the personal, 'Virginia Woolf detested Venice.'

That snobbish body would detest any person or place she considered 'underbred'. Venice is supremely vulgar.

Tamsin is saying, 'I guess you guys don't watch *Doctor Who*? Well, in one episode, Doctor Who and her team time-travel to Villa Diodati on the ghostly night in 1816 when *Frankenstein* is born. It turns out the person whose visions are making all life and history vulnerable is Shelley. He's like the "guide". When it's suggested he might be sacrificed to save the rest, you get his "Defence of Poetry", arguing poetry is a mirror making beautiful what's distorted. His thoughts will inspire centuries, so his words like matter. Save the poetry, save the universe. See? Yet when it comes to the ending and the need, like in an upmarket funeral, is for fine lines to intone, they don't use Shelley's utopia but Byron's dystopia, "Darkness":

> The winds were wither'd in the stagnant air,
> And the clouds perish'd; Darkness had no need
> Of aid from them – She was the Universe.

Byron can lay it on.'

Fran's impressed at Tamsin storing so much English men's poetry. A vision of her as a memorising forties' schoolgirl with crooked or no teeth – some girls had them all pulled, so the false would deliver film-star smiles. She blinks away the vision.

'I've been to Villa Diodati,' says Thomas

'Yikes, on another grant,' laughs Tamsin showing a set of level white teeth.

Did anyone have teeth like this when Fran was a girl? How do they do it?

'Well, yes. It's suburban now.'

'I'd better read up on it all. I've been to Venice only once, as a student, for half a day on the way to Yugoslavia. It rained.' She didn't mention how the water stabbed through Andrew's black umbrella.

Thomas looks at her complacently. 'Reading up's the way.' He shrugs. 'Remember, Byron's Venice was created by Ann Radcliffe. She'd never been there and *she* took it from Dr Johnson's great friend, Hester Piozzi. Then Byron creates Venice for everyone after, including the art critic Ruskin and Turner. So the city's always already written and read.'

Fran raises her eyes, as Jane Austen so often does under that symmetrically curled hair.

What, pray, is the difference in memory between seeing a place and reading of it, looking directly or through an image? In the Middle Ages one might receive indulgence for sins by doing pilgrimage to a decent *copy* of a shrine.

To prevent Fran reacting to what she'll judge patronising, Annie butts in, 'We should *all* read Mrs Piozzi before going. Her Venice stank and was infested with beggars and filth; no cows, so no fresh milk. But she does glamour charmingly: lights and music in the piazza, swishing gondolas, laughter from cafés across the lagoon. Byron too sees ordinary within extraordinary. Venice is perhaps his most creative time: excess writing, excess sex. He wrote to his publisher John Murray, "There's a whore on my right/For I rhyme best at night."'

My John Murray, adds Jane Austen, was a rogue, he would have drooled over such salacious letters.

Murray was generous to you, mutters Fran, you and your brother miscalculated. You thought your copyright more valuable than it was.

Jane Austen is remembering her amazing future worth. In the long run . . .

In the long run we are all dead.

Murray wasn't infallible. He turned down *Frankenstein*.

'I thought we were going for Shelley,' says Rachel. 'Are you a bit enthralled by Byron, Annie?'

'Italy's always Byron's rather than Shelley's.'

Thomas's phone rings. He turns away to answer it, then stands up. 'Yes, yup,' he says at intervals. 'I'll see about it. Yup.'

Fran studies Tamsin, busy speed-tapping her phone. Remembering the quiz about old age, she turns to Annie and Rachel, 'Do you think she's writing a blog about elderly feminists?'

'She wouldn't get far with fringe people like us,' grins Rachel. 'If "we" were so powerful in the sixties and seventies, why aren't we in charge now, Tamsin? Have the Young throttled us?'

'But you are,' says Tamsin, surprised, her fingers momentarily still. She chuckles. 'You don't know your privilege. Those exclusionary binaries in race and gender, you still impose them.'

'Really? Is cutting off a breast like cutting off a dick?'

'Forget tits. You can't dig for the clitoris without like serious damage. No great tradition of Western literature to draw from, though.'

'Doesn't pee at a distance.'

'Gross,' says Tamsin, 'no penis envy I hope, Fran. Who wants that wobbly stuff to truss up?'

'Well the owners obviously do,' says Rachel grinning towards Thomas now pacing nearby, his phone at his ear. 'They talk of it enough. Remember Updike being called a "penis with a thesaurus"? I see the thing moving like a slug over the page leaving its trail of slime.'

'What would it write?' says Tamsin, 'pussy pages I guess.' She gets up, scratching her metal chair along the pavement. She touches Thomas as she passes. 'Ciao,' she says. 'Getting into practice.'

Thomas waves towards her back as she marches down the market aisle of ethnic food.

Glancing at the mounds of dark spelt and rye bread and the steel pans of Mexican beans, Tamsin is considering the temptation of old people sauntering along memory lane. If she's spending time with them, she'd better do research, find out about the Beatles and Buddy Holly or was it Tom Jones and Frank Sinatra? They probably aren't attuned to popular culture, except maybe Rachel, who's anyhow American and would have watched different shows. Though apparently the fat sexist guy Benny Hill was popular there too. They'll say 'saucy', 'smashing', 'nincompoop' and other cringe-making words. Is there a webpage giving expressions current in, say, 1968? 1972? She wouldn't quote them, God no, but she'd know what was meant if they used their antique argot. 'Bob's your uncle,' as Grandad used to say.

As Tamsin retreats Fran says, 'We can listen to her new speech, the way she says "book" and "yellow". Quite different from you and me, Annie, wider.'

'You and your vowels,' exclaims Annie affectionately.

I like it, says Jane Austen. The young should always differentiate themselves.

'Will the trip work, I wonder.'

'We need rules, like not paying according to what each eats in a restaurant?'

'Time alone,' says Fran, 'or we'll go mad.'

Annie grins. 'There'll be plenty of that. You're thinking of Shelley in that claustrophobic Welsh wasteland and no mobile signal. This is Venice, capital of the tourist world, with coffee bars, tacky shops and jammed canals. You can go off without us into the crowd whenever.'

'If we think of ourselves as in a kind of zoo, with enough water and one or two shady places to hide, we won't go far wrong,' says Rachel. 'A little screaming in private will be accepted. And we'll be fed. We can live without waving testicles.'

'Goodness, Rachel,' laughs Fran, then adds, 'I wonder why Tamsin sticks with us.'

Annie swivels her eyes to land on Thomas's fine form. He's just putting away his mobile phone.

'Hey ho,' says Rachel smiling. 'Plus, if she isn't studying our outdated feminism, she can contemplate our white privilege – or should that be "white living"?'

'You mean, she's coming to shame us?' asks Fran.

'We might just have to be sensitive, that's all,' says Annie

'Inhibited,' says Fran, 'tiring.'

'Consciousness *is* tiring,' says Thomas sitting down again. The words make Rachel smile.

'Do you suppose you were sexually abused as a child, Thomas?'

'Doubt it. I went to boarding-school, my classmates would have mentioned it.'

'That proves it. No need to panic though. Its properly repressed. Just try to enjoy your present consciousness.'

'Denial beats therapy,' says Fran as jangling Julie swims into mind. Will she accept being schooled by Tamsin? 'Cheaper too.'

'Therapy can be hard,' says Rachel, 'in New York . . .'

'Where you're always the hero, never a bystander,' interrupts Annie. She once rejected therapy, but now, occasionally, fancies a crutch. Too late? 'You know, Rachel, we used to joke that in Britain, instead of an unconscious, we had a deeply interiorized sense of class.'

'Gotta go,' says Thomas, 'sorry.'

'All this talk of zoos, past feminism, and outdated whiteness makes us – you, me and Rachel – sound like a failed species,' says Fran, 'the European bison, better the white rhino. Maybe we are. I know you don't like me saying it, Annie, but I feel older here. Yesterday I went into a new shop in Trinity Street to buy a cotton top, cheque book in pocket. The young assistant rushed over to ask what I wanted, her subtext being, Would I please get out of her space since the Old frighten off the glitzy Young?'

'Oh, God,' exclaims Annie, 'age again. She perhaps thought you couldn't pay.'

'But I had a cheque book.'

'Nobody uses cheques,' says Rachel.

'Shop with me next time,' says Annie.

'We'll go together, a group's intimidating. The staff will have to converge on us. We can invite Tamsin along – as an age-beard. We'll buy her a skimpy sweater as reward.'

'Lovely,' says Fran, much cheered. 'It'll be like having a bouncy grandchild.'

Tamsin returns with a bag of red and orange fruit. She's surprised to see them still there. The sky's clouding over. 'What you guys talking about?' she asks.

'Calibration,' says Fran, 'how to calibrate the mind, body and blood in our future trip.'

Tamsin drops her shopping and sits down in her old seat.

'Youth thinks it will always be welcome,' smiles Fran.

'Mostly right, I guess,' says Tamsin. She knows she's flattering them by being there. Though she doubts they know it. 'Thomas has left?'

'Yup.'

'I wonder,' says Fran 'what it would be like to be Thomas in his long-man, toned-thighs kind of body. To see the world from higher up, two rungs on the ladder from me. Yet there's no arrogance in the lad.'

'Lad!' laughs Tamsin, 'only you guys!'

Nonetheless, all look where Thomas had sat.

You're thinking of youth, says Jane Austen gently: remember the pains and errors of being young. A butterfly moment: you give pleasure to others more than to yourself. How do you know who's comfortable in their own skin?

20

Before Fran leaves for Norfolk to pack, put out food for an absconded cat just in case, dither over the watering system – whether to risk drought or flood – she goes with Rachel to King's Chapel: after all, both are visitors.

'Tamsin lives way down there,' says Rachel pointing along a straight road of parallel terraced cottages. 'She had Annie and me over. She said, "It's kind of awesome serving tea to you guys. I've even bought a cake."'

They chuckle over this young person who's taking up more room in their minds than either expected.

'What's the point of all that grass?' asks Fran, spying a green college court.

'So only a few can walk on it,' replies Rachel. 'You know that.'

'Clive James said that wherever there's quiet ivy there are raving nutters. True of big lawns.'

'The whole place is old-fashioned,' Fran goes on, relieved of Annie's restraining presence. 'Our idea of a university is such a con trick. I blame Matthew Arnold pontificating just when science and technology were taking over, then thinking up moral and ethical justification for studying "Humanities". Crazy to send children away from home and real-world handiwork for three pampered years when they should be turning into adults, to learn what? – nothing they couldn't get with a little instruction and visits to an art gallery or library. Carlyle made the point years ago: "The true university of these days is a collection of books." Serves us all right they're now using their "education" for cultural strolling or virtue what-notting. I'd close it down. Put the money into curing Alzheimer's and saving bees.'

One of the 'Fran-rants' Annie once warned her about, their oddity being a cheery delivery. 'There's a mission to seek and extend human understanding too,' Rachel smiles.

'Do you know,' Fran can't resist a pliant audience, 'English universities in our mediocracy aren't accountable outside themselves, they just tot up their unread pieces of research, their "outreach" hits.'

'Happy to get that off your chest?' asks Rachel. 'I go with Oscar Wilde, "Fortunately in England education produces no effect whatsoever".'

They fall silent. Jane Austen sniffs in Fran's ear.

'Well let's enjoy the Cambridge "experience" since we're both outsiders,' says Rachel.

Some faces open doors.

Soon they're sitting in the stalls in King's Chapel close to the choir of older boys and men. ('God, I would never,' laughs Annie on hearing. 'Grown men in frocks.')

Rachel stares at the little boys across the aisle. Between seven and ten she guesses. One with a chubby face and glasses moves his legs in and out, twisting his hands and nudging his neighbours. Does he know people on her side can see what he's doing below the shelf of his prie-dieu? But it pleases her that these boys dressed and singing like angels are children under their sheets.

She looks around at the audience, here to have a free glimpse of the usually ticketed architecture and hear the famous choir: does anyone think this motley crew of bored or bewildered tourists a congregation? She feels a little dizzy from looking up at the vaulted ceiling and Renaissance stained glass, all blue, green, slashes of yellow, with occasional red, too indistinct to be understood as stories even if she knew the Bible and saints better than she does.

Adjusting her neck back to its usual hinge, she notes a boy, two along from the wriggling one.

The Boy. Her eyes widen.

He's fair but not quite blond with dark blue eyes and wide, naturally smiling mouth. He's singing with none of the exaggerated gusto of his companions. Is there a twinkle in the clear eyes as he parrots the psalm? Might she catch his attention? If she succeeds, she'll smile and nod to show she's here for him, proud of him, knowing this whole show is to make him look aetherial. She shrugs, warning herself.

Again she glances at the rippling white of the bespectacled child, then back to her Boy. They lock eyes. She's unsteadied. She can almost feel herself stand up and shout, 'Look, there's my Boy singing his heart out.' Something violent churns in the pit of her stomach.

She looks away. Her face pales again, her heart ceases to pump too fast, returns to its usual syncopation.

In the reserved seats behind her to the right sits a woman older than herself – Rachel never thinks herself old as Fran so often does. Maybe the woman's a grandmother, maybe – the thought chills her – the Boy was looking at this shapeless, flaxen-haired blob.

Rachel has a decent bladder but the robed guy at the door made a point that no one will pee in his church, that NO facilities are available for anyone, even the weak and aged. This warning makes her bladder leap like a fountain. She can hold on, of course, but the emotional yo-yoing waters her lower parts and returns her to herself. She shifts on the wooden bench and moves her eyes from the boy. When she glances back, he's not looking at her or the baggy woman behind. He's just a marvellous child singing repetitive words without meaning for him or ninety-nine per cent of his listeners.

Goodbye, she mouths as, after the blessing, the children parade out, ghosts in their white cotton, goodbye my Boy.

'That was nice,' says Fran, 'though I thought the Psalm would never end. I used the time to make a to-do list before our trip, while trying to guess who the chap in the red brimmed hat in the window could be. By the way, sorry for lecturing earlier.'

Rachel's steadying herself. Can she convert her encounter into a short story? Uncertain: narrative isn't a prosthetic. It would in any case have too much sugar for the lime and salt. Rachel smiles to herself remembering the ingredients you must always balance.

Fran's in her cottage, thinking of Annie again – and herself. She likes bits of women, she realises, hair, an eye or breast, but rarely palpitates at a whole body. Is that strange? Knowing – and this was truly low – most of all she wishes to get into bed next to Jane Austen, doing nothing untoward, simply lying in spoon position, hearing from her a perfect phrase on the edge of sleep.

She sees her Author smile and – for a moment – feels warm and safe inside.

The landline phone interrupts. Fran expects Annie's voice. She's been unusually silent; Fran has been carrying round her mobile in her gardening pocket, just in case.

'Have you made provisions for if you pass?'

'Pass what?'

Understanding dawns. Interesting intransitive use, leftover from belief in immortality, passing from one state to another in death, which now, for most, implies no such move.

'Are you still there?' she asks her cold caller – why not 'hot'? Down the line a scrabbling of mice or shifting of papers, a slurp? Perhaps from some stuffy room in Ukraine or Bolton where canned fizzy liquid is drunk. She waits, breathing into the mouthpiece.

The voice returns. 'Have you given power of attorney to someone?'

'Ah,' says Fran, 'you have my birthdate.'

'Ma'am,' says the voice, 'you gave it as identity along with your mother's last name, first pet and place of birth. Incidentally, ma'am, you got that wrong on the second try.'

'I couldn't get my place of birth wrong,' protests Fran.

'Ma'am, it was misunderstood.'

It's coffee, not Coke, they're drinking, something hot in a cup or bowl. A new voice enters. Fran has exhausted Tanya or Kirstie. A male person, British-Indian? says his name is 'Maurice'. He offers help.

Fran puts down the phone. Not safe anywhere. She sees the nosy BT wire looping through the trees into her house.

Now of course she considers death. As if one needs nudging! 'Death is not an event in life,' Annie quoted Wittgenstein as she and Fran stood by his grave off Huntingdon Road; it was stained with the shit of berry-eating birds.

Fran takes out her mobile to tell Annie of the cold mortality call. As she begins, Annie cuts across, 'The Master's dead. He was ailing, people muttered he should go . . . now he has.'

She surprises Fran by wanting to talk. Curling her feet under her on the sofa, Fran says, 'Go on.'

'Well, a few of us lined up round the smaller court, gardeners and secretaries, you know. The coffin was supposed to pass through to its private funeral. The wait went on. People chatted in bursts about weekend breaks and teeth implants, whatever. A couple of Fellows stood further down the line, the rest stayed away.' Annie pauses, 'Fran, are you still there? You usually interrupt.'

'I'm here,' says Fran, cupping the phone between ear and shoulder, so she can look at the pile of bills on the floor waiting to be sorted.

'A man like a beadle strides out of the lodge, looks like a Lord Mayor's procession, then the coffin draped in patterned velvet, carried by six suited guys.' Annie decides to censor her response: that she'd come to be moved, quite liking the old boy. She'd put a linen handkerchief up her sleeve but hadn't used it. 'Behind the coffin, leaning on the arm of a tall young man comes the widow. With four perfect flowers sticking out of a bag of water. Can you believe – the hounds walk after her?'

Dogs and flowers were, Annie now considers, meant as a touch of domesticity.

'I wanted to burst out laughing, I had to hold myself rigid, the whole thing exactly like the opening of grand opera.'

She's mum about her other feeling: of being short-changed. By what? That at this solemn moment no one in the procession noticed her. Why on earth would they? While she watched herself rather than the dead.

She's said too much. She's restrained on email but Fran ringing just then has set her off.

'Good of you to go,' says Fran moving the mobile from her shoulder, 'but why did you?'

'Dunno,' says Annie. 'I suppose we want a bit of pomp and style after the messiness of dying. Memorial services are a bore.'

When both have been silent too long but Annie seems disinclined to hang up, Fran asks, 'What music would you choose? In the crematorium I mean, while people assemble. Can't decide between the end of Schubert's "Quintet" and Elgar's "Where corals lie" with Janet Baker. "Amazing Grace" by Treorchy Male Voice Choir? Maybe one single chord.'

Annie often plans her twelve tunes for an appearance on

Desert Island Discs – she's thought of leaving a final list in case her monographs achieve posthumous fame and her ghost is offered the coveted slot on Radio 4. She tries to imagine the crematorium: 'Perhaps Miles Davis or Leonard Cohen.'

Disrespectful of Europe, Fran thinks. 'Life's so important, yet a corpse weighs the same as a living body, a second before translation.'

'We don't know that, do we?'

We do know the corpse of a herring is iridescent long after death.

Part Four

21

My sea, remarks Jane Austen, is not lonely. My naval heroes force enemy ships to surrender, they wrest riches from storms. Its bluster gives bloom to my girls – dear Fanny Price on Portsmouth ramparts, perfect Anne Elliot on the Cobb at Lyme. Like your Cambridge, however, Venice is built on a swamp: at best one might say it fronts a flat lagoon. 'Lagoon' is a lonely word.

Don't stay if you feel like that, retorts Fran in the Marco Polo baggage hall. We were sad for poor Harriet Shelley in Elan Valley; it'll be sadder for Mary Shelley on the Lido. No opening for pertness and sardonic quips. (People get tetchy at airports.) I didn't tell you to come.

Italy with its pines and vices, Mrs Radcliffe's gothic town? Why would I not?

How quick come the reasons for approving what we like, smiles Fran.

The Author purses her lips. One cannot creep upon a journey.

The afternoon heat blankets the women as they deposit their holdalls and cases in their rooms: Annie and Fran on Giudecca Island where lodging is cheaper and the fish stew the best; Thomas in a shabby palazzo arranged by a colleague from Ca' Foscari, Venice's university; Tamsin with her cosmetics and blogging equipment, Blue Tooth Remote, tripod, ring light etc., in an Airbnb above a pharmacy in Cannaregio; and Rachel, braving their mockery, in a classy hotel by the Accademia. 'I have allergies,' she explains.

To Thomas, even here Shelley is more alluring than Byron – never the glow-worm he once pretended to be under the Byronic sun. (In any case, who was the sun in that duo? When Shelley died, didn't Byron take on his ideal visions and go off to death too? No, Annie had laughed when years back he'd tried out the idea in a seminar.)

In due course he'll seek traces in the gorgeous Marciana Library near the Basilica, then the far less grand Celestia and Polizia Mortuaria. His grasp of Italian handwriting isn't great, but initially he'll just look for names under the 'second Austrian Domination' – and be patient. Striding from each to each, he expects, despite his map app, to find himself on dead-end paths and hump-back bridges with shaky or no rails. But now, while his companions are still unpacking, putting clothes in wardrobes and drawers, setting up their facial and electronic equipment in Tamsin's case, he uses the last daylight hours to begin his search by visiting the Danieli Hotel on Schiavoni.

Where did the Shelleys go when they reached Venice? An Italian scholar claimed it was the Danieli, citing a visitor register (in his possession) to prove it. The place is pricey now, possibly always was: Shelley never pigged it, though not drawn, like Byron, to the luxurious in life or décor.

In the twilit interior Thomas mentions his interest. The receptionist is indifferent.

Many celebrities have stayed with us, he says staring at a group of glitzily clad Russians by the ornate stairway. No, he's sure the manager has neither time nor inclination to see him.

Thomas brings out the talismanic name: Byron too lacks power.

'I'm disappointed,' he says to the women when he joins them for a first dinner on Giudecca. Perhaps his low mood has more to do with Tamsin's absence, for Rachel has carried her apologies across the Canal: she has media to attend to. 'I'm not an ambitious young biographer like Richard Holmes planning a Shelley door-stopper, but a few new facts would help. The Danieli couldn't care less.'

'Maybe you didn't look expensive. Bet you didn't buy a drink.'

'My grant doesn't stretch that far. But they did confirm their records were given away or sold. According to Anna-Maria, the colleague who arranged my apartment, the Italian scholar with the register lives in Rome and visits Venice. She tried tracking him down for me but he's elusive. Does he have it, did he lose it – or burn it? Is it an investment gathering value? Did he invent it – or rather Shelley's name on it? I'm beginning not to care.'

'Not a scholarly position,' laughs Rachel. 'He's probably a Henry James reader and thinks you're an American scoundrel from *The Aspern Papers*, trying to filch his material. Remember, Aspern was really Shelley.' She pauses, clearing her throat, 'Actually, the Danieli only became a hotel in 1822.'

'Right,' says Thomas. 'Settles that.'

After a decent pause, Rachel changes the topic. 'I've been thinking how often the Romantics asked, "What is life?" We don't do that now.'

'Should think not,' says Annie, 'idle chatter of a transcendental kind.'

'But we do,' says Fran, struggling to swallow sardines in *soar* – disobliged by Jane Austen's snickering about stinking fish in Southampton – 'those self-help books and science-of-life courses.'

'All poetry,' says Annie, dying for a fag. She wonders why, with the windows open and a rich smell of coffee and garlic in the little restaurant, an aroma of Gauloises wouldn't enhance the mélange. 'Love, hate, joy, fear, all poetry.'

'If nicely expressed,' says Rachel, noting Annie's twitchy hand. 'Since we must devote the final days to Shelley and Mary, we should get going tomorrow on some sightseeing. While Thomas labours, of course.'

'Eating too,' says Annie. 'I've brought restaurant guides.'

'Throw them out,' says Rachel, 'never any good. They follow the peak.'

'I bet Annie could make this fish stew,' remarks Fran.

Annie chuckles. 'It's in the sauce. They must grind up all the old leftover fish and some spices and *ecco*! You couldn't easily make it at home, you'd need so many different fishy bits from sea-bream chunks to a topping of langoustine.'

'Maybe Waitrose will sell all the ingredients on one counter, along with the recipe on a laminated card.'

'So where's the fun?'

The talk bores Thomas. Was it a good idea to travel with these desultory old women – again? He excuses himself after the main course. The others exchange smiles as he leaves, tapping out a text on his phone.

That night Fran and Annie regret their island lodging with lagoon view. Outside their windows on the little ledge local youths settle to smoke and flirt to the sound of pulsing music.

'We don't have enough language to say fuck off,' moans Annie by email.

'No,' says Fran, putting her bedside light back on, then watching the shadow of a moth fluttering on her wall.

Despite the disturbed night she rises early. She sits at her window facing the lagoon, fascinated by a world at work.

Noisy rubbish boats pass in shades of green and turquoise, their minders in matching colours; red and blue worker-barges deliver fruit, armchairs, toilet rolls and bottled water; red and green service boats prepare to dredge and pound in stakes like sharpened pencils, their drivers enjoying the early-morning sun, one hand on a wheel, the other gesticulating with a cigarette into a hidden phone; taxis are groomed; smart boats ferry guests to and from expensive island hotels so rich buttocks never touch a public seat; stylish Guardia Finanza police speed after money launderers and tax evaders.

Fran watches as the sun rises farther making little orange puffs in the sky, complementing, not ousting, the moon. Exercisers emerge, rowing gondola-style in crooked lines or jogging along the ledge by the window, disturbing seagulls pecking at waste left by the revellers.

A boy in yellow vest rides his bucking blue-striped speedboat like a frisky horse, making a single river through the lagoon. In its wake, an empty cruise boat bobs sedately, two men smoking under the awning. Between disturbances the lagoon ripples and shimmers in tide-like patterns; water smooths and clouds over the detritus of bones, boats, plastic bottles and tin cans.

At the end of the platform a fisherman, heavy rumped like the Old Man of the Sea with red cap and bushy white beard, settles himself for the morning.

Jane Austen mocks this list of particulars. My vision was more abstract, more memorable. She pushes Fran towards her astute watching women, from Elinor Dashwood to the two Charlottes.

Fran waves away both Author and characters.

Yet she doesn't lack a literary companion: involuntarily she sees the rising sun with Shelley's eyes, bathing everything in 'aerial gold'.

Perfect, she thinks, everything's perfect.

Except for the lack of tea-making equipment.

Maybe Italians are so sociable they never believe a solitary person in a single room wants to drink morning tea alone or brew in the witching hour.

She stops watching as she hears Annie stirring next door. By now the sky is exhausting, too bluely close.

22

After breakfast, Annie and Fran walk towards the outer door of the small hotel. They notice a woman standing at reception. She speaks a Dutch-accented English. In her sixties, slender and straight-backed, she wears little black shorts over brick-coloured stockings.

'Stylish,' says Annie.

'Daring,' says Fran. 'I couldn't do it. Not even with those legs.'

Annie glances at Fran's uncompromising Toast dress and laughs. Fran laughs too and pats Annie's arm.

They meet Rachel and Tamsin by the wooden Accademia Bridge. Rachel knows Venice better than any of them but hides the fact. As a teenager she'd been wearied by a round of churches, art galleries and expensive sugary snacks which her ludicrously thin mother kept scoffing. She was urged on by the hired guide, probably cousin to the café-owners. Rachel took in the town when her child-mind was fluid and knowledge penetrated; now she's sad to find she feels so little before what everyone else admires. Experience can be burdensome.

They set off for the Peggy Guggenheim Museum, going down one alley, then another, past façades with statuary high in the sky for birds and angels to appreciate. When Annie asks the way, she provokes the invariable response, '*Sempre diritto,*' and a shrug.

Weary, they stop for coffee and unhealthy brioche, orange jam poked in its middle.

'Flour, fat, and sugar,' laughs Tamsin, 'we wouldn't touch it in England. I guess it feels like exotic here.'

'I love doughnuts,' says Fran thinking of Johnnie with strawberry jam up his nose.

'By the way, where the fuck are we?'

'Where we're supposed to be,' Fran chuckles under her breath forgetting Tamsin has young, unwaxy ears.

'Glad someone knows,' says Tamsin, waving her phone whose map has led them to this café in a *calle* ending in a canal with no side exit or bridge.

Rachel grins, takes a sip of her bottled water, then puts them right.

They arrive by the Museum. Annie has visited before, likes the building and its random contents. Rachel finds memories jangling: Peggy Guggenheim reminds her of her spoilt mother.

Fran interrupts her thoughts by making a fuss about leaving her backpack at the ticket counter though she carries nothing important in it. Annie pushes round her to give in her own bag. Feeling a little absurd, Fran hands over her backpack. They enter together.

Annie and Tamsin are keenest to respond, chat and judge, noting the likeable, the meretricious, the autobiographical. With a penchant for Rosa Bonheur's cows and Victorian genre paintings of workhouse paupers, Fran has so little sense of modern art that the abstractions, the clever plays of light and shade, of dark and texture, of white and white, leave her cold and inarticulate.

She likes only Magritte's night-time house under a daytime sky: full of insomniacs.

The galleries are crowded – not so Annie, Rachel and Tamsin notice, but Fran's twitchy. She watches girls with unbelievable teeth and straight blond hair sashaying through the rooms attentive only to their phones, snapping pictures and themselves.

One half of the world cannot understand the pleasures of the other.

You forget, remarks Jane Austen, that Claude glasses tinted a scene so it became a Gilpin picturesque for tourists. Any different?

Tennyson's Lady of Shalott watches life in a mirror until jolted by trivial Sir Lancelot, tirra-lilling by her island. The Lady stops looking in the mirror, only then discovering what eluded her all those spinning years: that the mirror makes better scenes than anything found outside, that some fusty notion of life being better than art has tricked her into destroying herself when she could have gone on spinning and singing and watching shadows into contented, undramatic old age.

Bring it up to date: the Lady stops looking into a mobile phone. What good does it do her?

Just remember to enter recto and exit verso if you want to stay on Shalott.

Annie interrupts Fran's reverie. 'You're not used to crowds. London exhibitions are far worse.'

Fran smiles but doesn't answer. As Annie turns to join Rachel in front of a Max Ernst monstrosity, she slips off to find the museum shop. Comfortingly familiar with its National-Trust-type mugs, tea towels, T-shirts and children's pop-up books, she buys a Jackson Pollock scarf, preferring the scarf to the picture. When in folds round her neck, it looks ordinary, but she's cheered by the extravagance.

Catching up with her outside the shop, Annie says affectionately, 'Poor Fran, you just can't bear being in a crowd, can you?'

They move out on to the terrace overlooking the Grand Canal to sit on a low step.

'Tamsin is good,' whispers Annie, 'just concise adjectives and no "likes".'

'Good at or just good?' says Fran.

From inside they overhear a woman – Japanese, with hint of West Coast vocal fry? – say clearly, 'You English-speakers can't bear to be without a subject, it makes you very important to yourselves.' Close by, a man takes photos of the opposite palazzi, then, when their eyes turn away, focuses on the upright penis of the boy astride the metal horse. As Tamsin, then Rachel, come out, he scuttles off.

Rachel's regarding Tamsin, 'I hear you're an academic influencer?'

'Well, yeah, I kind of market my niceness.'

'Goodness,' says Fran, 'does niceness sell?'

Annie smiles. 'Are you nice, Tamsin? We think you are.'

'Oh yes, well, kind of,' Tamsin chuckles. 'It pays. But doing it well can stress you out.'

'You do it well, I'm sure,' says Rachel, wondering whether to mention to Tamsin that she has a white oleander petal caught prettily in her hair.

Tamsin gnaws her lip, 'Yeah. Yeah, I do get hits.'

Fran looks vague.

'Light TV slots, TED talks, those things – I put myself around, you know, as a thinklister. Instagram, Twitter, YouTube. My marketing platform . . .' She stops and grins.

'Tiring when you put it like that,' says Annie, moderately impressed.

Fran studies Tamsin, puzzled. 'She can't be tired of anything. She hasn't had time.'

'Bruh, come off it, you weren't so very young when you were my age, you know it. Loads of poets have done their work by now, Keats, Chatterton, Keith Douglas, 2Pac, yeah Shelley too.'

'Is that why you hang round with us,' asks Fran, 'to get away from success?'

'Maybe.'

Annie wonders if it's the masked Venetian air that's paradoxically making them want to unmask, or seem to.

'Could you live without the stroking now?' asks Rachel, 'Isn't it addictive?'

'Dunno,' says Tamsin, flicking her head and making those eye movements, innate or learned, that so fascinate Fran. The petal stays fixed. 'I could go on living a little in the vlogosphere, I guess,' she chuckles, 'delighting my followers. But then maybe you think I've done too much niceness to power any more ambition?' She pauses. Annie and Fran puzzle over her tone. She's addressing only Rachel. 'I think, now you ask, I'd kind of like not to be an academic. It's so compromised.'

'What then?'

Tamsin bursts out laughing, her head thrown back further than seems possible to Fran. The petal is dislodged. 'Maybe a columnist on a bestselling daily, read by everyone, then tossed away. Be feared at parties when my logo enters the room – I'd fix the photo' – she runs her eyes down one arm. 'I'd be opinionated, snide, prejudiced, cruel, exorbitantly well paid and fed as I feed on friends, scandal and celebs. I'd drink blue cocktails with beautiful trans people, then like tell on them. I wouldn't be nice.'

'Heavens! You've thought it out? I guess if the shilling's there for the taking,' says Fran.

'Interesting,' says Annie seriously, 'very, but quite alien to you, and us.'

Tamsin laughs again, a little uneasily as she sees Rachel isn't responding.

Annie and Rachel begin talking about Peggy Guggenheim's untalented daughter, but Fran remains intrigued by Tamsin. 'Are you describing a sort of writing or investigating yourself in public? I want to understand.'

'Maybe, kind of, through an image.'

'Is that why you like Shelley, because he's always looking at images of himself in others?'

'What makes you think I like Shelley,' says Tamsin, opening her eyes wide.

'Ah,' says Fran, 'and he certainly wasn't nice.' She's absurdly pleased when her remark raises another great hoot of laughter in Tamsin.

She turns to find the other two have re-entered the Museum.

Later in the day, after smoking a few joints, Tamsin makes slow love with Thomas in the bare palazzo room with its tarnished mirrors and vast hard bed. The light is dim and yellow.

When they stop to regard each other, to her surprise Tamsin sees Thomas agonising. Strange! He's noticed a brown, voluptuous woman and followed a wholesome urge. She didn't repel him, unruly desire satisfied on both sides. She doesn't want sentimental sex. Nor he, surely. So why the abstraction? She squeezes his hand, 'You can't have everything.'

Outside the palazzo she's drenched by one of Venice's sudden tumultuous downpours. Hearing the rain belatedly, Thomas comes out on to the stairs where a window fronts a little square. Tamsin gazes up to see his face as the rain eases. She looks dazzling with her thick hair wet and glistening. She knows Thomas's guilt is swept away in her glory. She raises her arms to prayer position over her dripping head.

*

All five of them meet on the Zattere for dinner – of booze and carbs, as Tamsin puts it. 'Spare us gastronomy as culture,' she says before Rachel opens her mouth.

This time they sit outside by the canal. Annie isn't yet holding a cigarette, but knows she can: all the difference.

Fran dislikes the taste but enjoys fizzy prosecco popping in her lungs. It makes a shower of sparks, iridescent and evanescent and organically astounding. How vivacious, she thinks, knowing she won't sleep a wink after it.

A gigantic ocean liner passes by dwarfing them all, its cargo of insects gazing across the miniature town. Beside the great ship a small speedy boat dashes along, a wasp buzzing round an elephant. Its bow wave bounces the moored boats, making them dance and jitter in the sparkling water. The liner's gentle swell merely sloshes the bank, wetting the bottom of Tamsin's canvas bag and Thomas's trainers. Neither notices.

'The long light really shakes,' says Fran still thinking of 'The Lady of Shalott'. 'Did Tennyson ever visit?'

'Yeah,' says Thomas, 'when old. Came for Shelley. He was disappointed. He'd waited too long to see Venice. Its art didn't move him, or his eyes were too dim. The canals seemed less picturesque than the pictures he'd long contemplated. How could he like it?'

'A common problem,' says Rachel, knowing it works both ways: see it too early and in the wrong company – or too late. Beautiful Venice – blowsy, vulgar and tedious.

'Tennyson didn't stay in the Danieli but in a new hotel on the Lido. I like to think of that tremendous beard lounging on a sunbed in up-to-date accommodation. In the evening he was rowed out in a gondola to watch the sunset, think of Shelley and remember love and youth.'

'Did he find Shelley?'

'No.'

Tamsin is touching her bare toes to Thomas's calf under the table.

23

'Must get Byron and Shelley together,' says Thomas as coffees arrive – with complimentary limoncello. He feels the warmth of Tamsin's feet up his legs and into his groin.

Two poets: a dance duet, with Mary Shelley's stepsister as conductor, the wild child.

'I see the women as just so many holes and orifices in this story,' says Fran.

'Crude,' smiles Rachel, wrongly assuming metaphor, 'both poets treated women as more than just wombs and cunts.'

Jane Austen sniffs: she deplores bad language. She settles herself for a rigmarole.

Rachel clears her throat. There'll be no unnecessary dialogue: quicker to tell – a power shared by fiction and non-. Take it or leave it, scan or skip.

A woman after my own heart, whispers Jane Austen. You can make tragedy into comedy and vice versa with a verb.

The men meet in Switzerland. It's 1816, the dark summer of nightmares, sexual imbroglio and *Frankenstein*. Too famous to need relating. Some interaction before, since Shelley had sent a poem or two – it was that way round: Byron the lord, the cynosure, and four years senior.

Summer past, Shelley and his 'Godwin girls' return to England while Byron travels to Venice. He takes various lodgings, then settles in Palazzo Mocenigo on the Grand Canal.

He's in Venice for the sex – allegedly, the small city hosts twenty thousand prostitutes – and the anonymity. Courting celebrity, like all celebrities Byron is angry when criticised. He tired of shocking the English in Switzerland where he'd become a tourist attraction spied through telescopes across the lake. (Don't be fooled: Shelley and Byron are always aware how they play to the home audience.) In Venice the noble rakehell is quickly an object of fascination – English visitors nobble his gondolier or wait for him on the Lido where he rides. Soon Shelley is in Italy too – post-war England being no place for a political visionary. Also, he believes his health improves abroad – and living is cheaper.

On 23 August 1818 (note the date) Byron takes Shelley by gondola to the Lido; horses are waiting. (On this occasion they forget, as they don't always, that one is a lord, the other mere son of a baronet.) It's the first of many rides along the dunes, during which the poets yacket away on art and philosophy, luxuriating in contrary views. Later, in one of Shelley's best poems, the pair become –we simplify here – the idealistic, progressive

Englishman Julian – himself – believing in man's power through his own mind, and the charming, sceptical Venetian nobleman, Maddalo – Byron, the brilliant, bracing nihilist.

Having had time through the centuries to peruse a little of Shelley, Jane Austen remarks, I would judge 'Julian and Maddalo' his best work, the most realistic and human, the least turbulent and windy.

You judge by yourself, mutters Fran.

Really? Do I expose my nakedness on paper? Blame others for my life's pain?

Fran's attending to Rachel, not Jane Austen.

'Both are geniuses,' says Thomas. He has an aftertaste from the limoncello. He decides he dislikes it.

'And hypochondriacs,' says Fran.

Jane Austen applauds. I have already invited your Shelley to Sanditon. She claps her hands, revealing again an author's self-centredness. He will be joined by fat Byron as plump Arthur Parker with a talent for rhyming.

Tamsin notes Thomas's irritation. Biography isn't her 'thing' but, though never final, never simply true, it must be told, aslant of course – and best without Fran's dated judgments. 'You go on, Thomas.'

Each is intoxicated by the other. But, possibly, here in Venice just now, Shelley's not as impressed with Byron as Byron with him. Remember, Byron has entered his most extravagant and promiscuous phase and there's always a Puritan streak in Shelley. He finds it hard to fuse the beautiful and vile.

Byron, he thinks, has surrounded himself with whores, garlic-smelling countesses, and Italians of 'dwarfish intellect': so his view is distorted and he apprehends the nothingness of human life. He's deeply discontented.

'See: something of England travels with Shelley, however he intends ridding himself of its grey ethical dust,' puts in Annie.

Both are charismatic, seductive in being and talk. Neither gay though Byron had his teenaged loves – what to do in an English public school? – and perhaps reverts at his Greek end – but there's attraction.

'What's the word for "erotically charmed by intellect"?' asks Fran. '"Homosocial" sounds like jocks slapping each other on the back in a pub after a rugby match.'

Ignoring Fran, Annie snaps, 'We don't need to buy into this myth of friendship.' She pats down irritation. 'Charmed for a while but also critical, even hostile, at least Shelley is to Byron. Why not? He'd be stone-dead not to feel competitive with a man of wealth, rank and fame, especially later with his own good poetry unremarked or unpublished. He writes (but doesn't present) a sonnet to Byron, as passive-aggressive a piece of envious praise as you'll find. As for Byron, he denies he's intimate with men, his friendships being mere man-of-the-world ties. In the beginning he is influenced by Shelley's visionary stuff, OK, but he soon tires of being proselytized by a man who thinks himself morally superior – in private he mocks Shelley as "Shiloh", remember Joanna Southcott's fake messiah-son?' Annie shrugs. 'Like me, I guess he thinks Shelley's work feverish.'

'On the contrary,' says Thomas, 'his poetry has an equanimity . . .'

'Enough,' interrupts Rachel. 'I'll continue.'

Despite being of 'dwarfish intellect', Byron's final semi-official lover, the Countess Teresa Guiccioli, is observant. She finds Shelley sympathetic and sickly: he's tall, bent, bony, his features delicate but irregular, a mouth ugly in laughter and spoilt by teeth. (Remember, Shelley's no longer the gorgeous youth of Elan Valley.) He has freckles from too much Italian sun, abundant hair greying and unkempt, a voice almost strident. His extraordinary dress is a schoolboy's jacket, unpolished shoes, no gloves. Yet he must always seem, she writes, the most accomplished among a thousand gentlemen.

'Only an elegant, convent-raised Italian lady would mention shoes and lack of gloves,' says Fran, 'what strikes me is that word "schoolboy".'

I'm relieved, mutters Jane Austen, nobody sketched me so minutely. An artist lives in his work.

The appreciation's mutual, for Shelley sees in Teresa a woman to tame weak sexy Byron. Sadly, Lord Byron isn't as in love with his reformation as Shelley and Teresa are.

To her surprise, Fran catches the eye of an elderly man on the next table, cradling a brandy and glancing at the *Gazzettina* folded beside his plate. She's happier sitting here with her friends than she's expected: contentment makes her smile. 'I do love the speedy boats, especially at night,' she remarks as one swishes past.

Encouraged to use his good English, the man responds, 'Some days away young men from Mestre went joy-riding. At three o'clock in the morning they killed two fishermen. They were sitting on the lagoon by Poveglia.'

Not a bad way and place to go, thinks Fran, though premature.

Annie notes Thomas's impatience. Though a father and not so young, he still shows the intolerance of youth, cringing at ordinary remarks of ordinary people passing the time. He'll need to restrain this squeamishness if he wants to be a popular teacher. You have to say and listen to the obvious every day, year in year out, and with a smile.

'It's good, Fran, you've continued accosting strangers,' whispers Annie beaming at the man, then ending the talk by looking away. 'You're blossoming now you've something other than falling leaves and rabbits to look at.'

Fran grimaces.

'Near Naples, Shelley visited a macaroni factory. He was impressed by its production,' says Thomas.

'Awesome.'

'Did he take samples?'

'Imagine, the Shelleys eating macaroni cheese,' says Fran. Before Thomas can huff a reply, she excuses herself to visit the 'services'.

Hurriedly she uses the malodorous toilet while, blessed with better stomachs or bowels, the others finish their limoncello. Thomas orders a brandy to take off the taste.

Fran hopes when she returns there'll be nothing smelly about her person, though something of herself lingers in her nostrils. As she approaches the table, she finds the talking has grown excited. A momentary melancholy touches her: all because she's been absent this fraction of time. Tamsin turns mischievous eyes on her.

Oh to be dust in sunlight. We are chance atoms. Mine was only ever a gentle sorrow, says Jane Austen.

Never quote Shakespeare without quotation marks, mutters Fran. Yet the idea amuses her.

Dinner over, the friends saunter towards the vaporetto stop. Thomas, Rachel and Tamsin stand on the bobbing pontoon to wave off Fran and Annie. What desire lines will coalesce in the next hour, wonders Fran, remembering with a smile her pained suspicion in Wales. Will there be danger in any promiscuous tangle? A little drink, then more drink, lust surfaces, trails off, becomes modest, weak, easily snuffed out, but perhaps remembered.

Wheels within wheels, says Jane Austen.

'It must be odd for the boy,' remarks Fran.

'We're out of the game,' says Annie. 'Let's watch the fiery

Shelley sunset tonight and not think of bodies and houses under the water, just what's on top.'

24

Infant mortality has been falling since the mid-eighteenth century and will go on falling – but who cares about statistics when finding their first baby dead in its cradle?

'They're so very young,' adds Rachel, 'remember that. Almost children.'

Rachel, Annie and Fran have gathered for *alfresco* lunch near the Arsenale. Thomas arrives from rifling disappointing archives in Celestia, helped this time by his Ca' Foscari friend. Tamsin comes after a morning online, taking advantage of the better WiFi in Thomas's palazzo.

'I don't see . . .,' begins Fran and stops.

At seventeen, Mary Wollstonecraft Godwin (soon to be Shelley) became what till recently was called an unmarried mother. She was more than twenty years younger than her own mother, Mary Wollstonecraft, had been when she gave birth to a daughter, then promptly died. The second Mary was seduced (or seducing) beside the first Mary's grave in St Pancras Churchyard. The seducer (or seduced) was Percy Bysshe Shelley, a beautiful married man of twenty-three.

Born 22 February 1815, two months before term, Mary's first baby is named Clara. Despite his failure with Harriet and Elizabeth Hitchener, Percy Bysshe still hankers after communes, sexy couplings that now include Mary's stepsister, with whom he was probably . . .

We don't know for sure.

An Oxford pal is roped in for Mary. But, despite being born of two great libertarian philosophers, when it comes to the crunch, she favours the monogamy scorned by her lover as tantamount to prison.

Mary Wollstonecraft also believed in monogamy. Both Marys think it better for babies. But, as Harriet's experience showed, Shelley isn't much interested in babies as people. (Fortunately, Mary follows her dead mother's advice and breastfeeds.)

Eight days after Clara's birth, they move lodgings to avoid being fleeced by the landlady. Four days later, Mary finds the baby dead.

She grieves in dreams: in one her baby wakes, it had been cold and needed only rubbing and warming by the fire to live again. This heartbreaking plea for attention and proper care goes unheeded by Shelley and her stepsister.

Name-sharing when the elder sibling dies is commonplace. So, when the next girl is born on 2 September 1817, she too is 'Clara'. Circumstances are more propitious. With his wife Harriet drowned in the Serpentine, Shelley, arch hater of marriage, is free to marry again and make Godwin, famous fulminator against shackling matrimony, the happy father-in-law of a baronet's heir. (How he crowed!) For Shelley, the new child, the fifth he's sired (a boy, William, precedes the second Clara), hardly impinged. No more than with the first Clara does he see the new baby as an impediment to moving where and when he will.

'I read an anecdote,' says Annie to Rachel. 'Shelley leaps over a wailing toddler, a friend asks whose child it is; Shelley, its father, replies, "Don't know."'

It should be stated here that the stepsister, daughter of the second Mrs Godwin, had arrived in the Godwin family as plain Jane. Not to be outdone by a mother who transformed herself from a serial fornicator into a respectable widow to marry the famous bereaved philosopher, Jane recasts herself as a romantic heroine with a French tinge: Claire.

Jane is a good name, remarks Jane Austen, though I'm not vulgar enough to display it on the cover of my books. I am a Lady and an Author before I am 'Jane Austen' – anonymity has its power. Of course, I tried other titles: I might imagine myself 'Mrs George Crabbe', I admire clever poets.

But Jane's a sturdy English name. I gave it to my secretive beauty in *Emma*, Jane Fairfax, who does her own hair with skill and plays the piano brilliantly. Plain Jane she is not.

Fran notes her Author's occasional prolixity.

Claire dislikes being outshone by beautiful, clever, interestingly born Mary. She may share a bed with her sister's lover – remember, we don't know what they did there, not at this stage – but she'll never be the poet's wife. She equalizes by nabbing the most famous author of all.

Aged just eighteen, she's impregnated by Lord Byron.

He's scandalised England with his cruelty to his wife and rumours of incest with a half-sister; he's about to leave the country for good and doesn't care what he does for recreation in those final dreary weeks. He won't resist a teenager flinging herself at him: he never pretends to care for her.

Shelley's impressed by Claire's ingenuity. The link with Byron excites him. But, if he *has* been donating his sperm to both stepsisters, then who exactly is fathering her foetus? With no available DNA, speculation's pointless.

Move on a little and we reach the stepsisters as mothers of three living children: William born to Mary in 1816, the second Clara born in 1817 – and Allegra born to Claire the same year, and, we have to assume for purposes of narrative, Lord Byron.

'*Frankenstein* says a lot about a mother's feeling for dead children and unsanctioned childbirth,' remarks Fran.

'Or fears for the living,' adds Rachel. 'What's meant by the Creature murdering his little 'uncle' William?'

William! Her father and her child.

Do Byron and Shelley ever share truth, simple factual truth? Shelley paints a winsome picture of the children: Claire's Allegra and his William are 'fast friends', making a secret language; they puzzle over the 'stranger' (Clara) 'whom they consider very stupid for not coming to play with them on the floor'. Mary writes: William won't go near Allegra and if she approaches him 'he utters a fretful cry untill she is removed! – but he kisses Clara – strokes her arms & feet and laughs to find them so soft and pretty'.

Despite her wildness, Claire understands the stain of illegitimacy 'unbleached by nobility' – she may or may not be aware of her *own* dubious birth. Baby Allegra needs protection. Byron does a deal: he'll acknowledge and pay to raise the child – so long as he never meets the mother. Allegra must be brought to Italy.

'To give him his due,' adds Rachel, 'Shelley's troubled, knowing about – though not always appreciating – mother-love.'

A fine country for holidays, for good food and frescoes, Italy in high summer is no place for pale English babies before vaccines and antibiotics. All three children – Clara, Allegra and William – will die there.

The sun bothers Annie, whose Virginia-Woolf hat is more decorative than functional. She moves her chair. Fran in the floppy reversible National Trust sort feels the sun only on her back. Tamsin is a little apart working through her phone and intermittently watching passers-by. Rachel and Thomas sit in shade, their energy in narrative mode.

What exactly do we know, Rachel?

According to agreement, once in Italy a nurse delivers Allegra to Byron. The rest of the extended 'family' settles in the spa town of Bagni di Lucca near Livorno. It bustles with English expatriates and fashionable visitors, the most illustrious being Princess Pauline Bonaparte.

The rented house, 'Casa Bertini', is rural and Shelley's as excited by nearby streams, waterfalls, and transparent pools as he'd once been in Elan Valley. Loves the shifting, transforming light.

Despite his attraction to women, he never finds their company enough. As with Harriet, so with Mary, so – he realises – it will always be. Besides, Claire is sulky and complaining without her daughter.

Away in the Venetian palazzo, the Byron bastard is caressed and indulged. She's enchanting, but soon spoilt.

Thomas interrupts to intrude new information from Anna-Maria. To curb these faults, Byron will later dispatch the child to a convent, to be raised conservatively as an Italian girl. 'I'd followed the line that this was cruelty from a voluptuous father tiring of a toy. But Anna-Maria, who was born close to the convent, says the place had an excellent reputation. And listen to this,' Thomas drains his third double-espresso as Fran watches impressed – she'd levitate if she drank as much – 'all documents and personal belongings of Allegra's were taken shortly after her death – despite the nuns' reluctance – to Florence by an English Lady. Who was she? Claire, later the prey of trophy hunters – and Henry James? Anyone else?'

Jane Austen intervenes. Spoiling's no problem where there's quickness to support it. My Emma learns some sense and marries a man not universally liked by posterity but a worthy spouse for the times.

Please be quiet, Fran whispers back. This is Shelley's day, or rather, Clara's – 'little Ca' they called her.

'We didn't come for Allegra, but we can't help knowing her fate in Harrow churchyard, Thomas. Despite Byron's instructions, she was buried in an unmarked grave.' Nobility doesn't always bleach the stain; it seems, whatever snobby Emma thinks. (The snub's been counteracted by the Byron Society – so much more populous than the Shelley one. Both of course dwarfed by the Jane Austen . . .)

In memory of
ALLEGRA,
daughter of LORD BYRON
and CLAIRE CLAIRMONT
born in Bath 13·1·1817
died Bagnacavallo 19·4·1822
buried nearby.
Erected by the Byron Society
19·4·1980

'Who?' says Tamsin. She's been preoccupied but now can't help smiling: the night was athletic.

Back to 1818. The nurse who takes Allegra to Byron tells disturbing tales. She hints that Byron is raising the child to debauch her. Actually, she's more concerned with herself – has the famous Lord swooped on her, as was his custom with servants, then ignored her, abandoned her? No knowing.

Claire's alive only to Allegra: she must rush to Venice. Shelley needs little persuading – that old tug between men. Across two hundred miles.

So, leaving Mary alone with servants and infants, Shelley and Claire depart from Casa Bertini for Padua, then Venice. They hope to persuade Byron to let Claire see her daughter regularly.

How could they expect it, especially without cover of wifely Mary – this pair of possible lovers so indecorous in licentious Byron's traditional eyes?

They enjoy the trip. Then, failing to understand the depths of Byron's aversion to Claire, they take a gondola and arrive in Venice – in a storm at midnight.

'Such children!' exclaims Fran.

Annie regards her. Something about this pair's affecting Fran. What?

Next day Shelley goes to Byron alone. The talk's good-humoured; Byron offers Allegra back, then agrees she may visit her mother. There's a rub: he assumes Mary is here, that Shelley and Claire aren't scandalously alone. He invites Shelley to settle his entourage in his own villa outside Este in the Euganean Hills forty or so miles from Venice.

'You know,' adds Rachel, who'd rather spend a week with Claire than a month with Mary, 'years later, when the men are dead, Claire fantasizes a harem-commune where sexes are reversed.'

Mary's idea of heaven is a garden and *absentia Clariae*.

Entranced as usual with each other, on this first Italian meeting the two poets are rowed to the Lido to ride and talk. The experience is so riveting Shelley forgets Claire waits for news. Maybe he's beginning to compose his celebrated 'Julian and Maddalo'.

Back in Casa Bertini Mary is lonely and uneasy, but her life is dominated by little ones. She writes to Shelley: Clara is 'well and gets very pretty'; she 'already replies to her nurse's caresses by smiles – and Willy kisses her with great tenderness'.

Too pathetic to read these letters, knowing the axe will soon fall.

Shelley returns to Claire from his exhilarating time with Byron. The deception must stop. He writes that Mary and their children should leave Casa Bertini 'instantly' for Este – where he and Claire stay – together. (Did Mary's heart sink, or wasn't there time?)

Fran interrupts again. 'Poor Mary trying so hard to keep a father for her children.'

Rachel touches Fran's hand where it lies on the table. Fran looks up, surprised.

August is the hottest month of the year in Italy; baby Clara's teething, and the travelling will take at least five gruelling days. Shelley knows this, but Claire must be indulged and Byron soothed.

'I travelled from Nigeria alone with a teething child,' says Fran; 'people were annoyed by the crying.'

Mary protests, the child is sick. Shelley is adamant. (We aren't yet out of patriarchy, however sexually liberated these clever women seem.) 'You can pack up directly you get this letter, and employ the next day in that,' he commands. Mary must organise departure, settle the household, sort out rent on the villa, pay debts and servants, travel and manage everything. Alone.

Instructions are imperious and detailed. Shelley will send money to the post office in Florence.

'He could have gone to meet her. It's abuse,' Rachel adds, turning away.

'Word's overused,' says Fran. 'When I was young it meant being very rude, now half the time it's sexual assault on a child or just some husband preventing his wife going . . .'

Rachel glares so fiercely Fran stops. 'Would kicking a pregnant girlfriend down marble stairs fit your criteria?' She sniffs to dampen her words. 'Some things are indelible.'

Fran's silenced – in part because she heard 'inedible' and is pondering whether the inedible would be ineditable. She hears Jane Austen muttering *sotto voce* about people with their pushy misery.

The day after packing up the house, Mary (and the children) must 'get up at four o'clock, & go post to Lucca' to arrive at six. She will use another three days to get to Este. The peremptory tone softens with a little tenderness for his abandoned family, but baby Clara 'cant recollect me', he writes.

'True but she can suffer for him.'

The packing and journeying will take ten days in all. Meanwhile, in Byron's villa, Shelley and Claire (with Allegra) enjoy the sun and its golden magnificence. Probably they enjoy the sex too.

We don't know . . .

Mary obeys, packs, closes the house, gathers the beloved children, bouncy William and pretty Clara. On 30 August, her twenty-first birthday, the day when in 1797 her mother Mary Wollstonecraft began her ten days of dying, Mary is ready to leave Bagni di Lucca. Three days after receiving her commands, she's in Florence to pick up money – and passports: Italy is much regulated under Austrian rule.

Florence to Bologna is seventy miles and can take over sixteen hours on the road; Bologna to Este near one hundred, requiring more than thirty-three hours by mule-drawn coach over rough mountainous terrain. As Shelley well knows, his little family must stay at inns where lice and bedbugs wait to attack a human body.

Jane Austen shakes her head. This emotional telling is too raw. She wouldn't narrate the tale this way. She'd be more austere, avoiding redundancy – or just tell another story on the edge. She mentions this to Fran – in a kindly way.

Rachel knows the tale is almost too painful. You don't have to be a mother or sense impending doom to wish to avoid detail. She'd never allow such affect into a short story. The genre controls the author.

Unlike Rachel and Fran, Annie and Thomas are more interested in verification than particulars. Tamsin studies the reaction of the older women. Snowflakes.

Poor Mary grows increasingly distressed on the arduous journey, the teething baby no doubt wailing and little William whiny and wondering why, why.

'This is just story-telling,' snaps Thomas, surprising himself, 'we need to get on.'

Just?

After four days and three probably sleepless nights journeying from Florence, on Saturday 5 September, almost exactly one year after Clara's birth, Mary arrives at Byron's villa. On the way the little girl has picked up dysentery or typhoid. Shelley's concerned – but more so for Claire, who's ill with something – we can only wonder, perhaps crudely – and has doctors' appointments to keep. As ever he's also much taken with his own ailments. He's suffering from food-poisoning: blamed on 'Italian cakes'.

On 13 September, he writes to Byron from Este that his little girl has been dangerously ill – so he's 'detained an anxious prisoner here, for four or five days longer. She is now better, & I hope to be able to see you at the end of the week.'

Alarmed yes, but also disappointed he can't be with Byron – living with one's family isn't commonly described as being a 'prisoner'.

Especially in such a charming villa.

Clara is not 'better'.

Nor apparently is Claire. On 24 September an appointment is made for her to visit her doctor in Padua at 8 o'clock. Mary should chaperone her and bring little Clara so Shelley can meet them and take them on to consult Byron's doctor in Venice. (How the constant care and chivalry for Claire will have racked Mary!) 'You must therefore arrange matters so that you should come to the Stella d'Oro a little before that hour,' he writes to his wife, 'a thing only to be accomplished by setting out at ½ past 3 in the morning'.

As well as the sick child, Mary is to bring manuscript pages of his new poem.

'It's breathtaking,' Rachel comments. 'It is, isn't it?'

Thomas exhales loudly. 'Shelley couldn't know how sick the baby was. He's a visionary, not a clairvoyant. The point is to travel in the cool of the night.'

'Off to get fags,' says Tamsin, 'you guys carry on.'

He knows the child's been ailing for weeks. Does he remember his first Clara dead after a house-move?

'If you say he was a marvellous poet, Thomas, I may do damage,' says Rachel. She gives a mordant chuckle.

(The adjective is Fran's. It derives from Latin 'biting' but she can't uncouple it from 'death' in comic mode. What is it about Rachel? The pregnant girlfriend – a novel, a memory?)

Clara is now so thin that, according to her mother, friends in Bagni di Lucca wouldn't know her. By the time Claire, Mary and Clara reach Padua, she's critically ill. Claire returns to Este while Shelley carries Mary and Clara on to Venice down the Brenta river. Rest, quiet and stillness would have been more healing for the little mite.

Fran looks away, brushing aside the gentle warnings of Jane Austen. If she isn't telling the tale, she's taking it on the chin, swallowing it whole. Each hears the story in different keys.

Late afternoon, they arrive in Fusina, ready to cross to Venice. The child – what did they expect? – is convulsing.

Austrian soldiers stop them going further; Shelley's forgotten the passports. Ever the patrician when dealing with the lower orders, he's forceful: the soldiers retreat before 'his flashing eyes and vehement eager manner' – and perhaps the child's obvious sickness. In the gondola crossing the lagoon (a whole hour), Clara deteriorates. Shelley deposits Mary and the baby in the hallway of an inn.

Which inn? The Danieli? Or the Hotel or Albergo Grande Bretagne? It doesn't matter – but why not Palazzo Mocenigo? Shelley spends most of his time there anyway, why can't Mary stay? Must she keep away because Claire is exiled?

Shelley sets out to find Byron's doctor. He's not at home. By the time he returns, Clara's 'in the most dreadful distress'. Inn servants have found a local medic, who says what any onlooker could say, that there's no hope for the little girl. 'In about an hour,' Shelley writes, 'she died – silently, without pain, and she is now buried.'

How does he know what pain the child suffered and had suffered in those excruciating days?

Mary writes in her diary, 'This is the Journal book of misfortunes.' Reticence is Mary Shelley's hallmark.

But there must be secret blame. On whom should it fall? Probably on all, herself as well as Shelley and Claire. A mother's business is to keep a child alive.

25

Shelley writes to Claire in Este that Mary sank into a kind of despair but is better next day.

Really? Soon he's complaining she's cold and distant.

Does he feel guilt? How not? Especially after those (speculative) nights of illicit love in Byron's villa. Yet, his overwhelming concern is for Claire: his grieving wife must, he writes, do all she can to persuade Byron to let Allegra remain in her care. A demand for a saint: to help with another's child after yours has been sacrificed.

'Byron knows the Shelleys' poor record in child-raising,' adds Thomas. 'Allegra would probably "perish of Starvation, and green fruit", he writes, mocking his friend's dietary fads.'

Rachel rises from the table, swigs her water bottle, and briefly walks off towards the canal, wishing she were a smoker to hide her reactions. She returns quickly, there's no stopping this story. Tamsin's taking her time.

Shelley's loss and sexual frustration (Mary, we assume, refuses sex) don't hinder his work. Indeed, they're good for it, like promiscuity for Byron.

> Most wretched men
> Are cradled into poetry by wrong,
> They learn in suffering what they teach in song.

Shelley continues working on 'Julian and Maddalo' and his great visionary poem *Prometheus Unbound*.

Mary's *Frankenstein* is subtitled 'the new Prometheus', so Shelley may be answering his wife's implied reproach to the visionary, selfish Dr F and his carelessness with the Creature, his only 'child'.

Thomas adds, 'He also writes "Lines written among the Euganean Hills" to catch his bleak mood, his "pulsing pain" in the "sea of misery":

> Day and night, and night and day,
> Drifting on his dreary way.'

The quotation makes Jane Austen's high nose twitch. My poets – Cowper, Crabbe, Gray – knew sadness as much or more. They hurt far fewer people.

> To each his suff'rings: all are men,
> Condemn'd alike to groan,
> The tender for another's pain;
> Th' unfeeling for his own.

Tramp, tramp, thud, thud, mocks Fran. No one reads this stuff now.

Jane Austen shakes her head, her curls remaining fixed.

Fran clears her throat, 'I know what you're trying to say, Thomas, that poetry, great art, can come from human suffering. Where the art is great, the suffering, even of another, might be worth it.'

'*You* want me to say that,' says Thomas annoyed. 'I merely point out that at this time and in this place, Shelley produces great art. I make no moral claim.'

'Can't countenance it,' says Fran feeling reckless. Dishonest too, for she's aware that bits of this Euganean poem now reside in her skull as vividly as Wordsworth's bothering daffodils.

Thomas subsides, smiling, 'Oh well, Shelley anticipated your attitude: "I am one/Whom men love not."'

'Right,' says Annie, 'so life goes on afterwards, as it has to.'

'I couldn't bear to visit Fusina,' says Rachel.

One does not love a place the less for having suffered in it unless it has been nothing but suffering, whispers Jane Austen.

It isn't *our* suffering, Fran retorts. Less easy to manipulate another's, and from two centuries back.

'What Shelley wrote after the death of Clara is undeniably great,' Annie continues. She seems the least moved and yet, thinks Fran, if anyone can be accused of dumping children for her own work and ease, surely it's Annie.

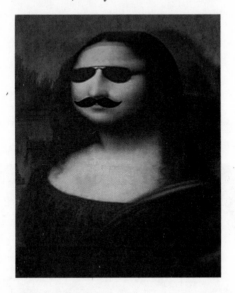

Tamsin saunters back with cigarettes and a bag displaying a bearded Mona Lisa with shades. Annie looks coldly at her. Tamsin grins back.

'I prefer the bag to the painting,' says Fran. The (much admired) expression reminds her of Jane Austen's in Cassandra's portrait.

Mary and Shelley return to the villa in Este.

Men are good at achieving aesthetic distance, perhaps objectifying a suffering separate self. Little mention in letters and diaries of that tiny life so speedily snuffed out.

To give Shelley a more sympathetic response, let's flit forward nine months to the death of Clara's brother, William, 'Wilmouse' as they called him, of malaria at the age of three and a half. He too died to convenience his father. They were in unhealthy Rome in summer; Shelley insisted on staying because his portrait was being painted.

> The babe is at peace within the womb;
> The corpse is at rest within the tomb:
> We begin in what we end.

The sorrowing mother is numb with grief. Shelley finds her demeanour unappealing (again).

'*Mater dolorosa*,' Rachel ends, eyes lowered.

Fran and Annie exchange glances. They're like parents wondering whether to adopt: Fran smiles to think of tall, self-assured Rachel succumbing to their care and constraint.

Mary tries to control her grief, at least after Clara's death – another story after beloved William's. Then – so Shelley thinks – or rather, *you* think if you read poetry as autobiography – she hated him and wanted him castrated.

With Claire uppermost in her husband's mind and perhaps heart, Mary may at this point have noted how precarious her hold is on her poet. Remember Harriet's short tenure. She may be assessing her marriage realistically, accepting that the old vibrating empathy between the genius and herself is past, their worlds colliding.

Byron suggests she copy out a manuscript for him, by way of distraction.

Annie interrupts the silence. 'This is the very afternoon to visit San Michele, isle of the dead.' She waves the cigarette she's been carefully holding away from the lunch table. 'Dark tourism. We might find something about burial habits in Venice in 1818. We've not seen Clara Shelley's grave. The Lido, they say, but we don't know for sure.'

Tamsin laughs, 'You guys are spending this gorgeous sunny afternoon in a cemetery?'

'Yup,' says Fran, cheered by the idea of an outing. 'The boat goes from the top of Venice.'

'I could swim it,' says Thomas, who admires Byron's wild athleticism.

I am relieved that rigmarole is over, remarks Jane Austen. Allow me to quote a more controlled account of death from my childhood tales: 'The Vessel was wrecked on the coast of Calshot and every Soul on board perished. The sad Event soon reached Carlisle, and the beautiful Rose was affected by it, beyond the power of Expression.' Please keep this in mind when you come to dispose of Shelley.

They trudge up misattributed lanes and filled-in canals towards Fondamente Nove, passing Tedeschi, former Austrian post office and surveillance centre, now a consumer emporium. Arriving at the boat stop, they look across at San Michele's brick walls, symmetrical decorations, and dark yews: they find the place – as Rachel could have told them – un-Romantic.

Fran senses Jane Austen's amusement, You expected to feel solemn awe I suppose. Like Catherine Morland anticipating Northanger Abbey.

Thomas has done his homework on Protestant corpses.

Venice had a long-established colony of German-speaking merchants. They worshipped discreetly, but had problems disposing of bodies. Churches, *scuole* and other pious institutions which interred Catholic dead baulked at heretics.

In 1647 Germans were given a special '*arca*' for their corpses, then in 1717 Swiss Protestants requested the island of San Servolo. The Senate refused but allocated them a (poor) plot on the north of the monastic island, San Cristoforo.

After Napoleon conquered Venice, along with most of Europe, he proposed a modern civic cemetery on San Cristoforo (disliking the stench of Venetian corpses) – with walled areas for '*culti non cattolici*'. The Austrians were more ambitious: in the 1830s, construction of the modern island of San Michele began, taking in San Cristoforo. Walled-off sections accepted unbaptized infants, Greek Orthodox, and some resident Protestants.

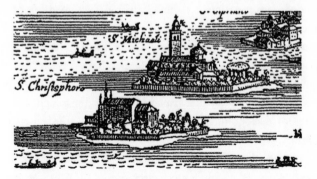

As they approach San Michele, Tamsin snaps a photo of the neo-gothic walls (post 1870), then turns her mobile camera towards Thomas, who pulls a lock of hair over his forehead and grins.

On land, they walk desultorily in different groups, first along church cloisters, then out among graves. Fran savours the quietness. She spies Tamsin and Thomas entwined between tombstones. Perhaps they'll enjoy a Shelleyan moment in a graveyard less dank than St Pancras.

Rachel likes the stillness within the light: how little is needed in these sunny places to catch patterns. What pattern in a life, how make the real, the whole, from a pattern? A story, a poem?

'Don't care for it,' says Annie, 'those walls of the dead with little pots of gaudy flowers, looks Hindu.'

'Catholic,' says Fran.

'Not Protestant, you mean?'

'Not tasteful,' says Rachel joining them, 'but, in the sun with only the shadow of trees, they have something.'

In the island's pokey office, they ask after Protestant graves. The bored official flicks long purple-painted nails to direct them to *'recinto evangelico'*.

'Sounds like preachy Nonconformists.'

'Let's get it over with,' says Annie turning away. She's flooded with nostalgia for the wifely, old-fashioned life of the heterosexual couple. She's fond of Fran, but travelling with women instead of a man – dare she admit it? – disturbs her, people look at you differently. Despite being (probably) the centre of the little group of five, she feels unsettled. Jane Austen may whisper to Fran that friendship is the finest balm for the pangs of disappointed love, but Annie can't quite access this comfort. Not yet.

She sets off quickly while Rachel and Fran clamber over hillocks and graves, taking a more circuitous path. All three arrive at a shabby corner of the 'evangelical' section. Tamsin and Thomas are already there, staring at tombs of Joseph Brodsky and Ezra Pound, both adorned with humidly wilting flowers. Thomas knows almost nothing of either.

Tamsin grins at him, '"I sat on the Dogana's steps/For the gondolas cost too much that year." That's all I can quote. It's poetic because Pound was a poet, see.'

She chuckles. Enchanted by her words, they all laugh.

'Shit,' she says, 'I remember another bit: "peacocks in Koré's house, or there may have been" – that's got a lilt.'

'You're a wonder, Tamsin,' smiles Fran, looking at Thomas as she speaks. 'So much lodged in that head – you'd think it'd be too heavy for your long neck.' She flushes at having made so physical and possibly unseemly a remark.

Four workmen are sweeping up leaves with besom brooms. They chat together in a slow quartet. Not catching the Italian – maybe Venetian? – Fran and Annie recollect the chorus of gardeners in *Richard II* who comment wisely on the sorry acts of their betters. Perhaps these gardeners have the wisdom of the place, unavailable to visitors.

For pity's sake, don't let Fran try to engage them!

Rachel makes a quick swoop round other tombs. She reports that the earliest date from the later nineteenth century, 'way beyond our period'.

'Let's try the Greeks. Perhaps they dumped some Prots in with them,' suggests Tamsin.

Annie's dejection has given way to weariness. She wants more alcohol: a large glass of white wine by shimmering water would cheer her. When they arrive at the Greeks, she perks up at the sight of Diaghilev's tomb, a pile of mouldering ballet shoes on top.

'Jeez,' says Tamsin, 'a bit gross. They're tiny. Are they from dead infants?'

They look in different directions, seeing nothing but tombs busted by tree roots, stones toppled over, writing defaced by years.

'I think we're done,' says Thomas, feeling the weight of women, even perhaps Tamsin. Elan Valley again – and the London flat with Kiran, the girls and sometimes his mother-in-law. Does he seek female groups – reprising the family he was so keen to leave? He smiles at the notion of Tamsin as a facet of his overwhelming mother. Shelley and his women? You don't hear a lot of his mother.

They set off back towards the vaporetto stop, finding the cemetery as much a maze as Venetian *calli*. They trail round in irritated circles.

'Hey guys, lost in the land of the dead, nice one,' whoops Tamsin.

They spy a burly man and hurry towards him. The German points to a map in his thick guidebook. To Fran's weary eyes it seems a board of snakes and ladders. Thomas bends over the page talking the German he prefers to Italian – and indeed to English. The men smile at each other. The exit is behind them.

Before leaving, they make a final stop at the office to see if more can be learnt from Purple Nails. She's been replaced by a middle-aged woman with black dyed hair and bright orange lips reading a *libro giallo*. She doesn't look up. Fran's turn to ask about graves before 1820 – in halting Italian.

Irritated, the woman glances at her, 'All here,' she says in English and returns to her novel.

Tamsin steps forward, 'I think Protestants were buried on the Lido after 1684 too. Like before San Michele was established?'

'No Protestants on the Lido, only Catholics,' says the woman, her eyes fixed on her page.

'Fuckwit,' says Tamsin smiling.

'And Jews,' adds a young man, entering behind them.

Thomas turns to address him, 'There was a Protestant burial ground where there's now an airfield.'

The Italians exchange glances and smirk. 'No,' says the young man, 'only Catholics and Jews.'

Returning on the vaporetto, they're sardined within a party of Chinese tourists clutching glass baubles, vases and trinkets bought in Murano and likely imported from their homeland. Thomas looks behind at Annie and Rachel caught between children playing games on their mobiles. 'Those officials on San Michele are wrong,' he says over his shoulder.

'So why didn't you argue?' asks Annie

Thomas shrugs against Tamsin's head. 'Not worth it. They knew nothing and were interested in less.'

By the window Fran hears Thomas's response, liking the idea of less than nothing. Feels positive. The thought makes her light-headed. I need food and a glass of fizz, she thinks.

Rachel pokes Annie, 'I could murder a beer.'

26

Next morning Fran looks out of her window to find a scruffy barge tied to the single cleat. Two people – father and daughter or a couple? – come out of a small cabin, remains of bread and coffee visible on an upturned crate. They undress without embarrassment, do an all-over wash from a bucket, then stuff night things into the cabin, carefully padlock it, and leave.

Annie joins Fran to watch. 'I suppose they're going to find a café to defecate in. At least I hope that's where they put their shit.'

'Gypsies,' says Fran. 'Or hippies. I like them.'

The couple return, a dog barks from the cabin. They set about cleaning and mending the loose planks of their little house.

Mole in *The Wind in the Willows* mends and paints his dark, lonely home before feeling the call of spring.

Up we go!

On the quayside the pair deposit leaking bags. They stain the white stone. Then the young woman carries the bags towards the rubbish dump, dripping oil as she marches over the humpback bridge. She returns to continue housekeeping.

Fran's eager to talk to them, but her language is too poor. She tries grinning through the window, but no substitute for words. She goes outside with Annie to nod encouragement whenever eyes meet. Clothes, tools and pans clutter the narrow quayside.

At a late breakfast, they find the staff outraged. 'They're not from the island,' shouts the waitress over the noise of a coffee-grinding machine. Her English is good: she's been a barista in Bromley. 'They must go,' she says as the grinding subsides, 'their mooring is illegal. The owner calls the police. They make big mess.' She sniffs crudely through her arched nose. They sniff better in Italy, Fran thinks.

Annie's looking at her phrase book. 'I can't hold even the simplest conversation in Italian,' she wails. 'I despise people who go to other people's countries and don't become fluent in words and ways. But here,' she throws down the book so it touches the edge of her saucer, wobbling dregs in her cup, 'the words I memorised slithered off as soon as we landed in Marco Polo.'

'We suffer from British-educationitis,' says Fran. 'Learning the future perfect before mastering how to buy a pound of salami or the polite way to ask youths flirting outside our window past midnight to shut up so their grannies can sleep.'

'It's metric here – and in England,' laughs Annie. 'It's something to know grammar. You're right, though. In our day it was considered enough. Speaking was for foreigners. Besides, we pride ourselves on being monolingual.'

'What if one gets a heart attack here? What's the word for it? And what if they're on strike again or the mist's so thick vaporetti don't run?'

They ask the waitress what happens when Giudecca is cut off. She stares into her coffee machine and barks, 'Always one boat to Zattere. *Solo Palanca.*'

'Sounds like Chiron announcing a stop-off at Purgatory.'

Back in Fran's room, while Annie studies the guidebook for the Lido, Fran continues watching the gypsy boat. Urged by the hotel owner or police or just feeling the coldness of his welcome, the man is trying to start the engine.

Sputtering, then silence.

'Isn't it marvellous to see so much going on?' says Fran.

'Hmm,' says Annie taking out a Gauloises and waving it at Fran's window. Thinking better of it, she replaces it in its box. 'I once stayed in a bedsit overlooking the Old Kent Road. Not unlike.'

'I wonder what Agafia watches.'

'What is it about Agafia?'

'Envy I guess. The self-reliance.'

'She had God,' says Annie, 'remember that. Have you been noticing Tamsin and Thomas?'

'You know I once wondered about Rachel. But she's too old.'

'Not that again,' laughs Annie. 'Thomas and Tamsin don't hide much. I guess by now they've exchanged "the kiss of love when life is young", the nearest earthly thing to heaven Shelley could imagine. Shelley didn't stick around long to find what happens next. Maybe a bit tricky for Thomas.'

A burst of sunlight dazzles the glass in the window. A knock on the door, Rachel enters, astonishing them both.

'Gorgeous here,' she says.

Fran smiles. 'Go on with you. Not your sort of place.'

'No, well, where is?'

She plops down on the bed, one buttock on Annie's open phrasebook. 'I popped into the Danieli last night after what Thomas said about it. My mother and I stayed there decades ago when she was a troubled teenager.'

'*She* was?'

'Yup, Mother never made it to adulthood. I however was always grown up. Anyway, we stayed there, very grand and sombre. We ate oysters, lobster and little quails, an *amuse bouche* of pea cream and lagoon shrimp, and all manner of good delicate things, nothing quite having the perfect taste. Then Mother binged on sugar outside in the *campi*, as well as pills and alcohol of course. She wanted to seem literary and arty and kept saying, with her mouth full of shellfish that would soon be in the toilet bowl, how fascinating it was that George Sand and Alfred de Musset stayed there, in room 10, I think she said. No reason. I had the brochure too and I remember saying, Proust and Balzac as well, and Shelley and Byron in room 13, figuring she'd read none of them and no one knew where any of them stayed – in the last two cases, certainly not here. "Clever little mouse," she said to me holding my arm as we stepped down the golden stairway, supposedly doing a mother-daughter thing for onlookers. Actually, she was unsteady and wanted my support.'

Annie's astonished: even when directly questioned, Rachel's been reticent; why this now?

To Fran the reminiscence sounds rehearsed.

'Time for the Lido,' says Annie after a pause. 'Shall we go to your place for coffee en route?'

Visualising her four-poster bed with its Fortuny brocade hangings, the red velvet chaise by the high window, the ornate mirrors, Rachel replies, 'Nah, easier to go direct to San Zaccaria before we lose steam.'

'Have we everything we need by way of texts, info and paper hankies?' asks Annie.

Fran invites Jane Austen along, using the jocular tone she associates with the sisterly letters.

I didn't deal in dead babies.

Persuasion? Sir Walter Eliot's dead heir.

Never born.

Mrs Hall producing a dead child because she may have seen her husband?

No private correspondence can bear the eye of others, begins Jane Austen.

I'd never sink to that.

'Sink to what?' asks Rachel.

'Just a passing thought,' answers Fran. She blows her nose.

Life's in dialogue, remember, Jane Austen says helpfully. You have others here to obscure the chatter.

'We have to go by the Anglican church for Thomas,' Fran reminds Rachel and Annie.

When they arrive at the *campo* beside little St George's, Rachel walks off to look through a reflecting shop window. Unexpectedly, Shelley's troubling her. He thinks he can arrest moments with words, but is careless of the particular moment of a child's life. The real palpable living thing doesn't affect him, just the being of his mind, the being in words: desire and regret rather than experience. Is this a way to live? Recollecting her own emotion before the unknown choirboy in King's Chapel, she presses her hand on the glass.

'I can't take another pious interior,' exclaims Annie, waving a hand towards the church. 'You go Fran, it's your world. What's the point anyway?'

'Not much. Just possibly there might be records of dead Brits.'

Fran enters alone, makes enquiries and learns the place became an Anglican church only in 1892. She returns with one modest fact: the tombstone of Consul Joseph Smith on the wall is from the Lido burying-ground.

'I'd hoped for better things from the Anglican community,' says Thomas when he hears.

Prone to flooding and always windswept, the Lido was never desirable for burial, its sole advantage being its inclusiveness: anyone could go under there. Yet, the excluded are segregated: Protestants and Jews of course, but also Muslims and condemned criminals.

I never wanted that pompous tomb and plaque in Winchester, Jane Austen interrupts. I wished to be laid to rest in the modest Chawton churchyard where my mother and dear sister would have joined me when their time came.

The dead don't choose, whispers Fran, a grave's for the living.

A strange idea: you deny the will of the dead to dispose of its most intimate possession.

'Whenever I get information from Italian officials or scholars,' grumbles Thomas as they assemble for the trip, 'it turns out wrong or obfuscating.'

'Maybe our truth isn't theirs,' laughs Tamsin chewing.

Where does she put the used gum? Does she swallow it – how would it move through the intestines? Or does she discreetly spit it out, wrap it like dog poo to throw away later? Fran's puzzling the questions when Tamsin blows and pops a bubble, releasing a smell of chemical strawberry.

They laugh. 'I guess you guys want me to be younger than I am,' she says moving the wodge of gum into her cheek. 'I got this bubble gum specially to complement my uptick.'

'The fact is,' announces Thomas, 'that 1818 is from an in-between period. Current arrangements on San Michele date from the late 1870s. The layers of history in this town are scrambled.'

'Same everywhere,' says Fran. '*Bubbles* advertises Pears' Soap. Then Pears is taken over by Sunlight Soap, so Millais's picture is in the Port Sunlight gallery on the Wirral. You wouldn't expect that, would you?'

27

The vaporetto to the Lido across the Bacino and southern lagoon is exhilarating. They stand on the platform, unusually free of tourist groups; water and wind swish past.

It's a holiday, thinks Fran. I am on holiday with my four friends. Five Go Adventuring.

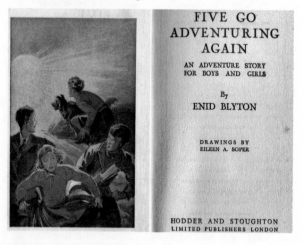

Thomas waves his hands in excitement. 'I've got a footnote,' he exclaims, 'or something for *Notes & Queries*. Look at San Servolo island over there. Scholars think this is where Byron and Shelley meet the Maniac in "Julian and Maddalo". But the poem describes only *one* belfry tower, clearly there are *two* there. The madhouse must be on the other island way over there, see, only one tower.'

'This really matters, Thomas, unlike the Danieli?' chuckles Fran.

'It most certainly does,' snorts Annie.

Indeed so, whispers Jane Austen, it matters in art whether there are hedgerows in Northamptonshire. Less so in life.

Emma's apple blossom in June?

Some moments call for your 'soft-focus'. Would I be 'everybody's dear Jane' without it?

'All art as fabulous as the island of Shallot,' insists Rachel. 'Words have to have autonomy.'

If she had a couple of double gins inside her, Annie might have responded, 'Fucking creative writing!'

The boat stops at Santa Maria Elisabetta; they alight before realising they could have stayed on until San Nicolò, nearer the burying-grounds. But the walk in the morning sun is pleasant.

Dodging cars, buses and hired tricycles, they pass hotels, cafés, bars, beaches with different coloured parasols twirling in the breeze, shops selling bikinis, cigarettes and ice cream.

Yet, as they go beyond the most commercial areas, nearing their goal, they feel something wild lingering – as if to say, this string of leisure joys just might be washed clean away with a great wave of water.

Like Rhayader if the stone dams fail.

Thomas reiterates his warning. The Jewish cemetery is set apart and guarded, but much of the area for other aliens was dug up to create an airstrip. All they'll get is atmosphere – and little of that. 'Show them your pictures, Tamsin,' he concludes. 'Old Protestant tombstones are stacked behind the Jewish cemetery on the edge of a new Catholic one. Not easy to get there but someone took pictures. These and Fran's British consul are all we've got.'

'Right,' says Tamsin cocking her head. 'The images show a few tombstones restored with funding from Venice in Peril and the French Committee. There's like more info on the web, but,' shrugging, 'it's kind of boring, antiquarian stuff.'

'In short, we've nothing to see here.'

Contrariwise, all to imagine.

'Forget the artefacts,' says Rachel, 'get back to the story.'

'Yeah, the dead baby,' says Tamsin. 'I'm up for it. I should but don't care for archives, Thomas.'

'I bought you an ice cream in payment,' he replies, a loving look sliding into his face for all to see.

'OK,' says Annie, turning away.

Tamsin bounds on ahead, her brown soapy-smooth body in its tight white shorts the very image of vitality and joy. Fran drags her eyes sideways.

'First step, the record. The baby dies. Not a new-born but a child, more than a year old. A small, but not very small body.

You wrap it in a sheet, a blanket, an old shirt? You hire a gondola to row you and the bundle to the Lido.'

'All this in a town full of rules and regulations,' Fran interrupts Rachel, 'where Mary and her dying child were stopped at Fusina for lack of paperwork.'

Jane Austen clears her throat, I gave the opinion on England and its neighbourhood of voluntary spies to my hero Henry Tilney, not entirely trustworthy but an effective storyteller and a man of common sense. I would expect that Venice, a city of masks and spying, would be thick with surveillance. You do well to doubt this improbable, indeed absurd, story.

Shelley, Mary, Byron, a whole party of other men and women – or just Shelley with his bundle? – walk on the sand, perhaps in wind and rain, perhaps in baking sunlight which must even in so short a time attack that tiny body. Or is it night-time so they see by flares and torches?

Tamsin catches the last words. 'Prot burials at night,' she says. 'Found that on my archive morning, well, in Rome anyway.'

'Whatever the climate and light, someone digs a hole in the sand and puts the child in. Can we see women at the scene?'

Rachel is imagining too keenly. Annie frowns, 'Is this being done as history or fiction?'

'Or vision?' says Fran. 'Shelley imagines his own death in a desert place under a great moon.'

'Did he,' pursues Rachel, 'think of his baby as "A fragile lute . . . quenched for ever,/Still, dark, and dry, and unremembered now"?'

'Doubtful. He kept the better poetry for himself.'

'The best lines are these,' says Rachel:

          'Heartless things
    Are done and said i' the world, and many worms
    And beasts and men live on.'

'He can hit the nail when he wants to,' says Fran, touching Rachel's arm.

His own imagined death is a peaceful fading, nothing as undignified as pain and filth. Little Ca dies in agony, in convulsions. But the burial place fits Shelley's visions of poetic deaths, liminal spots of water and unstable land.

'Precarious,' says Fran.

Uneasy at the sistering, Thomas says, 'Let's try to look at it from Shelley's point of view.'

That, thinks Fran, is rather daring in the circumstances.

'Shelley and a couple of friends, maybe Byron, along with the British consul or a clergyman and a grave digger, would have gone to the Protestant place on the Lido by night. A hole is dug in the sand and a baby inserted. The hole is filled. Then all, including Shelley, return in the gondola to – somewhere. Shelley has a drink perhaps, watches a Venetian sunset.'

His tone surprises Fran and Rachel. Matter of fact, outraged, querying?

Jane Austen whispers, At last you may be getting somewhere in this macabre business.

'So,' says Fran, 'you continue your poetic career. There will be another child to kill before you're through, this is the second dead one.'

If you discount the child drowned in the Serpentine in Harriet's belly.

'God!' Tamsin sniggers, addressing Annie. 'You guys used to preach that scholarship needed detachment. We never believed you.'

'Venice doesn't let death settle,' says Rachel. 'Remember Henry James, who drove (so some assume) Constance Fenimore Woolson to suicide? He tries to dispose of her dark silk dresses by having himself rowed out onto the lagoon in a gondola, then throwing them overboard. They billow out and won't sink, floating on the surface around the boat. Filling with water like live bodies.'

'You supplied that image, Rachel,' chuckles Annie. 'No evidence Henry James thought of dresses as living or dead bodies, he was just nonplussed by all this female stuff. Though he could have given them to the poor; drowning them is pretty theatrical.'

'Mary can't have come, I feel sure,' says Fran. 'Italy will be the graveyard of her children. She must fear for little William. Does she recall Harriet's son and daughter? They survived babyhood because their genius father absconded.'

'Not for the burial of course, women don't,' says Thomas. 'But a couple of days later she went to the Lido and met Byron. He may have comforted her by the little grave. Why are you making these men into monsters?'

Annie's bored. She says, 'After Shelley dies, Mary recaps the storm of misery that's engulfed her life in Italy. She remembers Clara asleep "on bleak Lido, near Venetian seas". That settles the place, if we ever doubted.' She wants to walk to the seaside and let hot sand run between bare toes.

They arrive at the locked gate of the Hebrew cemetery, stare through, then scramble across scrubby terrain along barbed wire where the desecrated Protestants might have been. The going's tough and they give up – far too easily, as Thomas assumed they would. But he's been humoured for most of this trip by his female retinue and won't insist on their persevering. He dampens down the desire that often rises embarrassingly when he thinks of Tamsin, even within this odd quartet.

They regain the road, retrace some steps, then turn off towards the shore through prickly undergrowth. The smudged and mottled sand is matted with thistles and amphibious weeds. Nearer the sea the sand becomes light and fly-away.

'Wherever Clara was buried, it must have been in restless sand like this,' says Rachel. She walks on ahead, then turns to address the stragglers. 'It's a terrible place to be left, by so much water, the lagoon one side, the sea on the other. When he describes watery death, Shelley thinks only of himself, not his child.'

Distrusting the accelerating emotion, Thomas answers levelly, 'She'll be buried in the cemetery, why ever not? But it's true, we have no account of it. Letters and journals are missing. So let's return to Shelley and Byron on the Lido. Perhaps they ride where the baby will be buried, then is buried. "Julian and Maddalo" is finished long after the first intoxicating outing, so it remains strange that dead Clara makes no entry. The only child in the poem is Claire's daughter, the lovely "toy", his "special favourite".'

'Allegra, who's caused such misery to Mary, the child his own has been sacrificed for,' snaps Rachel.

Thomas had intended using this trip to impress Rachel, but their views are diverging as they hadn't in Wales. He's not ingratiating himself. He turns the subject, 'Yet there *is* a sense of death in that poem, a swirling of sand and sea that suggests human dissolution, even if not focused on the dead baby. Remember, the poets go off to a lagoon island to meet a "Maniac". Confined and maddened, the Maniac already seems drowned, his hair swaying in the spray.'

'Another Shelley clone with the usual sad, gentle face,' sniffs Fran.

Annie steps in. 'You know Byron wanted to be buried on the Lido, at least when enthralled by La Guiccioli. He found a good epitaph in a cemetery in Bologna: *Implora pace.*'

How often Annie slides towards Byron, Thomas notes again. Byron, the celebrated, charismatic and cruel. He smiles perfunctorily.

'You know the nation's favourite epitaph?' asks Fran. '"I told you I was ill."'

From behind, Tamsin touches Thomas's arm, 'Hey, you're right, the Maniac's kind of dead, and the two poets feel good after their ghoulish meeting. I guess like going to a funeral makes you feel more vital.'

Rachel is silent. The Maniac's long moan heaps blame on the woman. Her angry grief makes her want to castrate and mutilate the beloved; supposedly it's sent him mad. Such double-dyed, multi-gendered guilt and hypocrisy! How difficult, sometimes, not to abandon Shelley altogether. 'If "Julian and Maddalo" doesn't deliver a burial ceremony for little Clara,' she says brightly, 'should we go back to Shelley's visions of his own?'

Thomas shrugs, his eyes on the strip of skin where Tamsin has rolled up her shirt to reveal a glinting navel jewel. He touches the phone in his back pocket, wishing he could record every inch and moment of this elastic, electric body.

'The real one? OK.'

For Shelley this stormy death was transforming, for us an interruption.

28

In July 1822, Shelley is drowned on the opposite coast of Italy: the bay of Lerici in the Gulf of Genoa. He's anticipated his death in poems of pale poetic *alter egos*. 'If you can't swim / Beware of Providence,' says Byron–Maddalo to Shelley–Julian.

'Let's stay with "Lines Written among the Euganean Hills" composed after Clara dies,' begins Rachel. 'He becomes a "tempest-cleaving Swan", welcomed by the sea

> with such emotion
> That its joy grew his, and sprung
> From his lips like music . . .'

Inevitably after so much anticipation, you might suspect his end determined. Friends confirm his wish to drown at sea.

'Abandoned Harriet drowned herself in a London lake,' Fran interrupts. 'Mary Wollstonecraft (his mother-in-law, remember), also abandoned by her lover, as good as drowned herself in the Thames. A pattern? Though the sea beats a London lake and river, more poetic to go out with the tide.'

Rachel isn't listening. 'Unlikely he sabotaged his craft – and not even a genius-poet could raise a storm. He could, though, take advantage of it.'

Thomas is bursting to interrupt. Shelley knows about boats, for God's sake. He's building a steamboat with cylinders, boiler and ironwork. He's only stopped by lack of funds (as usual).

But *this* is a sailboat formed for the excitement of storms and tumbling speed.

He knows about sailboats too.

Little rain for weeks. The weather sultry in that ominous Northern Italian way. Enough to make the most light-hearted dismal. Shelley and Mary are not getting on. He's writing powerful gloomy poetry – of no financial worth (though deep in debt) – and beautiful love lyrics to another woman. He wants to buy Prussic acid – not for immediate suicide, mind. Having just dangerously miscarried, Mary's depressed and irritable. Shelley may leave her. (Post-Shelley, she'll massage these last days.) Remembering Harriet: rejection falls heavily on women. (Death not so much.)

The voyage out lacks incident, not the voyage back.

The boat's a double-masted ketch, adapted for speed. A friend and a teenage boy as deckhand accompany Shelley – had he pierced holes, as some critics suspect, he'd have been a murderer.

On that day, from being serene, the sky frays, clouds scud and hide the sun: thunder, fog, everything the heavens can throw descends.

Is there such a storm?

Sails become too full; some are hastily furled. The boat goes sideways on the wind.

An Italian captain offers help. It's refused.

Did this happen?

In mist and smashing rain, the boat is rammed by another vessel for robbery.

Perhaps – or is this an extenuating lie devised by the man

who helped modify the heavy boat for speed, fatally wounding its structure? He's the only source.

So many questions mark an insecure narration, a too passionate involvement, interjects Jane Austen. Like my Marianne Dashwood accosting Willoughby at the London party.

Fran bats her Author away. Emotional fashions change. Marianne Dashwood's an online heroine, the scream you muffled is now heard loud and clear.

To Rachel's surprise, Thomas mutters, 'You know – I'm not now sure. Why the Prussic acid? Does Shelley carry it onto the boat?'

It takes a young man to suspect another's fatal enthralment.

Thomas smooths his hair and smiles. Unlike fiction, biography is ragged.

Shelley drowns with the others – how little we care for them. He's swollen into meat for sharks and dogfish . . .

'The fish he most hated.'

Eight days on, the corpse washes ashore, face and arms eaten, flesh and bones decayed. An old rag retains its form longer than a dead body, Byron will note.

The black single-breasted jacket though torn is recognised, the shirt, bits of buff-coloured nankeen trousers, black boots and silk white stockings.

Both Shelley and his wife Harriet, long in the water, are identified by what they wear.

In the jacket pocket – handy proof that art, or artefact in this case, survives human mortality – the leather binding of Keats's *Lamia*, damaged when perhaps Shelley pushed at it while drowning. In the instant of real death, might death be less alluring, willed or otherwise?

*

The hot time of the year, the remains putrefy. Genoan quarantine laws demand covering in lime and quick burial. Leftovers are dug into the sand, an old pine root marking the spot.

In Elan Valley there was a dead tree . . .

It's too close to the lapping sea. So, a month later, the stinking bits are exhumed to suffer pagan burning before assembled friends. Laid on an iron furnace under logs of wood, with wine, oil, salt and frankincense to counteract the smell of putrefaction. Edward Trelawny, corny old raconteur, impresario and technicolour literary liar, who will dine out on Byron and Shelley the rest of his long life, concocts last rites.

Byron is hot – noonday sun is fierce, fire intensifies the heat. He swims off.

Annie interrupts Rachel. 'Years later Louis Eduard Fournier paints him in Byronic posture on a cold windswept (English?) beach. He contemplates the pyre with its body of intact head, hands and feet – in fact hands and feet were severed and no flesh remained on the blackened skull. Fournier adds a kneeling Mary in the background. She wasn't there.'

Trelawny claims Byron complimented him on his pagan incantation, 'I restore to nature through fire the elements of which this man was composed, earth, air and water; everything is changed, but not annihilated; he is now a portion of that which he worshipped.' Byron's compliment is implausible.

'The fire takes time to catch,' says Thomas. 'Then it burns for hours, the lime producing phosphorescent blue flames. Shelleyan radiance. Bones fall apart, remains are cooked in their own oiliness. Atoms disperse into the air, a single bird flies away. A nice touch.'

A curlew, a vulture?

Annie looks quizzically at Thomas, 'Yeats says, "The living can assist the imagination of the dead." Trelawny, Fournier, now you.'

Jane Austen grimaces. A sad, slightly ridiculous account. No irony needed, no joke, but some discreet distancing. Death is common, fabling commonplace.

'One day Byron will remark that his own brains are boiling, "as Shelley's did" when he was grilled,' adds Annie.

The conservative newspaper, the *Courier*, is even less decorous: 'Shelley, the writer of some infidel poetry, has been drowned: now he knows whether there is a God or no.'

'Yeah,' says Tamsin, 'his mates like get bits as keepsakes. Mary wrapped the heart in silk gauze. Trelawny burns his hand snatching it – so he claims, though no one saw him. More like a liver.' The offal ends up in Bournemouth.

'Trelawny takes a slice of jawbone with teeth sockets for himself. Later, fragments of skull circulate, to be kissed by fans.'

My point about reliquaries, says Jane Austen. These friends sound a little touched. It's as well I had a Christian burial. We're not Catholics or Hindus.

A lock of your hair – rather discoloured by yeast – was recently auctioned in Gloucestershire, whispers Fran.

Quite different. Hair is given voluntarily as gift for rings and lockets. What you describe is irreverent, morbid.

You didn't give it, Fran retorts, you aren't Marianne Dashwood. Cassandra snipped the hair when you were dead, before the coffin was closed.

The Author is silenced. Then she remarks, There's a place for reverential curating – a pressed violet, Crabbe's bright blue damselfly – but not human parts.

'I'm amazed,' says Fran 'there was anything of Shelley left to bury in the Protestant cemetery in Rome. Our baby girl remains intact.'

As far as we know.

If death is harsh, once dead everyone can seem at peace. Like her father's spirit, little Clara's goes to

> some world far from ours
> Where moonlight & music & feeling
> Are one.

No one follows this. Is the tone right, for once?

Fran feels a prick of emotion and wonders if she's trying to channel the sad dead grandma.

That's what comes of living in your head and the dribblings of books, warns Jane Austen, now recovered from the taunt of purloined hair.

Yet Fran's heartened by the idea of Clara's splendid lineage. Buried in an unmarked grave perhaps, yet still granddaughter of Mary Wollstonecraft. Something, yes?

Granddaughter too of a baronet, the kind of classy thing that matters in England.

Annie's trying to dislodge a linseed stuck between her back teeth since breakfast. However she swishes her tongue, she can't move it. 'We could designate a spot,' she suggests. 'Like they do in colleges, deciding on a room to claim for a famous author. National Trust houses with beds Elizabeth or Mary Queen of Scots slept in. Like Rachel said about the Danieli.'

Suddenly turning from the sea, Rachel startles them all by squatting and setting down her water bottle. 'I've brought candles and matches.'

'Go ahead,' says Thomas walking slightly apart with Tamsin, who's been checking her phone.

Rachel fixes her candles in the sand and tries to light them, while Fran and Annie stoop to shield them from the breeze.

'What are those old women doing?' a child's high-pitched English voice rings out.

The mother walks behind Annie and Fran without their seeing her. 'A ceremony of some sort,' she says, embarrassed. 'Come away, Imogen.'

Yet she herself remains close. 'My father-in-law wanted his ashes thrown off Bardsey Island,' she says to their backs. 'We had to hire a boat and go to all sorts of trouble. By the end we were so cold we didn't care. We threw the ashes overboard, but they blew back in our faces.'

Fran turns, smiling, 'He's still with you then.'

'Sort of,' laughs the woman. She takes the child's hand and pulls her away.

The candles have flickered out, Rachel walks to the seashore, carrying her sandals. When she returns, Fran notices her toenails are varnished green. Her groomed face is untethered.

'I know that, whoever came with the corpse to the Lido – and I accept, Thomas, that all would be done properly – it can't have been Mary. But let me for a moment imagine that it was and do another death.'

They're silent. Fran looks encouragingly at Rachel. Annie lights a cigarette and pats the air to ensure her smoke goes seawards like Shelley's floating ashes. Thomas exchanges glances with Tamsin, who's circling her head on her long neck.

The bundle is wrapped in blue cloth. Mary holds it to her breast like the baby it is, while Shelley digs the sand, just far enough from the sea to avoid water gushing in. He goes deep if not six feet. The bundle is small. Only the lull in digging tells Mary he's finished. He's a little exhilarated as well as sweaty from the effort – he always responds acutely to heavy exercise. Distressed too – Mary and Shelley, deep down one single 'tempest tost' bark. Her head is close to the body she clutches and she doesn't look up to catch his eye. After the stillness and silence has lasted too long, she steps forward, too hollowed out to cry. She kneels beside the hole already filling with fine sand and, stretching her arms from her breast, lowers the little child down.

Suddenly Rachel's kneeling by the snuffed candles. 'My baby,' she sobs, her head bowing forwards. The sand absorbs her tears. 'My baby,' she moans again.

I knew where it would end, sighs Jane Austen.

Back for the night in the hotel, Fran and Annie see a gap on the waterfront where the gypsy boat had been. Petrol stains the flagstones. When they meet the waitress, they ask what happened. She shrugs. She doesn't know whether it was the police or just locals who edged them away, out into the lagoon. They made no fuss.

After their motor refused to start, a local man kick-started it with a lead from the hotel. Off they chugged in their little house, travelling the blue water, criss-crossing proper paths laid out for civic boats. Wet washing flapping from a string line, the ragged dog standing on the stern.

What sort of dog? It'd be a lurcher in England.

Fran's sad she missed their going, though perhaps one glimpse of the older man stripping to a kind of thong and soaping himself so frankly was enough. The mess would have grown, making more indelible stains. But still, she's a teeny bit envious, as she is of Agafia. That ability to want and stand a loose, uncomfortable, free life.

Agafia doesn't live in the sun by a famous lagoon but in the tundra – though that too is hotting up with global warming. After thirty years of isolation, she goes on encouraging the Rapture with her ritual of bows and prayers.

Fran looks towards the darkening water: lagoon, Lido and Elan lakes all wishy-washy in her mind. It must be heart-breaking to wait like that.

Have the gypsies been hurt by their lack of welcome on firm ground? Wanderers are always resented by the securely settled. Remember the Romani suffering their Devouring?

Bet the old man can whistle through a fish scale.

Annie's unmoved, 'Just messy travellers.' She's recollecting with distaste the scene on the beach, Rachel doing a Trelawney. Theatrical, like the Master's thespian cortege. Her own griefs are the most pressing, but she's kept her equanimity; she'd never stage such intoxicated shows. Why be so censorious? Is she affronted by other people being moved by themselves? 'I must go to bed,' she says, but stays sitting in Fran's room. 'Do you think Rachel has a shrink?'

'Dunno,' says Fran. 'Julie once went to a class where she had to imagine her young self, meet her on the road, then embrace her as everyone wants to be embraced by grown-ups.'

'The baby she buried might be herself, you mean?'

Fran shrugs. She remembers the feel of her hands on Rachel's warm back as she knelt; the others shifting their feet away from what one critic, attuned to Jane Austen's mockery of silly novels, called 'the distraction scene'.

Annie still sits on Fran's bed as light finally fails. If they hadn't such a horror of sentiment, she's sure they'd be holding hands.

Fran smiles and stretches out an open palm.

Part Five

29

'Is it too neat a structure?' asks Annie. 'Making a life based on pooled damage?' She waves her cigarette through the window, then stubs it out. Smoke wafts back into the Cam riverside café. 'Just because we've spent some hols together, beguiling ourselves with dreamy Percy Bysshe, doesn't necessarily mean . . .' She shrugs.

'Damage pooled might be damage squared,' warns Fran.

We none of us expect to be in smooth water all our days, says Jane Austen.

'I wasn't great at math but I see no reason it can't cancel itself out,' chuckles Rachel. 'Minuses multiplied. We wouldn't have to live entirely with the absent if we had other company.'

Annie and Fran are apprehensive. Rachel's running away with the idea.

If no one runs, we all stand still.

'Come on,' says Rachel, 'everyone who's arrived at our age has bruises. Let me try putting it together. So, I gave birth to a dead baby, I'd been kicked downstairs, I went through childbirth when he was already dead. If I hadn't had a bulimic, alcoholic, drug-addled mother who makes analysis her life's meaning, I might have sought more help and not taken it so hard.' She smiles to leaven her words, the others look down, hoping she'll not make each of them a calamity paragraph. She goes on, 'Fran's husband drove his car into the water, his car becomes like Shelley's boat with speculative holes, but . . .'

'He didn't take the car,' interrupts Fran. 'I asked him to go, well once, before he did.'

Startled by the new variant, Annie says, 'It doesn't upset Rachel's point.'

The wet days, the Welsh mud in the seams of her hiking boots, still haunt Rachel. 'I guess I think of Fran's lost husband in Elan reservoir.'

Fran scowls. Mildly amusing to create a past; uncomfortable to meet it alive and talking.

'I destroyed my father,' says Annie. 'Is that what you want to say, Rachel? I haven't told you this, Fran, but I guess now . . . You knew Zach never got the Honorary Degree. A small thing but it rankled, ate him up, he wanted to be part of the Oxbridge world while despising it – he called it a court-orchestra – he even flirted with a skinny Dame Professor to get past the Council. Well, I kiboshed it with hints of plagiarism. OK, Fran, that doesn't grab you, you don't care a fig for our cliquey clubs and honours. You want me to say I didn't pay enough attention to my children.'

'Some confessional orgy,' Fran smirks to hide alarm.

Clumsy, whispers Jane Austen, giving her full-on sardonic look. Keeping back, then tendering truth is not a fictional crime. You live in your story, you adapt to its manners. No human being has omniscience, not even an Author.

Fran sees tears in Rachel's eyes. As likely to be for Percy Bysshe's teenage brides, their lost babes, Annie's abandoned children, her absent fatherless boy, as for her own stillborn child. It's the way of feelings. What's Hecuba to him or he to Hecuba/That he should weep for her? says Hamlet, surprised.

She tries to remove the created memory of Andrew's floating, then sinking body but finds the image smudging. Rachel carries off trauma, if that's what it is, so much better, she thinks, unaware of her new friend's hidden crutch: *Sweetpapers*, those stories that stylishly skewer a narcissist mother – note, reader, the aggressively fond dedication – and dissolve vindictive men.

(Had Annie seen this while on the Shelley trail in Venice, she'd have recollected his hostile praise of Byron, whose power tramples Shelley into a 'worm beneath the sod'.)

The conversation wanes. Rachel wipes her eyes, 'I tear easily,' she says, 'ignore.'

Is this what happens to women's talk with no man present, they speak over each other, echo, agree, get emotional and fall silent?

Jane Austen explodes. Sentimental claptrap! Women are rational creatures. They may be more inconsequential in mixed company, but imbecilities are not limited to one sex.

You try to make a new family and it acts just like the old one, thinks Annie. What a surprise! Nietzsche despised the family's crushing traditions. Would they be reconstituting them if they set up together? Would they fall into the mawkish piety he predicted? Or would they try to do a Virginia Woolf and tesselate themselves into the body of one complete human being? Merge identities?

Unlikely.

'We should stop whingeing about the past I guess you're saying, Rachel.' Hoping to erase her earlier discordant impression, Fran adds, 'Yes, but sometimes there's an eruption if words aren't allowed out whenever – you know, so long rehearsed and perfected.' She smiles at the slight raising of Annie's left eyebrow. 'There'd be a thinning audience, of course. Maybe we could learn not to cry at our own pathos. I don't mean you specifically,' she adds, catching Rachel's wet eyes.

As a child I composed an Ode to Pity, remarks Jane Austen. Sweetly noisy falls the silent stream. I dedicated it to my sister because of her pitiful nature.

'We should do laughing,' announces Annie. 'I remember you telling me about that laughter-therapy group up there in darkest Norfolk, Fran.'

Giggling, chuckling, guffawing, snorting, chortling, cack-ling? The young giggle, the old cackle, the semi-old chuckle.

'We could have a chuckling room.'

Fran picks at her teeth. The Polish poppy-seed cake sold in this ethnically interesting café is full of compacted lumps of seed the size of raisins. She'd mistaken them for chocolate drops. The unseemly act reminds her of Annie more discreetly dislodging linseed from her teeth before Rachel's 'ceremony of innocence' – as she now refers to the candle-scene on the Lido.

Noting Fran's preoccupation, Annie begins. 'But there's a neatness . . .'

Fran stops teeth-picking to interrupt. 'OK, a lost man, failed motherhood, defeated dad, absconding husband, dead baby, sorry Rachel, too frank I know, but there it is, it's a curious coincidence.'

'A pattern,' says Rachel, 'we make it.'

'Sounds like most of the disasters are mine,' notes Annie, sniffing to hide displeasure. 'I mentioned our idea vaguely to my brother. He said, Why don't you girls just check into an old people's home?'

'Sort of what we're planning.'

Rachel glances at Fran. Annie catches the look. 'She's always downbeat. Fran has a secure provincial background, it makes her seem gloomy or stick-in-the-mud, even when she isn't.'

Fran smiles. She thinks of her adult life – moving to and round Nigeria, back to Europe, criss-crossing Britain for temporary jobs, moving houses, struggling to integrate herself and Johnnie, making and leaving friends, coping with precarity and wrong turns, all while Annie took a sedate carriage ride from Primrose Hill to Cambridge with a detour to Paris. She grasps the role she wants in the group. The indulged misanthrope, expressing in words the facial expression of Cassandra's portrait.

Jane Austen smiles, knowing as Fran knows, that, below

layers of discontent, even sometimes despair – mainly the fault of insomnia – she's quite a cheerful person. Occasionally, Fran's mortified at her inability to provoke bewilderment.

'Would you be hungry for America the Beautiful?' she asks Rachel.

'A little hunger's good. I'd be satiated if I didn't miss a meal from time to time. Also, I like being sort of baffled by the place I live in.'

'You mean England's like a missed lunch?'

Annie says, 'You know, Fran and I are very fond of each other.'

'Oh, I guessed that, kind of sisters. More? I can live with it, with you. Polyamorous.'

'Pollyanna? Making the best . . .' begins Fran before suspecting her mistake.

She blushes. She's never been the sort to wonder about Jane Austen's sexuality or consider what two women sharing a bed for part of their lives might or might not have done beyond keeping each other warm in the cold season, that lovely confidential spoon position.

Jane Austen's shoulders giggle; the dead are always young. As well speculate on the Mad Hatter and March Hare, what they get up to with a dormouse in a teapot.

Yet one idea always startles Fran. Cassandra thinking her sisterly love so great that God punished her by giving Jane an early death. She shakes her head: better remember the pair as young women dressed middle-aged, exchanging private jokes while squashing pattens into the mud of Hampshire footpaths.

Grief can confuse the mind, says Jane Austen softly.

'Seriously, Rachel, would you really leave behind all that superabundance?'

A genuine question, posed mainly to raise the topic of each one's special wants.

Does Fran wish to engross Annie, not share her, even with Rachel? But would Fran be enough for Annie without anyone else – and, surprising herself here – would Annie be enough for her? What does an urban woman know of ground-love? London, Birmingham, Liverpool: all predators.

Rachel thinks of the money clicking over from Chase Manhattan to Lloyds even now. Is this what makes Fran (and Annie) uneasy?

'It isn't and wasn't all superabundance. I missed the gold star as a child.'

Are you proposing to shack up with this pair of losers? she can hear her almost comatose mother sneer.

'What of Thanksgiving,' pursues Fran, 'cinnamon apple pie, bagels and lox, 4th July, T-shirts and shorts on sexy summer days, the Bloomingdale wardrobe?'

Rachel smirks, aware only Annie and she know most of her clothes are a great deal pricier than Bloomingdales'.

'Tamsin can make any of us feel frumpy.'

'Thomas too,' says Fran. 'By the way, what did either of them get from those Shelley trips? Oh, I guess. Plus, Thomas used up some travel money and got a journal note.'

They fall silent. No need to say: what did we?

'If we were – not saying are – living close or close-ish in Cambridge, we could rent a room cheaply to Tamsin,' says Rachel. 'Talented young woman.'

'What a strange word – sounds like a biblical allergy. But yes, Tamsin warms us all.'

Annie remembers Thomas's elated and stricken expressions.

Jane Austen groans by Fran's elbow.

'Thomas has just risked his marriage and home.'

'Chaos is irresistible.'

'It isn't though, is it? Just routine for Tamsin, fun. Why do we make her a child when she's absent?'

'It's infidelity.'

'Goodness. How quaint. He won't abandon Kiran.'

'I was thinking of the reverse.'

'The young live in a foreign country, remember.'

'Perhaps she goes for older or attached men like she enjoys old ladies, parental substitutes.'

Rachel visualises Tamsin's grin on hearing this. Might she catch an expectation of hurrahing youth in a new story? She doubts it, knowing her thoughts are dated. She holds a residual sense that youth ought to be just a teeny bit subservient to age, and no longer is.

'She'd be a reproach,' says Fran. 'She's away in her techie world where the young are vastly superior. Fingers twinkling over tiny keys, influencing, Snapchatting or whatever. We've nothing to offer.'

'A nice room.'

'She'll be impatient with us, and we'll be irritated. We may have learnt control, but Tamsin?'

'We could warn her,' says Fran.

'She's not likely to say, I could tolerate you old bags as long as you give me cheap lodgings while I glitter my image and compose inflated grant applications – Annie of course providing the mother of all references, like she did for Thomas. Still, there are gestures we can read and maybe she can't, yet.'

'The young know better how to manage a face. We didn't study ourselves in selfies.'

'Do they keep taking them till they look right, then adjust expression to fit the snap?'

'We could ask. A lot we'd like to know.'

'Thomas doesn't take selfies,' says Annie, 'but you can't talk to him even on a phone without recalling his whole body.'

'Wow!'

30

It's best, remarks Jane Austen, to keep ailments private. Old age, frailty, decline and death: it is no use to lament. As I remarked shortly before dying, I never heard that even Mary Queen of Scots's lamentation did her any good, so could not expect benefit from mine. We are all sorry, and now that subject is exhausted.

The Author flexes her fingers inside an expensive pair of red leather gloves. As a child she went gloveless, but maturity brings covering of parts.

'My father died of boredom, I think. Listening to my mother's aches and complaints and what her sham of a gold-digging shrink said. She posed as unhealthy when she must have the constitution of an ox. She's ninety-seven.'

'What did your dad do?'

Rachel shrugs, 'Made money.'

Annie has been giving serious thought to arrangements, the inhibitions needed for communal living – if – and she's not entirely sold on the plan – they try it. Some difficulties might be countered by feminine pleasantries. But what of infatuations, ephemeral or more? She recalls the raw, dumbfounding heat she once felt and wanted to inspire in greedy-eyed men but never knew for sure she did. Frantic grief is better understood, more overwhelming than joy. Both subside, Fran would say. Yet, Annie asks, 'What if one of us attracts an admirer, a suitor, a beau of either sex?'

'Fat chance. But, if it happens, you take a gun and yourself down to the end of the garden.'

'Oh goody, we can talk in metaphors.'

'Just keep it outside, you mean, like cats?' says Annie, who believes all animals outdoor creatures. Extend her views to human animals? After a pause she says, 'I like hot baths, I want to be the colour of a lobster when I emerge. I must have a big bath just for me.'

An undignified image startles Fran: Annie pleasuring herself under the cold-water tap after the broiling, legs up the tiled wall.

She's always assumed her friend had passing affairs at those extended conferences in Vancouver or Palermo. Mum's word for fumbling with or without intercourse – 'hanky-panky' – always intervenes between Fran and solemnity in sex.

Blow-jobs, big cocks, mum-porn, jiggle-balls.

Jane Austen makes a noise between a sigh and a snort. My contemporary, the Marquis de Sade . . . She pauses. You think you add possibilities; you forget what you have lost.

'I shower every day,' says Rachel, 'sometimes twice.'

Fran's silent; often in winter she takes only two showers a week so as not to tax her inconstant, noisy plumbing.

Unlike sex, poor personal hygiene is unspeakable.

'One of our first bathrooms in Philly had fuchsia and black tiles and diamond mirrors,' says Rachel – 'people came specially to see it.'

They chime on pleasantly enough over the weeks into late autumn, making plans in the air, on Facetime, by email and on an occasional postcard, none being quite sure she wants them carried out but certain she wants the others to want them. Real or experimental theatre?

Rules too – such as:

We must

* not emerge until ready to address the day. No slouching in trodden-down, sweat-grey slippers,
* keep accessories (and impatience) in our rooms,
* clean public spaces (or employ a less educated, more

poorly paid Eastern European to vacuum and dust?
Exploitative? Too much like a hostel?),

* avoid plug-ins that make a house smell like a Turkish taxi,
* talk a lot, often simultaneously, linear time being
uneconomical among friends.

Jane Austen finds this list hilarious. All things are relative
except decency and morality, she says at last, wiping her eyes.

'Since we won't share lavatories, the most important place in
the house for chaos and disruption will be the stove,' says Fran
during an arranged meeting at a café in Ely. Her head holds
images of Dad cleaning up after making his sticky honeyed
hams. 'Watch out for cooked sugar. Olive oil supposedly healthier than lard but just as greasy. Like drying the loo seat if you've
misjudged, the stove must always be wiped after use.'

Annie ascribes this distasteful simile to Fran's living alone,
her irritation when anyone stays and splatters a fried egg. 'We'd
have our own bedlinen,' she says, licking cream off an opal ring
on her middle finger. 'No sharing. I hate fitted bottom sheets.
They stretch over corners like membranes on bones.'

They've ordered too many cakes. Only Fran feels the need to
eat more than she wants. If they hadn't been squishy, she'd have
squirrelled one or two away in her bag – then forgotten them.
'I do have some odd habits,' Fran begins. 'I . . .'

'I know,' interrupts Annie. 'She listens to the *Shipping Forecast* in the morning *and* at night.'

'We must avoid too much empathy if we're shacking up.'

'No letting off steam then?'

'Venting,' says Rachel, more linguistically up-to-date thanks
to her creative-writing students, 'it's OK if you ask permission
to reach out.'

'Takes away spontaneity.'

'Reach out?' says Annie, 'I had in mind spilling out.'

'Listening is emotional labour,' chuckles Rachel, 'if you're really going to max out.'

'Could we stand her?' asks Fran

'She's teasing,' says Annie, 'I hope.'

'Sometimes I do feel like an angry ship in a bottle,' admits Fran – she's being too serious – 'but the main point is to let things simmer, die down and cool, not be brought to the surface and stain everything at once.'

'As culinary image, this isn't quite working,' says Rachel, 'but I'm all for self-restraint in company. If anyone wants to confess in a church or pub, she'll feel free. If you need a channel to the outside, I'll be that channel.'

Fran thinks of Agafia pulled into the World when desperate to return to her own nothingness. A recluse will always relapse.

'We love you for your quiddity, Fran,' says Annie, noting the withdrawing face. She touches Fran's arm.

'For your neuro-diverse characteristics,' says Rachel. 'Oysters and sparkling wine?'

'Only at weekends. Need to be rationed.'

Rachel and Annie laugh.

Jane Austen cracks one of her thin-lipped smiles.

'You old Puritan.'

'The pair of you are so English,' says Rachel, then pauses. 'Could we, truly, can we make this "new found land"?'

Desire, petty jealousies, and fears will all be unsettling.

Rachel is still the keenest. In a new variant of old anxiety, Fran wonders whether Rachel really wants to live with Annie alone, herself merely thrown in. She tries to check the thought. It's the kind that, uncontrolled, scuppers things. Perhaps before – and if – she leaves Norfolk, she should take one of Julie's Mindfulness courses to stop thinking what she thinks.

'I have to retire next year,' says Annie. 'I could stay around supervising bits and bobs, go to the Library, be greeted less and less in Waitrose by old colleagues, squeeze myself sometimes into pre-prandial sherry, not so bad a life.'

'I could go back to Saxtham and put organic mulch on the veggie plot, take in another cat, do community cleaning, glass-eel rehabilitating, you know.'

'Creative-writing instructors are always wanted, for lovely sunny places like Mexico and Barbados.' Rachel swivels her head a couple of times. 'Or we could try.'

Annie has more to give up than the others. 'Are we being utopian? What do we really think of this? We've spent the past year contemplating failed communes. Would we be doomed by what we know?' As she speaks, she realises she yearns to live with Fran. Who'd have thought?

Tea over – paid for by Fran because it's her turn – they walk into the Cathedral Close, then circle the cloisters and as the light begins to fade cross into the sloping park heading for the station. The air has the slight chill of fading autumn. Judging by most previous years, the season will plod on into mist and murk without the drama of old snowy winters.

'We, um, could start by renting somewhere. None of the complication of owning. A few personal pieces but live with the original floral curtains as background,' ventures Fran.

'God no,' says Annie. 'I must have decent blinds and wall-paper. We could make a joint prescription, unnegotiable demands, something to carry round in a handbag, so we make pets of each other's monsters.'

'Does she always talk like this?' Rachel asks.

Fran's still gratified she's presumed to know more of Annie. It's true, 'going back a long way' counts. Though there are times when, perversely, she wishes her friend hadn't visited her parents in the bungalow. Residual snobbery? She can't tell, for Annie had been polite. Why translate courtesy into condescension?

'I have special china for Christmas,' says Rachel, 'It's still in sawdust.'

I can always find another cottage if needs be, thinks Fran.

'Great,' laughs Tamsin when she hears, 'I'll be eternally young. At home I was the grown-up beside my little brother Kwa. Here I'll be Petra Pan outside the window tapping or clawing. Or rather inside when you guys find a grand place. I'd make it Herland of Colour. Dunno about the parthenogenesis, but, yeah, aesthetics, woven tunics and fast running.'

'Not my vision,' laughs Fran. 'I had in mind something cosy like sticky-toffee pudding in winter.' No, she thinks, not quite like that.

With nothing materially utopian to offer but never to be side-lined, Jane Austen interjects: Indulge your imagination in every possible flight which the subject will afford . . .

'D. H. Lawrence proposed an intellectual community in Florida or Samoa, somewhere like luxurious and warm. They'd live his phallic philosophy of male and female unity.'

'If I remember rightly, Tamsin, he couldn't keep it up,' says Rachel. 'Sorry, unfortunate expression. His views darkened, he went back to hierarchies and strong male leaders.'

'Oh, we may have leaders,' Annie sings out, 'so long as they change from day to day.'

Fran looks at her friend and, not for the first time, wonders if she's had plastic surgery, some lifting or filling, secretly in one of those summers when she'd been taking long research trips without Paul? Did she always have such prominent cheek bones?

Annie sees Fran's expression disengaging: will her friend gradually turn into a boxed-set-watching, crossword-doing old baggage, morosely greeting anyone returning from a ritzy outing in Mayfair?

Rachel glances at both women: if she had to choose only one – and surely that won't happen – it would be Fran. She has a smile in her voice, sometimes.

'I wouldn't want to belong,' says Fran out of nowhere. 'Well not in a treacly way.'

'Before we commit, should we seek advice? Maybe a therapist, a counsellor, a life coach, a style guru?'

'Oh my God, a fortune teller!' exclaims Tamsin. 'I know about astrology. Mum was always reading out her horoscope to Dad while he looked at the cricket results on the back page. Tarot! My friend Harmony . . .'

'You have a friend called Harmony?'

'Well yeah, her parents thought Melody too common. She's a City trader.'

'Counterpoint might be classier.'

'I'd go for Fugue,' says Fran. 'No one inexpensively educated would know how to spell it. When I tired of it, I'd become an expletive.'

'Good-oh,' says Tamsin, pirouetting round on flashy striped trainers. 'It'd be like College with cheaper rent and people to fuss over me and my lovers.'

'Would the children come to stay?' says Fran.

'What children?' Tamsin rubs the bottom of her nose with the end of her forefinger.

Fran and Annie look at her, impressed. Children, life's centre, the *raison d'être* of the female body, reduced to a throwaway line.

'Oh, I see,' says Tamsin. 'You guys have kids?'

Daniel and Esther.

Does Annie regret ignoring them during those hungry productive years? They have good jobs in California and Hong Kong. If there are wounds, no one need open them. Esther was – and presumably still is – what used to be called 'highly strung'. Fran doubts she'll be happy anywhere, but, with perpetual sun and multiple therapies, she'll approximate it in Santa Monica. Daniel, the nervy bullied teenager, now at Investec earns twice or thrice what Johnnie earns. Is Annie embarrassed or proud? Left-wing principles stop at the nursery door. For Christmas, his wife sends identical calendars of the children to Fran and Annie. That tells you something. Who else is on the gift-list?

Dear, dear Johnnie.

'Don't worry, they're older than you and far off. We could have a home-warming party. Let everyone in, then show them the door.'

'A barbecue,' says Tamsin, 'with a brazier too. I know where the Uni keeps one for strikes.'

Thomas is at Annie's to bless the enterprise, which he only half assumes a joke. 'Why linger, why turn back,' he quotes. He seems excited. The women look at him, a little uncomfortable. Is it Tamsin's involvement? 'Shelley's radical commune was to be an enclave of beauty, a love-haven, a Paradise of immortals.'

Yes, thinks Annie, it *is* Tamsin. 'I don't think we were aiming for anything so exalted,' she laughs, 'just a quiet grouping of ladies, spinsters or spinsters manqué. An odd hotchpotch, very English, not untroubled or overblown, trying something, for us, a little different in twilight.'

Fran and Rachel heard that: twilight. Did Annie really say it?

'How big will this house be?' asks Thomas. 'Nantgwillt, Villa Diodati, or Palazzo Mocenigo?'

'My cottage has two little staircases,' says Fran.

'Happily,' says Annie, 'no chance of us moving in there.' Then, seeing Fran frown, she adds, 'And no corridors: good communes need corridors.'

Thomas grins round, then lets his eyes rest on Rachel. In Venice he'd been repelled by her emotional incontinence – it had reminded him of his mother and mother-in-law, Kiran sometimes. He wonders – never publicly of course – whether women are indeed more hysterical than men. Yet, apart from this one stagey moment – creative camouflage for something else? – Rachel's a good mate. He likes her the better now he no longer needs to court her. A deeper session of Googling has revealed that her connection with Princeton is through her family's major benefactions. Good, for, unlike Tamsin, he isn't a natural networker.

Not the time of the White Male, especially an 'old fogey', as Annie once called him. He'll wait for the wheel to turn.

His grin widens at the thought of Tamsin: a gift from the women she's labelled the 'Three Witches'.

3I

Fran's in Norfolk preparing the cottage for sale, knowing it will take time to shift. She's moving any cuteness from living spaces; the pink china pig and Johnnie's blue owl go from the fireplace. Outside she's cleaned the teak banana bench on which the hawk had shat, bought new bushes to look pretty by spring, rewilded a sunny verge with native seeds, rooting out modern hybrids that might repel the sophisticated second-home buyer.

Every plant in the garden must be hardy or easily replaceable. All will be tidy. The wild strawberries are gone.

Jane Austen is again muttering about fruit, set off by the mention of strawberries. Mrs Jennings stuffing on mulberries, Mrs Norris's apricot no tastier than Dr Grant's potato, General Tilney boasting of pineapples, Mrs Elton gorging on Donwell's gourmet strawberries.

Why this displacing of vulgarity onto fruit? smiles Fran. You never saw Bosch's fleshly nudes devouring gargantuan strawberries.

Shakespeare called them wholesome berries. I am always with the Bard.

Did you know your 'amiable' Anne Boleyn had a strawberry birthmark proving her a witch and St Hildegard of Bingen rejected fruit that creeps with snakes and toads along the ground?

Fran hums now as she pulls up nettles and dead plants, murmuring, 'Sweet place, all nature has a feeling, landscape listens.' Despite her poetizing their earthy pull, she knows the cottage and garden have demanded too much maintenance: her trees are overbearing, her flowers too needy. The trip to Venice had dark moments but on the whole, even with a tendency to overcloud in memory, it had been more than usually bright.

She sees Jane Austen strolling by the bare apple tree quoting lines from Cowper's 'Sofa':

> The sloping land recedes into the clouds;
> Displaying on its varied side the grace
> Of hedgerow beauties numberless.

It's winter, thinks Fran, but no matter. Words and things don't necessarily coalesce.

She ambles over to meet her Author. You haven't always made my life better here, she says, with your caution, civility and repression, your maddening romantic endings.

As ever, you misinterpret me, replies Jane Austen serenely.
You were never a good close reader. Besides, we have all a better
guide in ourselves, if we would attend to it, than any other
person can be.

Fran walks swiftly back into the warm house mumbling what
not even she can hear.

The mobile phone rings. She struggles to remember where she
left it. Like her gardening jumpsuit, her long cardigans have
capacious pockets so she can carry round useful items. But the
phone almost always rings elsewhere. She locates it in the downstairs cloakroom next to a face-down open book. She presses the
Talk button.

Silence. Could it be another cold call about funeral plans or
life insurance? She's ready to press 'End' when she notices the
number. Annie.

'Horrible.' The voice is raspy, distorted. For a split second,
she thinks – absurdly – they don't want her.

'Tamsin is dead.'

Fran slumps onto the lavatory top, steadying herself against
the thin windowsill. What, how, when and – especially and for
ever – why?

'Knocked off her bike on the Newmarket Road. She had
lights on. A car flung her onto a cement barrier. A hit and run.
He didn't even stop . . .'

Fran thinks wildly of Shelley's boat, perhaps run down in
the mist by someone who sped from death. Literary thinking
collapses. Why's Annie talking about blame? She shouts at the
phone, 'It doesn't matter about the driver.'

The parents come to Cambridge, along with Tamsin's young
brother, a tall lad in his late teens. What had once been Tamsin
lies in a funeral home near Mill Road; after private cremation

her ashes will return with her family for burial in Leicester. To the surprise of her friends, the parents have allowed short visits to the Chapel of Rest.

Fran is looking at Tamsin's corpse – the way one stares at a road accident, a body pulled from the sea, nobody known. Has the face been adjusted? Surely being thrown into the air and against cement hard enough to kill would distort every feature into agony and shock.

She tries to think appropriate memorial words: she shall not grow old, never old . . .

The hair's not right; its electric coils are damped down, almost straightened. To her horror, Fran feels a sudden squirm of desire. Necrophilia? Or is it only now she can gaze with impunity? Again, that unruly urge to giggle. It makes her shiver and sway.

Annie takes her arm, 'I think we should go. The parents don't want us here.'

They're looking over with suspicion, even dislike. Fran hopes she can talk later to the mother and dispel a little of what she must feel.

'See,' says Rachel as they leave, 'those young men are coming to get a last yearning look. For how many was she the love of his life, I wonder? There was a guy with the parents and brother, maybe the boy next door who's waited ever since she quit Leicester.'

A little ceremony is arranged at the College – a 'life-celebration'. The parents are bewildered in the alien town; so, urged by the Tutor, Annie takes some charge. She suggests informality, people speaking ad lib.

As Thomas begins, she sees her error.

'The soul of man, like unextinguished fire, / Yet burns towards heaven with fierce reproach,' he's saying. 'Tamsin is a rare spirit, someone whom nothing should ever satisfy, too much for the world.' He glances at a card in his hand and recites, 'If thou wouldst be with that which thou dost seek!/Follow where all is fled!'

Fran whispers to Annie, 'It's about Shelley, someone should stop him. He's near sobbing, don't let him break down; the parents have their heads in their hands.'

Before anyone can interrupt, Thomas ends.

'Phew,' exclaims Annie under her breath, 'say something, Fran.'

'I too would like to read a poem. Tamsin once quoted this to me from John Clare, whom she loved:

> The winter comes; I walk alone,
>   I want no bird to sing;
> To those who keep their hearts their own
>   The winter is the spring.
> No flowers to please – no bees to hum –
>   The coming spring's already come.'

'Not sure that was much better,' whispers Annie.

'I really wanted to use those Byron verses she quoted to us – remember we were surprised? About darkness, "She was the Universe".' Fran chokes on her words.

The boy from home gives a poised smile to the mother, who looks gratefully at him as he recites the appropriate poem: 'Remember me when I am gone away.'

Then Kwa reads something they assume is a lyric from a popular song and plays a recording of soupy music of the sort Tamsin might have liked at age ten. Fran jiggles her leg to the crude rhythm to show willing. She looks at Annie's loud blackness. The feathered hat focuses attention on her. Was she once an emaciated goth in torn black down the King's Road?

It is, Annie had said, a hat for the occasion, understated and sombre.

The College Tutor makes a dignified speech and Harmony sings an African folksong to a guitar. 'She'd have to with that name,' whispers Rachel.

The mother, darker than Fran expected and with no hint of Tamsin's beauty, begins to talk, then dry-eyed till now, cries to interrupt herself as her little white pot-bellied husband arms her away. Rachel too is crying. She cries easily, she's said. It makes an impression on the parents.

At the end they speak to the family.

'She didn't like our home,' says the father, 'not now. Even the garden was too tame.' Suddenly he breaks into a gasping sob, his belly shuddering.

'It was the Brussels sprouts,' says Kwa – was he controlling a snigger, a wail? 'She didn't like the stalks you left in the garden.' The mother pats his arm, then holds it tightly, pulling him to her.

He springs free, 'She didn't like Brussels sprouts either. She left them on the side of her plate at Christmas.'

'Hush. Don't mind that.'

Thomas has been crying but has the presence of mind to mutter to the parents, 'My condolences . . .'

'Tamsin will go on being our "influencer",' Rachel says.

The word feels in quotation marks; Fran wishes Rachel hadn't used it. Yet what to say? She'll live in our hearts? Worse. So sorry for your loss?

As you see, whispers Jane Austen, sometimes silence and deep feeling sit best together.

Only sometimes, thinks Fran. Sometimes, only the ornate, the flamboyant, the baroque will do.

'The canapés are good,' says Annie.

'I don't think the parents wanted this. How did it happen?'

'Harmony and Jason agreed.'

Harmony and Jason whom we never met till now.

Fran thinks, the mother must feel as we do, left out. She's fussing about the car her husband parked in the wrong place, the College carpark being too difficult to manoeuvre into. She's suspicious of these white women older than herself. What was Tamsin doing? What were *they* doing? She addresses Annie, whom she takes as the ringleader with that hat: 'She moved away from us,' she says simply, 'when she came here. We hardly saw her. It upset Kwa.'

'She really hadn't,' Annie responds quickly. 'She was just in the long phase of "young adult". She spoke warmly of her home and your big garden.' Not strictly true but properly said. 'She loved you all very much.'

Wrong, thinks Fran, too possessing, too condescending. 'We were just sort of aunties,' she butts in. 'So very sorry for your loss.'

The mother clutches Fran's hand, 'She respected you.'

Fran hears frost in the expression. She squeezes the hand. 'She tolerated us,' she says with what she hopes is a deprecating smile. She pulls Annie away, 'We're only bit-part players here, if that.'

As they walk off, Annie chokes, 'Why Tamsin? It should have been Thomas.'

32

You chose to live with women. Friend and sister were soul mates in that Chawton cottage you preferred to Manydown Park, your one real chance of marriage to a proper house.

Jane Austen sniffs. I favour the term 'companions'. Very dear companions.

Yet you throw your girls to husbands as if you can't stand them an instant more after they've caught their men. Nothing but flippancy to send them off.

The rich afterlives rest with you, smiles Jane Austen. In Texas, California, the Arctic, Pakistan, my girls have fought vampires and werewolves, solved crimes . . .

Just our bagatelle. *You* leave only one female grouping, one! If I wrote a sequel, I'd follow Maria Bertram and Aunt Norris.

As I've said, you like to dwell on guilt and misery.

Because Mrs Norris is thrifty, bustling with energy and anxious to fend off young rivals, you flatten her into a villain. But going into exile with a beloved niece shows heart. Why should these women torment each other? What's so hard about exile with every comfort? They'll have a nice house – Sir Thomas Bertram could do no less – they'll be in another county, let's hope a mellower one than stony Northampton (Sussex perhaps or soft Wiltshire), Maria is young, handsome and disgraced, just the type to attract a saucy charming man. Why on earth shouldn't she have a second spring? And why shouldn't Aunt Norris, loving Maria even more in her disgrace, turn a blind eye – or for that matter gleefully keep both open?

Your whimsy.

Really? There's love on one side – common enough in ties across generations: Maria has security of affection. You think you can sniff out an adulteress, but that supposes a woman turns into a different creature after illicit sex. Beneath your cynical good humour, you're waspish and intolerant: it's we who've given you our liberal views.

You are misguided on matters of importance, says Jane Austen stiffly. You've caught the arrogance of the Present, its moral bankruptcy. I might not come with you to – wherever you presume you're going. (After all, she has millions to haunt – no reason to stick around with people who wilfully err.)

We've created each other, whispers Fran, we must stay together.

Not quite, snaps Jane Austen, her words and presence fading into the blankness which a perceptive successor compared to a spoon held up in the sun.

Go on, grins Fran, you can't resist house-hunting. Not Emma Woodhouse or Elizabeth Bennet, but know-all Diana Parker bustling round Sanditon for lodgings, that's you.

I thought you'd never guess, chuckles Jane Austen returning to focus.

Of course, you'll come, exclaims Fran. Three women to-gether – and no mother. You'll share a room with Percy Bysshe, a big one, nothing improper, single beds. A Venetian window to look through, you gazing on earth, he at clouds. Mr P.B. Shelley and Miss Jane Austen will find each other unprepossessing but will chat amiably, both being bred as gentry, constrained by manners, the politesse of their rank.

Or maybe you'll stay in the garden: conservatives always lurk there.

A year passes. The loss of Tamsin becomes a duller ache. Silently each thinks of that bewitching body avoiding the shrunken face, drawn lips, the bony frailty, sag and colourlessness of old age – only to be burnt to ashes. No wonder an occasional desire to giggle afflicts them.

'She was never going to live with us, but she'd have stayed a while and added diversity,' remarks Fran.

'We have that,' says Rachel, 'mammoth differences between any two people. Diversity's inbuilt.'

Having swallowed the insult of a shared bedchamber, Jane Austen can't resist quoting the Favourite Book: People themselves alter so much, that there is something new to be observed in them for ever.

On the contrary, Fran thinks, people are remarkably repetitive.

The visit from Tamsin's parents doesn't materialise, so plans to laugh warmly over smiley photos of their daughter as infant on the beach at Skegness or as teenager receiving school prizes are in abeyance.

'I guess they didn't like us,' says Rachel.

'Can't blame them.'

Nor has Thomas been calling on Annie in Cambridge as much as before.

'We didn't pay a lot of attention to his inner life. I assume he was describing that with his Shelley talk,' Annie answers when Rachel quizzes her.

'It wasn't his inner life that attracted Tamsin,' says Fran. 'They probably hung out with us for each other. They liked our background noise.'

'Human relationships are just so much performance,' shrugs Rachel

'Should warn you that kind of blanket remark gets up Fran's nose,' chuckles Annie.

As Tamsin's digital executor, Harmony has given the Black Diva material to Thomas, who's crafted it into a blog ending with Tamsin among the tombs of San Michele. He spends more time in London than he used to, feigning monogamous love until it becomes real again: then his long-suffering wife no longer need threaten to leave Thomas coping with three children. Yet, whenever he's on a train and sometimes in the car if the back seat is empty of small bodies, he finds Tamsin's thighs wriggling through his sinuses. He crosses and uncrosses his legs.

*

Fran's in Norfolk. The cottage is on the market, but without a 'For Sale' sign on the roadside. Who except joggers and horses pass by? She's touched up windowsills with fresh paint and replanted outdoor pots.

Into black binbags she's stuffed her attempts at writing. The activity satisfies more than pressing Delete.

For a day or two before rubbish collection, the binbags might be dragged back down the newly laid brick path, then bashfully repossessed. But they aren't. (Had she meant proper business, she'd have made a bonfire like Cassandra or Sylvia Plath. Or John Murray burning Byron's memoirs – might these have said something of Shelley's dead children? They can't all have been about scabrous sex.)

A house without a past is more saleable; yet the cottage languishes. Not in the choicest location, it must be viewed to best advantage before sugar-beet harvest, when fields aren't being sprayed with chemicals, when hawthorn foams over the grass or cowslips shine and birds sing merrily from the mossed roof. It saddens Fran that a place she's valued attracts no one else's love.

Are Agafia and she eccentric because they care for the tundra and dull level fields where normal people crave Caribbean beaches?

Once in a bleak 4 a.m. mood Fran catches herself almost wishing the place would burn down, taking with it her encroaching 'stuff'. Never with her inside.

'I used to pray our house would burn,' Annie'd said, 'so Mother and I could bolt and leave Zach to the flames.'

'Burning to death?'

'Yes, well, going out the back anyway and not coming home, ever.'

We've lost men and learnt a lot. Fran sighs.

You do know that when Elizabeth Bennet announces she never knew herself till she'd read Mr Darcy's letter, there's . . .

Oh no, groans Fran, not irony again.

Not quite, but points of view may err. Time shuffles off every mood and perception. Nothing is finally learnt or defined, certainly not the self.

Fran expels breath loudly enough for even a shadow to hear.

The sun steps out so brightly it clatters right through the kitchen window and lights up the cleaned but smudged stove. A visceral, intrusive, wonderful sun.

Goodness, says Fran, thinking her exclamation right for once, how I shall miss this place! Just agricultural tenements gentrified and painted, not even pargeted, but still.

Neighbours too. The Reeves in the crooked farmhouse:

she'd helped their girl with English essays when she twice failed GCSE; in return she's had home-baked cakes, string beans, plum tomatoes and beetroot, and been invited to the Guy Fawkes' party round an enormous sparking bonfire. The Lambs and the Riches, and Jenny from the new houses near Waitrose. They drop in from time to time, chat over tea, and stay that bit too long. Dave, too, who does casual work clearing drains and removing jackdaw nests from chimneys.

Such luxury to live here.

There's nothing like staying at home, for real comfort, announces Jane Austen.

Mostly it's the plants and creatures. The copper beech by the gate – stealing sun off the unused front door where otherwise she might sit to drink a morning coffee – opens soft tawny leaves, unfurling gold, then bronze; the pear tree serving mushy yellow fruit. The tactile greenness, the quiet mossiness on roof and walls, the fungus in soft clefts, even the absconded Jeoffry, who turned khaki to disguise himself against the foliage. Moles, badgers, hedgehogs in hibernacles, foxes, hares, beetles, worms, bats (not 'as blind as' after all), secret seeing through eyes myopic or hyperopic, compound or simple, binocular or monocular, catching infra-red or ultraviolet, open before birth like the leveret. Rabbits, squirrels eating the tulips, the bushy-tailed fox prowling for hens and human rubbish (never threatened by hunting dogs). The dull mallard beside her flashy drake, tadpoles and sticklebacks, newts – or ewts as they more memorably used to be – in the pond.

'Ewts,' Fran says aloud.

Not all always unmissable, not all 'real comfort', not when winter wind grows malicious, ditches overflow, gutters and drainpipes gurgle, and long algae make the pond green as gangrene. Grass freezes. Rats and mice think to come in from the cold. Then you may want human company.

If and when you do move, says Jane Austen, you should leave Agafia behind.

She never needed me.

'It's dangerous being a loner,' Annie says yet again in an unexpected phone call. 'It does real damage.'

She's thinking of herself: it's not a general truth.

Fran opens her mouth to speak, then closes it, warned by her Author's honest, kindly face. Remember, if things go unto-wardly one day, they mend the next. There will be little rubs and disappointments, but we find comfort somewhere.

Fran brushes prudence aside, 'Are you saying I shouldn't be there?' she says.

Jane Austen sighs at the foot-shooting.

Before Fran can protest idea and idiom, Annie answers, 'I think you'd struggle – and so would we.'

Stung by 'we', she should respond, 'But I will try.' The words don't come. 'Yeah,' she says.

Affability and condescension, murmurs Jane Austen. My Lady Catherine, your Annie . . .

Fran faces a bitter day, unsolaced by blackbird, beech tree, newts or the lovely word 'akrasia'. In the evening she's once more on her prosthesis, the magic phone link with Annie and Rachel.

She raises a second worry to dampen the first: 'I don't like to intrude, but I have very little pension and haven't yet sold the cottage.'

'Should say,' says Rachel – and to Fran she seems speaking from an immense high-ceilinged hall – 'I have enough money. But nothing's secure. Just so you guys know. There's a brother, I don't mention him a lot, but he exists and with a trio of unbalanced kids and two ex-wives to support.'

'Too much,' laughs Annie, filling the triangular lines, 'you are our Aunt Betsey Trotwood, Pip's Magwitch, Jane Eyre's uncle from Madeira. I knew you were OK, I didn't know you were rich. Could we accept imbalance?'

'Not asking you to. It would be an arrangement of shares. Not mega-rich. I just mean we can have a place big enough for our eccentricities.'

'I'd feel guilty,' says Fran.

'She's objecting before accepting,' says Annie. 'I know Fran. She's leaping into this.'

The sadness of 'we' evaporates. Fran smiles through her polished window at a rabbit's rump about to scurry into the undergrowth near where Jane Austen is wagging an elongated finger.

Quantum entanglement, says the Author.

33

The cottage has had an offer, so Annie and Rachel make the trek up to Norfolk for a last time. A smell of fertilizer attacks Rachel's nose and Annie sniffles at something natural and grating from the garden.

Fran suggests tea and Chelsea buns or Chablis and olives to her guests. She'd prefer the former but knows the latter might make agreement easier though it's only five in the afternoon. She hopes the wine is approved. It's way more expensive than her usual plonk.

'Do you think Thomas will visit?'

'Dunno. We'd have to cook him tofu and lentils,' says Annie. 'Maybe he'll come to talk of Tamsin – and his career.'

'It's an odd idea. Did we women have "careers"?'

'We'll consider the point while sewing a joint patchwork quilt,' says Fran, 'or decoupaging a folding screen for the sitting room.'

'Living room,' says Rachel, thinking of *Sweetpapers*; one much praised story turned on the semantics of domestic space.

'Drawing room,' says Annie

'The parlour then.'

For all their rules and semi-serious requirements, they've resolved on only one thing: to look down at themselves with unfiltered gaze if needs be, but to stick with soft focus when the eye travels out. A good resolution.

Hope is a Christian virtue, whispers Jane Austen.

Fran smiles as she washes down her Chelsea bun with the remains of the Chablis.

As the years pile up behind, if indeed they do in this ensemble, light will darken for all of them, none being young; each will have less and less to clean about themselves and perhaps take less trouble with what remains.

A bit mawkish, interrupts the Author. Cowper makes the point decorously:

> not a year but pilfers as he goes
> Some youthful grace that age would gladly keep,
> A tooth or auburn lock.

But Fran's incorrigible. They'll ignore (with difficulty) the snot, the dribble, the twitch, the sag, the stained blouse, the rumpled flesh, the lax bladder, the wavering bowels, the compromised brain, the preoccupied look of the aching, the knowledge it can all only get worse. What courage old age requires!

Not yet of course, absolutely not yet. However, best be prepared. Let them think these things ahead of time: no need to say them, though Rachel being American and with a greater tendency to spade-calling (with vocabulary to support it) will sometimes declare the obvious, making Fran laugh nervously.

There will be dying, there will be dying, but there is no need to go into that.

'I've always thought about death,' says Fran. 'I've got asthmatic lungs. It's an exciting disease, you never know if the breath will stop.'

'I have allergies,' says Rachel, 'I don't find them exciting.'

'Lungs are the self.'

'My mother has asthma,' continues Rachel. 'Or does whenever life falls on top of her. Her rasping breath shattered any argument against her faked ailments. When my brother wanted to experience puberty, he was upstaged by Mother and her super-charged breath. That was the only clever thing he ever said.'

'Hypochondriasis was a disease causing belly-ache, anxiety and obsession. The sufferer needed stimulation and agreeable company to recover,' says Annie. She delivers snippets of history promiscuously now she's deprived of respectful students.

'Mother always talked of her body parts, so they could each be separately and expensively served.'

'In some gentry circles it wasn't done to describe any parts. A maid dressing Mrs Piozzi's hair burst out laughing at the idea a lady said her *stomach* ached.'

They fall silent, Annie thinking of Mrs Piozzi's wish for cows' milk in Venice. She exhales and says, 'Will we be too compet-itive for communal living? The eighteenth-century commune Millennium Hall was run by do-gooding women, not ones who tried to excel at yoga. Absurd, but it's a character defect. What do I do?'

'Avoid yoga?' says Fran.

'Be stern with yourself,' says Rachel. 'If you get handed a coffee mug second on three consecutive mornings, retire to your room and do private postures with thoracic breathing.'

'Or get cross and protest, that'd be healthier,' says Fran.

'It wouldn't because you'd both be nice about it, and I'd feel ashamed.'

'Yeah, well, we'd hand you the mug first next time.'

'I'd resent that too.'

'For sure you're unsuited to community, Annie. But you're in and you make a mean guacamole with tabasco sauce.'

'We should have slate tops,' says Annie briskly. 'They wipe down.'

Fran and Rachel glance at her. Annie, always centre stage: why not? No one wants to live with cold eyes.

'Where do we go?' begins Rachel. 'Wet Wales is out, much as Fran wants it – well as long as she's thwarted.'

'Actually,' says Fran, 'I'd quite like to live in Ambridge.'

'Easy. Add a C and we stay in Cambridge.'

'No, Cambridge is Tamsin. Wherever we settle, we'll plant tulips and anemones for her, she's always Mayday.'

'Sentimental but true,' says Annie, abruptly aware she doesn't want to stay a moment longer in her town. Why be vindictive towards a place that's fed and clothed her so many years and whose old-stone beauty still stuns her?

Something to do with Paul and 'happy heart'? We won't go there. 'I can't take the country,' she says, 'my eyes stream. You've seen, Fran.'

'Nor I mean streets.'

'Oxford?'

'More snobbish than Cambridge.'

'Cotswolds? Frosted hips and haws, medieval clay, lambs and catkins, very fashionable. All rural trappings, converted chapels serving lattes and avocado toast.'

Annie gives an artificial cough, 'Remember, Rachel and I need a library.'

'Need?'

'Want – with heating and squishy chairs – and books. How about London? Near the Tube, maybe a park with ponds.'

'By the sea,' says Fran.

'I'd be out of place in a resort,' says Annie.

'The very place to be out of place. Tourists make one think one belongs, knowing where loos are.'

Crankhumdunberry? suggests Jane Austen reverting to childhood. Pammydiddle?

'The house will be new to all of us, so derelict we animate it by decorating from top to bottom,' says Rachel. She's assuming leadership in the search, having less emotional investment in English earth but (potentially) more financial. 'Got it: a place near fields, water, people, emptiness, libraries, cafés, the Tube.' She pauses for smiles. 'Each will have her room, a necessary sense of ownership. Shared spaces will be neutral – but not grey, ecru or cream.'

Annie shrugs. 'No fear of soullessness. Leave a scarf or smeared wineglass and a perfect room's tacky.'

'A house from birth,' Rachel continues, 'not a fancied-up barn or Manhattan-type loft-conversion – a house intended for what it is, in unashamed bricks or stone.'

'A surprised house, sheepishly tangled in Virginia creeper and wisteria.'

Annie's contribution to the new life will be uncompetitive yoga in the early morning, so she'll become placid and ruminative later in the day. She'll be released from peer pressure and, though she keeps this from Fran, relinquish the need ever again to pretend she likes Jane Austen's banal and overrated books – insufficient fibre she's always thought. She'll loaf with rubbish novels and the whacky Booker shortlist if she wishes.

As for Rachel: who sees what expatriates intend for their future? Even the planets don't know. One day her companions will read her pseudonymous short stories – witty, unsettled and addictive, the *Washington Post* called them – and understand a little more about her. Well, as a writer.

Fran determines to construct a new personality. Less apprehensive of exclusion now, she aims to speak in a thoughtful, slightly guarded way. It will take practice. As she moves towards a new decade, she'll stop drawing attention to age – losing even the residual hope of the response, 'You don't look . . .'

Noting one or two omissions in Fran's plan of reformation, Jane Austen says, If I come, I shall – as you once suggested – remain in the garden, refreshing myself with the fruits of others' labour. Wherever we are, the bells of the Church of England will ring out cheerily.

Fine by me, says Fran, though more plangent these days.

She packs up her editions of the sacred works in their different formats: reprinted paperbacks in new covers with bonneted girls looking through saucy modern eyes; annotated hardbacks with Hugh Thomson illustrations; comic versions of *Pride and Prejudice*.

You'll look well out there by the hollyhocks. You can serve expensive teas on rosy plates when the sky's blue. Celebrity has responsibilities.

I am no enthusiast of hollyhocks, replies Jane Austen, a Victorian taste. I will need pinks, sweet Williams, columbines, cornflowers, Cowper's ivory-pure syringa, his laburnum rich in streaming gold. Fruits and flowers, she murmurs again, flowers and fruits.

Moved by Shelley's gardens of amaranth and asphodel, his unseen sweetly singing, sad skylark, if she wanders among Fran's flowerbeds Rachel may tame any jumble with a hint at colour-coding – but she'll be no Henry Tilney imposing taste on Fran's myopic eye. Home is collaboration.

'Our time is past,' says Fran, already back-sliding. She sits sipping white wine in Annie's house, perfect and ready for wide-angled sale shots.

A little exasperated, Rachel responds, 'That's giving too much to what doesn't exist. The now's the thing. Our time's inevitably now.'

'Sounds a bit alternative,' says Fran, feeling so warm towards Rachel her face reddens.

'Shelley had a ring on which was engraved *il buon temp verra*,' says Annie. 'Come on, guys, we all know the answer to happy life: focus on trifles.'

'Watch grass grow, be overtaken by clover and moss, listen to a house groan and moan.'

'Find content in the paltry.'

'See a pigeon's sheen.'

'Make commonplace miraculous.'

'Shucks,' laughs Rachel – she'd recently used the exclamation in a story set in 1955. 'Do we have the shoulders for it?'

'We'll bring our solitude along,' says Annie with such gentleness the others smile.

'And authority?' asks Fran. 'Will we divvy up duties? In the Jane Austen household one becomes the housekeeper, another the caregiver.' She leaves off the creator, the author, the genius.

'I don't know about caring,' says Annie, 'but I can organise.'

'And cope with our inefficiency?' laughs Fran. 'Would you feel the impulse to criticise?'

'I'd repress it. I was trained in repression. I forgot the lesson but can recap.'

'If we call laziness sloth, we can luxuriate in it. Idleness slows time and fends off ageing.'

'Self-pity?'

'There'll be a drinks cabinet. We can retire when pricked by shards of devouring memory.'

'Ah, we can talk in quotes as well as metaphors.'

But not adverbs, thinks Rachel. 'We must have a table for an ice bucket,' she says.

The strange vision halts Fran, then she chuckles, 'Absolutely, non-negotiable.'

'A painted birdbath for Fran, handcrafted by refugees,' says Annie. 'Rachel will do the good cheer. She's had an easy life, why shouldn't she be cheerful?' She stops, remembering the scene on the Lido.

Rachel recalls those lunches in the Danieli, the deeper resentments of childhood.

No reason to eschew a regular course of cheerful orderliness, says Jane Austen.

Orderly cheerfulness? Fran blushes to find herself correcting her Author.

'And you, Annie? What's essential beside the bath?'

'Nothing. We'll all be displaced, that's the point. We'll have a shed for things never unpacked like family photos, heirloom tablecloths, domestic detritus – and a bench to sit on for contemplating the closed crates.'

'You can leave things behind too. Bits of yourself, I guess,' says Rachel. She's a little uneasy: the jewellery inherited from her grandmother is lodged in a New York bank.

Fran doubts this, nothing of her left in Nigeria nor, she's discovered, in Elan Valley, though she'd breathed its air deeply. She's where she is. And yet, thinking again, she sees traces in the warm ham-smelling kitchen by the Long Mynd – she's brushed the earth there – and maybe by reed-edged Norfolk ditches.

She expects sometimes to pine for her floating cottage, especially on clear fresh harebell mornings. Then she'll settle for equable low spirits till enough contentment returns.

Annie will smile bitterly when she recalls her artisan house, half its value swallowed by Paul and 'happy heart'. Perhaps because she often inhabits New York in her stories, Rachel will regret nothing. None feels amputated by moving on.

They see a house on a street with camouflage trees. Like a Mediterranean villa in exile, thinks Rachel, who secretly fancies a stone hideout in the South of France. But one alien place is as good as another, so she doesn't protest. It would be tactless since she's paying the lion's share. She's glad when Annie and Fran reject it as lacking 'nuance' – Annie's word.

Waiting a little longer, they find somewhere more suitable, combining in various degrees the desired privacies, a garden sufficient for mistakes in placing foxgloves, hollyhocks and snake's head fritillaries, near enough to city sounds for Annie to breathe trafficked air in the evening and sip a decent cappuccino in the morning, a library not so distant, and a sense of water trickling somewhere. Rachel orders an expensive wooden swing set for the bottom of the lawn, so Thomas's girls will play happily when enticed to visit.

Fran grins. 'If he comes, he'll see three ageing women acting out a 1970s' Women's Lib refuge.' She'd have preferred a homemade high swing hung from the apple-tree bough to swish a child over tall grass. A grown-up too.

Rachel finds the tie between Thomas and Annie so interesting she's based a short story on it, set in Brooklyn. When, much later, the others discover this, there are words, then mutterings of betrayal, questions as to other depictions of her housemates.

Expecting the *éclaircissement* – she's increasingly praised for catching the zeitgeist for the older woman – Rachel will be easy in her answers: she's attacked nothing in them that had a claim to reputation, though she may have picked up an (endearing) foible or two.

Jane Austen approves. Claims to reputation are the dearest to the heart, they are what beauty is to the trivial, she announces.

Rather an eighteenth-century viewpoint, Fran whispers back.

But as long as Rachel doesn't stand on claims of 'simple honesty', she'll forgive. Annie needs more cajoling.

Rachel will sometimes be in her room on the phone to Miranda (her agent), discussing stories that mustn't track her down, not yet; Annie and Fran will have time together, looking or whatever. When her eyes aren't fixed on Annie, Fran sees that what she'd once thought a dilapidation in Rachel is mind poking through a cosmetically prepped face.

Occasionally Annie will savour a smell of cigar smoke, a heavy scent that Fran associates with burning autumn leaves, and Rachel with smooth thunderous evenings in Manhattan.

Only Fran feels the guilt of comfort, a yearning for a little dereliction, a little austerity. She's kept back some money from the disappointing cottage sale, just in case. Will Annie be loyal if her wants change, her friendship become less transactional, less a compact of convenience? Does either of them really know Rachel?

For now, she'll plant the new garden and be saddened her efforts aren't quite appreciated. If there's no proper pond, there's at least a hollow where, after rain, a trembling skin appears. She's no time for water features.

'None of us has ever swum in a river naked,' remarks Annie.

'I have,' says Fran.

'Me too,' says Rachel, 'bliss, in the New Jersey Pine Barrens, the water brown and most flattering.'

Truly, says Percy Bysshe, trailing his expensive blue jacket in the wet grass, a garden invites me to be elsewhere, see beyond land and water, the loveliness of fabled Eden . . .

Jane Austen smells gassy hyperbole and delicately holds her noble nose.

Fran comes out and moves the geniuses towards the far end of the lot where holly and briars flourish and overhanging trees make it almost always dark.

Is this a way to treat defenceless Authors?

Agafia was born in a hollowed-out pine washtub. She'll be thinking where to die in readiness for the posthumous Rapture. Please God, not in a distant hospital with cameras clicking. But she has no more control over her death and beatification than Jane Austen.

'If one of us dies suddenly – as can happen – what will you do?' asks Fran.

'Nothing,' says Annie. 'We're not family.'

It turns out they *are*, in a way. Just before they've time to feel truly settled, if ever, Covid-19 arrives. It's unheeded in reckless Westminster while it floats through homes and care homes with its spikes like one of Annie's yellow yoga balls. Now it seems they're a 'household' and will be locked down together, with a yard full of authors. How lucky is that?

'Or glimpse of distant upland pastures.'

One may end in fantasy, in one's own or another's book, remarks Jane Austen turning her deadpan face to her companion. She gazes through the Victorian illustration at upland pastures. Life's impossible otherwise.

Of course, dear Madam. We are both Romantics. Shelley smiles his sunny smile and looks up to the bright stars, beaming in daylight.

Illustrations

Hedgehog. Alamy.

Jane Austen's Writing Desk. (Courtesy Jane Austen's House, Chawton.)

Jane Austen. Cassandra Austen. National Portrait Gallery (NPG 3630).

River Wye. William Gilpin. *Observations on the River Wye*. page 20D. 2nd ed. London: R. Blamire, 1789.

The Vale of Nantgwilt, A Submerged Valley. R. Eustace Tickell, 1894. Sketches on pp. 92, 104, 117.

Jane Austen. Cassandra Austen c. 1804. Private collection.

Horses. Giulio Falzoni. In author's possession.

Tintown. Powys Digital History Project, Powys County Archives R/D/CL/1/20 and 21.

Byron's Room in Palazzo Mocenigo, Venice. The Stapleton Collection, Bridgeman Images.

Lobster Claw and Palette. Thomas Bewick Description of Water Birds, London, Longman and Co. 1821. p. 43.

Illustration and title page of *Five Go Adventuring Again*. Enid Blyton. Alamy.

The Funeral of Shelley. Louis Edward Fournier, 1879. (Courtesy National Museums Liverpool, Walker Art Gallery.)

Hugh Thomson illustration from Mrs Gaskell's *Cranford* (1898).

Where there is no attribution, picture or photograph is author's own.

Acknowledgements

Denied coffee and croissants in the library and bookshop cafés, in the March 2020 Lockdown I turned to writing a novel using only what I had to hand: memories, photos and leftover bits from earlier projects. Three female characters entered and stayed in the house over the next unsocial months.

As millions of readers have also found, Jane Austen's novels live in the head; I have allowed them and their author to appear, in part responding to and in part directing the thoughts of my most voluble character. Words attributed to this figment are sometimes from Austen's work, but not always.

In 2007 I published a biography called *Death and the Maidens: Fanny Wollstonecraft and the Shelley Circle*. This ended with Fanny's suicide in 1816, so I had unfinished business with the poet, who did not play an heroic part in this story of death and emotional carelessness. My biography came out at the same time as Ann Wroe's lyrical appreciation, *Being Shelley: The Poet's Search for Himself*. I have given a little of its enthusiasm to two of my characters, Rachel and Thomas, who between them describe pursuing Shelley through two pivotal moments in his life.

I am grateful to many people who have generously donated time and information. Nora Crook and Mathelinda Nabugodi put me right on some Shelley details (errors are of course mine, some intentional), and John Gardner led me to appreciate the poet as engineer. I have chatted about Jane Austen with so many friends over so many years it's impossible to recall them all, but I must mention Linda Bree, Diana Birchall, John Wiltshire,

Peter Sabor and the late Deirdre Le Faye (I doubt I'd have dared dramatize Jane Austen even as a shade had that great and exacting scholar still been alive).

Oddbjørn Sørmoen, John Millerchip and the Revd Malcolm Bradshaw gave me information on Protestant tombs in Venice and Anna Rosa Scrittori of Università Ca' Foscari provided material on Italian convents. I found Agafia Lykova on the web in the *Siberian Times* and on the YouTube video 'Hermit Agafia Lykova'. I already had notes on a few of the Radnorshire Transactions, but information about Elan Valley, its houses and local anecdotes, comes from the Powys digital history project and the excellent website https://www.elanvalley.org.uk/ discover/reservoirs-dams/lost-valleys. I prize a second-hand copy of *The Vale of Nantgwilt A Submerged Valley* by R. Eustace Tickell; at last I have found a way to insert it into a novel.

The Shelley quotations in the text are from *Shelley's Poetry and Prose*, eds Donald H. Reiman and Neil Fraistat (2002) and *The Complete Poetical Works of Percy Bysshe Shelley*, ed. Thomas Hutchinson (1965). For biographical material on Percy Bysshe and Mary Shelley I consulted *The Journals of Mary Shelley 1814–1844*, eds Paula R. Feldman and Diana Scott-Kilvert (1995), Richard Holmes, *Shelley: The Pursuit* (1974), John Worthen, *Shelley Drowns* (2019) and Iris Origo, *The Last Attachment: The Story of Byron and Teresa Guiccioli* (1949). Where Austen is quoted correctly – rarely the case – the quotation is from *The Cambridge Edition of the Works of Jane Austen* (2005–8). Scattered sayings and snippets of prose and poetry lodged in my bookish characters' minds come from Elizabeth Bishop, Emily Dickinson, John Clare, William Cowper, Thomas Gray, Alfred Tennyson, William Wordsworth, Lord Byron, Walt Whitman and Derek Mahon, as well as George Eliot, Charles Dickens, George Gissing, Mary Wollstonecraft, Muriel Spark, W.S. Gilbert, Henry Adams and Thorold Rogers.

I am grateful to the Zooming groups that supported sanity during Lockdowns; also, to Newnham College, Cambridge, for keeping its gardens open and its flowerbeds unusually stocked with lettuce and tomatoes. I owe thanks to Derek Hughes, Mary Colombi and Nancy Steiber for reading the manuscript. While the characters and events are fictional, the amateur photographs printed here are my own. Since they were largely unlabelled, some may seem a little random, with, for example, seasons confused, but I hope that most complement the text. I owe huge gratitude to Art Petersen of Alaska, who so kindly took time from editing his mammoth biography of Mollie Walsh to help make these photographs and other illustrations suitable for printing. Sarah Wasley, Rosemary Gray and Patty Rennie knocked the book into shape and Jeremy Hopes designed the lovely green cover. Thanks to all of them.

I owe most gratitude to Katherine Bright-Holmes, editor, advisor, encourager and friend.

A selection of Janet Todd's previous works

The Revolutionary Life of Mary Wollstonecraft (London: Weidenfeld and Nicolson; New York: Columbia University Press, 2000; London: Bloomsbury eBook, 2013)

Rebel Daughters: Ireland in Conflict (London: Viking, 2003); *Daughters of Ireland: The Rebellious Kingsborough Sisters and the Making of a Modern Nation* (New York: Ballantine Books, 2004)

Cambridge Introduction to Jane Austen (Cambridge: Cambridge University Press, 2006)

Jane Austen in Context, ed. (Cambridge: Cambridge University Press, 2006)

Death and the Maidens: Fanny Wollstonecraft and the Shelley Circle (London: Profile Books; Berkeley: Counterpoint Press, 2007)

Jane Austen: Her Life, Her Times, Her Novels (London: André Deutsch, 2014)

Lady Susan Plays the Game (London: Bloomsbury, eBook 2013; paperback, 2016)

A Man of Genius (London: Bitter Lemon Press, 2016)

Aphra Behn: A Secret Life (London: Fentum Press, 2017)

Radiation Diaries: Cancer, Memory and Fragments of a Life in Words (London: Fentum Press, 2018)

Jane Austen's Sanditon: With an Essay by Janet Todd (London: Fentum Press, 2019)

Don't You Know There's a War On? (London: Fentum Press, 2020)